THE
GRAIL
CONSPIRACY

THE
GRAIL
CONSPIRACY

LYNN SHOLES
AND
JOE MOORE

Midnight Ink
Woodbury, Minnesota

First Edition
First Printing, 2005

Book design by Donna Burch
Cover design by Kevin R. Brown

Library of Congress Cataloging-in-Publication Data

Sholes, Lynn, 1945–
   The grail conspiracy / Lynn Sholes and Joe Moore. —1st ed.
     p. cm.
   ISBN 0-7387-0787-2
    1. Women journalists—Fiction. 2. Jesus Christ—Relics—Fiction. 3. Christian antiquities—Fiction. 4. Americans—Iraq. 5. Biblical scholars—Fiction. 6. Conspiracies—Fiction. 7. Cloning—Fiction. 8. Grail—Fiction. 9. Sects—Fiction. 10. Iraq—Fiction. I. Moore, Joe, 1948– II. Title.

PS3619.H646G43 2005
813'.6—dc22   2005043770

Any Internet references contained in this work are current at publication time, but the publisher cannot guarantee that a specific location will continue to be maintained. Please refer to the publisher's website for links to authors' websites and other sources.

Midnight Ink, an imprint of Llewellyn Publications
A Division of Llewellyn Worldwide, Ltd.
2143 Wooddale Drive, Dept.0-7387-0787-2
Woodbury, MN 55125-2989, U.S.A.
www.midnightinkbooks.com

Printed in the United States of America

The authors wish to thank the following for their assistance in adding a sense of realism to this work of fiction.

Dr. Mark A. Erhart, Ph.D.
Professor of Molecular Biology
Chicago State University

Dr. Ken Winkel, Ph.D.
Director, Australian Venom Research Unit
Department of Pharmacology
University of Melbourne, Australia

Dr. Joseph W. Burnett, M.D.
Professor and Chair
Department of Dermatology
University of Maryland School of Medicine

J. H., whose professional ethics guided his decision
to remain anonymous

"The prince of darkness is a gentleman;"
—William Shakespeare,
King Lear, Act III, Scene iv

PROLOGUE

AFTER CREATING THE HEAVENS and the earth, God produced, in his own image, the first man, and named him Adam. He then commanded all the legions of Heaven, the Angels and Archangels, to bow before Adam and pay him homage and respect, for God was to give Adam control over all the earth and its creatures. But Lucifer, the most beautiful angel of all, became jealous and refused to bow before Adam. He gathered others around him who felt as he did, and they formed a massive army rebelling against the Creator. A vicious battle raged between God's angels and those who had turned their backs on Him. So much blood was shed that it formed two mighty rivers flowing across the scorching desert. In the end, the great warrior, Michael the Archangel, along with the Host of Heaven, defeated Lucifer and drove him and his rebels out of paradise.

The Fallen Angels, Nephilim as they were called in the Bible, were forbidden to ever enter heaven again. So they descended to the Earth and furtively walked among men. Down through the ages, their hatred grew, and Lucifer vowed that someday he would have his revenge.

But there was one among them who repented and secretly sought the Creator's forgiveness. His name was Furmiel, Angel of the 11th Hour. For his remorse, God agreed to give him mortality and let him live the rest of his existence as a man. Since Furmiel's spirit could never return to Heaven, God allowed him a daughter who would be taken at birth to assume her father's place among the Angels. But because God sensed that the time of Lucifer's revenge was at hand, he permitted Furmiel's wife to give birth to twins, the second daughter to live upon the Earth. She grew to adulthood unaware that the blood of the Nephilim coursed through her veins.

And because of that bloodline, she was destined to be called upon.

ABANDONED

"Get out!" The Iraqi driver's thin, high-pitched voice filled the car. Sand and dust spewed up as the vehicle skidded to a stop.

Jarred awake, Cotten Stone sat upright. "What?" She tried to focus in the gathering twilight.

"Out! I drive no American."

The radio blared the frantic-paced voice of an Iraqi announcer.

"What is it?" she asked. "What's wrong?"

The driver threw open his door and ran to the rear of the car.

Cotten tugged the rusty door handle until it finally gave with a squeak. "Hey, what are you doing?" she called, jumping out.

He opened the trunk and tossed her two bags onto the shoulder of the highway.

"You can't leave me here," she said, coming around to the back of the car. "This is the middle of the damn desert."

The driver cocked his head toward the voice on the radio.

She picked up the duffle bag that held her videotapes and chucked it back into the trunk. "Listen, I gave you all the cash I have.

1

I don't have any more." She turned her pocket inside out. It was just a little lie. She had squirreled away close to two hundred dollars and stuffed it inside an empty film container. Her emergency stash. "Do you understand? See, no more money. I paid you to take me to the border."

The driver jabbed her shoulder with a stiff forefinger. "End of ride for American." He yanked the bag out again and slammed it into her chest, sending her stumbling backward. Then he was around the car and in the driver's seat, grinding the gears and spinning the old Fiat around.

"I don't believe this," she said. Cotten dropped the bag on the ground beside her other one and threaded a loose strand of tea-colored hair behind her ear, watching the taillights fade.

The soft whisper of the desert wind carried the first chill of the evening as the January sky turned from rose to indigo. Cotten pulled the hooded parka from her carryall and slipped it on, feeling the cold already creeping through her.

She jogged in place, hands stuffed deep in her pockets. Darkness, thick as Iraqi crude, poured over the desert. Someone was bound to come along—had to come along, she thought.

Ten minutes passed with no sign of another vehicle. Finally, she grabbed the handles of her two carryalls and started walking. Gravel and sand crunched like glass chips under her field boots. She glanced behind, wishing for the glow of headlights, but there was only dark, barren desert.

"I should have known better than to trust that guy." Her voice cracked from the dryness. Whatever he'd heard on the radio must have spooked the shit out of him. Cotten knew U.S. forces were gearing up for an invasion. The rumors had been flying around the foreign press corps. for weeks as the war drums grew louder in Washington and London. It was no secret that there were already small insertion teams of American and British forces in the country. The invasion might still be months away, but it was hard to hide the buildup of forces in the Arab countries bordering Iraq to the south. The local Arab news buzzed with sightings of Special Forces and Army Rangers appearing and disappearing in the middle of the night. There were even strategic flyovers of fighters, Predator drones, and high altitude recon aircraft testing the vulnerabilities of the Iraqi missile and radar installations.

Cotten hoisted the strap higher on her shoulder. "It's your own fault," she said. "You're so damn headstrong."

A few weeks ago she had stood in the office of SNN's news director, Ted Casselman, and begged for the assignment to cover the effects of economic sanctions on the women and children of Iraq. It was an important story, she thought, and she didn't care how unstable the region was. Americans needed to see what sanctions did to innocents. And, she told Casselman, if the U.S. had plans to attack Iraq, she wanted to be there, right smack in the center of the action.

Cotten didn't mention that she also needed to put some distance between her and Thornton Graham. She didn't tell Casselman because she knew she would probably fall apart if she had to explain. The emotional wound was still too raw. Her request to do the story made perfect sense as it was—an eager, hungry reporter—and she wanted an assignment that would make world headlines.

The Satellite News Network didn't send rookies on assignments in such volatile locations, Casselman told her repeatedly. Yes, he conceded, she had talent and promise. Yes, he felt she could manage the pressure. And yes, he agreed that a Middle East assignment right now was a perfect opportunity to launch a successful career. However, not only was she a rookie, she was a woman, and a woman in Iraq in the current conditions was out of the question. Once the war started, the only journalists would be those chosen in advance by the military and embedded with the troops. And they would only be male. The rules were set, and the answer was no.

She became incensed and began a tirade about the unfairness of it all.

Casselman cut her off with another firm, "No."

After she calmed down, Cotten finally got him to agree to let her tag along with a group of reporters as far as the Turkish border. From there she could cover the plight of any refugees fleeing north once the conflict began.

He was furious when he learned she went on to Baghdad.

Then his call came this morning ordering her to leave. "Things are going to get dicey. Get your sweet ass out of there any way you can. And I want to see you as soon as you get back. Clear?"

She tried to reason with him and buy more time, but he hung up before she could make her case.

When she got home he was going to *I-told-you-so, I-should-fire-you* her to death. That was if she got home. Cotten shivered. She was stranded and freezing in the middle of the Iraqi desert.

* * *

Charles Sinclair stared out his office window at the sprawling campus surrounding the BioGentec laboratories near the University of New Orleans. The blue of Lake Pontchartrain lay beyond. He watched the small army of groundskeepers with their John Deere mowers and golf cart utility vehicles moving across the lawn and among the gardens— manicured and in perfect order. He liked perfect order.

The phone on his desk chirped, and he jumped, spilling a few drops of the chicory coffee onto the Persian rug.

"Yes?"

"Dr. Sinclair, you have an international call on line eight," his secretary said.

Sinclair punched the blinking button. He wouldn't take this call on the speakerphone. "This is Sinclair." The hiss of the connection annoyed him as he pressed the receiver firmly to his ear.

"We uncovered the entrance to the crypt two days ago," the man on the other end said. "Late this afternoon, it was opened."

Sinclair's knuckles whitened as he clutched the phone. "Ahmed, I hope you have good news." He paced.

"I do. Everything is just as Archer predicted."

"What did you find?"

"Many artifacts with the bones," Ahmed continued. "Armor, religious trinkets, some scrolls, and a box."

Adrenaline streaked through Sinclair's body making his fingertips tingle. "What does the box look like?"

"Black, no markings, about fifteen centimeters square."

Perspiration softened the starch in the white collar of Sinclair's Armani shirt. Static filled the pause before he spoke again. "And its contents?"

"I do not know."

"What do you mean? You were there, weren't you?"

"Archer did not open it. He and the others are packing to leave as we speak. We must abandon the site—the area is becoming too dangerous. Everyone is nervous. There is no time to examine—"

"No!" Sinclair pinched the bridge of his nose. "You go back immediately and get the box. Have Archer show you how to open it. Call me as soon as you confirm what's inside and you have it securely in your possession. Do you understand?"

"Yes." Ahmed's voice sank into the static.

"Ahmed," he said, keeping his voice low and controlled, "it is imperative that you complete your assignment. I cannot stress that enough."

"I understand."

Sinclair hung up the phone and stared at the receiver. The Arab could not even begin to understand.

THE CRYPT

SUDDENLY, THE SOUND OF an approaching vehicle caught Cotten's attention. Headlights danced in the distance along the uneven highway. At last, she thought. But what if it was Iraqi soldiers? She backed onto the sandy shoulder, her heart thumping up into her throat. Finally, when it was close enough, she guessed from the lights on the cab and trailer that it was a fuel tanker. She took a few steps forward, waving her arms, but the vehicle didn't slow. Shielding her eyes from the sand and gravel thrown up as the truck roared past, Cotten watched it disappear as quickly as it had appeared.

It probably wasn't wise to hail a ride anyway. No telling what frame of mind any Iraqi would be in at this point. She'd be safer keeping out of sight and making as much distance as possible before daylight.

After an hour of walking, Cotten plopped her bags down and sat on one. Her arms ached from the weight of the carryalls, and she shuddered as the cold penetrated her heavy parka. When she got back to the States, she was going to Florida for a long overdue thawing out. That was a promise.

Cotten emptied one of the bags, taking out anything she could leave behind. As she sorted through her belongings, she wondered if coming to Iraq had been smart. Maybe she'd made a stupid decision. She hadn't stopped to analyze everything, and then when Casselman protested, she got one of those dog-with-a-bone attitudes. There were other assignments she could have taken—ones of equal importance, ones that would have distanced her from Thornton.

"Damn, damn, damn," she said as she retrieved only the essentials: wallet, passport, and press credentials along with her still camera, lenses, film, and the plastic film container that hid her emergency money. She stuffed them in the other bag with the videocassettes. After taking one last look over her shoulder at the small pile of belongings left behind, she trudged on.

The moon rose and painted the desert with enough light to keep her from losing sight of the road. She wished for her sofa and comforter, a hot cup of Starbucks or better yet, a smooth Absolut over ice.

Suddenly, she stopped and blinked, making sure what she saw was not a mirage. There were lights in the distance. Not from vehicles, but from some kind of settlement or camp with electricity. She set the bag down and rubbed her shoulder and arm to get the circulation back. Taking out her camera, she attached the telephoto lens and brought the lights into focus. If it was an encampment of the Republican Guard or even the Iraqi regulars, an American woman traveling alone would stand little chance. Some of her colleagues in Baghdad had told her stories of the brutality, rapes . . . men who behaved like animals, like feral dogs.

She panned across the site. There were no obvious weapons, army vehicles, or anything that resembled a military installation. It looked more like an excavation site. Buckets, temporary tents, tables, spoil piles. An archaeological dig? Cotten guessed she was somewhere near one of the ancient Assyrian ruins scattered throughout the region.

Several old trucks were grouped near a crumbling stone structure. A handful of men moved in a flurry of activity.

This might be her opportunity to catch a safe ride to the border, she thought. She hesitated, wondering if she should take the chance. Finally she stowed the camera and headed for the lights.

Near the site, she saw men scrambling about, loading equipment and crates onto the trucks. The sporadic confrontations between the Iraqi military and the increasingly brazen, U.S.-backed Kurdish rebels had probably made the area become too dangerous for an archaeological dig.

She strained to hear their voices. Turkish! Not Iraqi. Relieved, Cotten entered the camp and approached one of the men. "Excuse me," she said.

He wore a dark shirt ringed with sweat under the arms. The stench from his body was sharp in the cold air. He glared at her for a moment as if wondering where she came from. "No English," he said, taking a crate from a wheelbarrow and throwing it onto the bed of the truck. If she hadn't leaned back, he would have swiped her with it.

Cotten tried to stop another man who sidestepped her and gave her an annoyed glance.

Someone tapped her on the shoulder, and she spun around. A short, stumpy man stood close.

"American?" he asked.

"Yes."

"Turk," he said, and smiled, revealing a mouth filled with crooked brown teeth beneath a mustache that hung over his lip like an awning.

"I need a ride," she said, pointing north.

He twitched his head toward the ruins. "Go see Dr. Archer, Gabriel Archer."

Someone shouted and, with a polite nod, the Turk hurried away.

A small group boarded one of the trucks. The engine coughed to life, and the truck pulled onto the road. There were still two trucks left, but they were quickly being loaded. Not much time to find this Dr. Archer and beg for a lift.

In the moonlight, she located the entrance to the stone structure. Wooden scaffolding shored up the walls and, as she entered, she ducked beneath a low archway. Just ahead, a string of bare lightbulbs dangled over the entrance and along a passageway beyond. She followed the passage until it ended at a set of steps leading underground. Buckets of dirt were stacked nearby, waiting to be hauled outside and emptied into screens. A gas generator rattled, powering the string of lights running into the hole. She leaned over the head of the steps and called out. "Hello . . . Archer?" There was no response. "Dr. Archer?" she called louder.

In the distance she heard the throaty diesel of another truck start up and pull out. Only one left.

Cotten started down the stairs. The icy air smelled old like a mausoleum. She'd only been in one, but that distinct mustiness, the dank odor of soil and rock, couldn't be forgotten. Even though she'd been a child at the time, she remembered her father's funeral: the sickeningly sweet scent of flowers, the strange acidic odor of chemicals, and the cold, stony smell of the burial vault.

The steps ended in a small room. She crossed it and peered through a short tunnel leading into an expansive chamber. There she saw two men. One was slightly hunched over and gray-haired, dressed in a dusty khaki shirt and faded jeans. He must be Archer, she thought, because the other man had the swarthy skin and garb of an Arab.

She squeezed through the narrow shaft.

Archer stood next to what Cotten thought was a crypt in the far wall of the chamber. She caught a glimpse of brown bones and a glint of metal. He held open a small box at which both men stared intently.

Cotten opened her mouth to call out.

Suddenly, the Arab pulled a gun from under his robe. Cotten froze as the man pointed the pistol at Archer. "Give it to me!" he demanded.

Archer closed the lid and took a step backward, keeping a firm grip on the box. His eyes widened, his face turned skeleton white. "You're one of them."

Cotten pressed back against a loose support timber. It shifted, and a small avalanche of pebbles and sand spilled to the ground.

The men turned at the sound and for an instant looked at her.

Archer dropped the box and grappled for the gun. He slammed into the man, and they tumbled to the dirt floor.

The Arab shoved the gun barrel against the archaeologist's head. Archer thrust up an elbow, redirecting the aim of the weapon just as it discharged. The blast was deafening in the hard-walled chamber.

The Arab straddled Archer, forcing the gun into the old man's cheekbone. With a loud grunt, Archer kicked his knee up, driving the Arab forward and ramming his head into the wall. Dazed, the man let up for an instant, and Archer scrambled out from under him. The Arab lifted the pistol, took aim, and Archer dove for it, crashing down hard on his opponent.

The gun wedged between them.

A second shot pealed, but their bodies muffled this one.

Cotten held her breath as both men lay motionless. The chamber fell silent except for the sound of her blood pulsing in her ears and the thudding of her heart against her ribs.

Then, finally, Archer moved, slowly rolling off the Arab. A red blotch stained the front of his shirt. More blood seeped from the Arab's chest.

Archer struggled to his feet and stood over the dead man. His chest heaved and labored as he wiped his face on his sleeve. He picked up the box, his tree-knot knuckles blanching as he clutched it.

He coughed and straightened, eyes fixing on Cotten. He squinted, staggering a few steps before slumping to the ground. "My heart," he said, grabbing his chest.

Cotten dropped her bag and moved cautiously, checking behind her. She stared at the body of the Arab as she stepped past him.

"What can I do?" she asked, kneeling next to Archer. "I'll go get help."

"No." Archer reached for her hand. A cough wracked him, and Cotten elevated his head in her lap.

"The box," he said. "Take it." He looked over at the dead man. "They will stop at nothing now."

"Who? What do you mean?"

His face twisted with a wave of pain. Hands shaking, he pushed the box toward her. His skin paled, his lips darkened. "You must not let them have it."

"What is this?" she asked.

His voice was weak, not much more than a whisper. "Twenty-six, twenty-seven, twenty-eight, Matthew."

"I don't understand."

He didn't answer, appearing to stare straight through her. Then Archer motioned her closer, and she leaned in to hear as he whispered.

She shook her head in confusion. "Please, you aren't making any sense. You want me to stop the sun . . . the dawn?"

He seemed to rally, lifting his head, his voice suddenly strong as he spoke. "*Geh el crip.*"

Cotten reeled. He couldn't have said what she thought she heard. It was impossible. Impossible. Archer had spoken a language she hadn't heard since she was a child. Only one other person had ever spoken to her in that language—her twin sister.

Her *dead* twin sister.

HOMECOMING

"How could you know those words?" Cotten asked, her voice shaky.

But Archer's eyes were already closed. His grip loosened, and his head slowly fell back, chest still.

Archer was dead.

The string of bulbs blinked, and then went dark. The generator must have run out of fuel, she guessed. Carefully, she moved Archer's head from her lap. She couldn't help him now, and with only one truck left, there was no time to waste.

Afraid she might trip over debris, she tucked the box under her arm and crawled through the blackness in what she hoped was the direction of the tunnel. Suddenly, the earth shook and the walls quaked. Cotten curled over her knees and shielded her head, waiting for the ceiling to collapse. Dust and sand filtered down, collecting in her hair and on the backs of her hands. Small stones pummeled her back. Had bombs dropped somewhere close?

The rumble subsided, and she continued crawling. Her bag wasn't that far away, but moving in the pitch-black room was slow going. As her hand touched the floor, she recoiled.

The Arab's blood.

Cotten cringed and wiped the blood off her hand on the dead man's pants leg. When she reached the wall she felt her way to the tunnel opening where she had left her bag. Her fingers groped through the nylon carryall until she found her penlight.

The bulb flickered when she twisted the tip and then died. "Come on!" she said, shaking it. It glowed again, but the light was little better than none at all.

Holding the penlight in her mouth, Cotten dumped some of the tapes and other articles onto the dirt floor and placed Archer's box inside the bag. As she repacked, the light died again. She swept her hand across the floor for anything she might have missed.

A second rumble rocked the chamber, followed by a third and a fourth. It was a distinct clap, one she recognized from when she'd done a piece on high tech Air Force ordinance: sonic booms from fighters breaking the sound barrier.

"Archer." A man called from the direction of the passage. "We can wait no longer." There was a pause. "Do you hear me, Archer? We go now!"

"Wait," Cotten cried, zipping up the bag and scrambling to her feet.

She stumbled through the dark until she finally reached the passageway. A truck engine growled to life and pulled onto the highway as she emerged from the ruins.

"Stop!" she yelled running toward it.

The Turk stood up in the back of the vehicle and waved Cotten on. When she was close enough, she swung her bag up. The Turk grabbed it, then reached out and yanked her up into the truck.

"You run fast," he said.

She gave a nervous laugh as she sank down, breathing hard.

"Where is Archer?" he asked, his voice faltering from the rough ride.

The canvas partially covering the sides of the stake body truck flapped, beating against the wood frame, and the motor grumbled, making it hard to hear.

"Dead. Heart attack." Cotten pointed to her chest.

The Turk shook his head and translated the news to the handful of men riding with them.

Jets roared in the darkness overhead and two pinpoints of orange light shot up along the horizon. She watched with dread, waiting for the missiles to find what she assumed were American fighters. But there were no impacts. The missiles drifted over the desert and burned out like shooting stars.

As the truck rolled north toward the Turkish border, Cotten crouched in a corner, her arms wrapped around her legs. She tried to make sense of what had happened back in the crypt—one man willing to murder a second for a box whose contents were unknown to her. Then the strange ramblings of a dying old man whom she would have thought delirious if not for one thing. He spoke to her in a language known only to Cotten and her twin sister—a sister who had died at birth.

* * *

Chaotic shouts jarred her awake. The Arabian sun, already high in the morning sky, blinded her as she sat up in the bed of the transport truck. Like swarming ants, the Turkish dig team clambered out the back. Cotten pulled herself up to look around.

Throngs of people lined the highway, marching across the rolling hills and out of the surrounding mountains. Refugees, she thought, fleeing before the war began. Women, clasping infants to their breasts and clinging to the hands of their other children, swept past the truck like the incoming tide. Cotten looked into their dazed faces. That was what Americans needed to see.

She grabbed her carryall and climbed down to the asphalt. Coming around the side of the truck, she saw more vehicles lined up, their engines silent, their beds and cabs empty. She realized they had finally reached the Turkish border, probably near Zakhu. A large Constantine wire fence stretched across the terrain, and the highway passed through a narrow checkpoint with barriers of tanks and armored personnel carriers. Hundreds of Turkish soldiers, all holding automatic weapons, herded the refugees into a bottleneck for quick inspections and document checks before letting them through.

Cotten hugged her carryall to her chest as she let the tide steer her closer to the checkpoint. When there were only a few ahead of her, she dug into her bag and pulled out her passport and press credentials.

"American press," she shouted, holding the documents up. "American press." As soon as she could get through the checkpoint, she'd stop and take some still shots of this scene. Black and white—powerful close-ups of faces, the wide dark eyes of the children, of mother's hands holding smaller hands. She could already envision them intercut into her video edit. No music, no voiceover. Just the stark frozen faces of despair and fear. It would be a brilliant, moving ending. No one would be able to watch and not get chills.

A young Turkish soldier saw her and waved his arm. "Come on, American. This way." He grabbed her by the shoulder and shoved her across the border into Turkey.

"Thank you," she said, but he was already inspecting the documents of the next in line.

Suddenly, another soldier took hold of her arm and pulled her aside.

"Papers!" said the Turkish officer.

"I'm an American," Cotten said, staring up into his cold eyes and his hard expression. "I just showed my papers to the soldier at the checkpoint."

"And now you will show them to me."

Cotten handed him her passport and press ID. "I work for the American news network SNN."

He opened her passport and compared the photo to the one on her press ID. "This way," he said, guiding her toward a truck a few yards away.

"Is there some kind of problem? I just finished an assignment in Baghdad, and I'm on my way back to New York. You have no—"

The tailgate of the large transport was down, and the officer pointed to it. "Place your bag there."

She had to remain calm. This was just a routine inspection. They had no reason to suspect she was bringing anything illegal into the country.

"Open it," the officer said, motioning to her carryall.

Cotten unzipped the top and spread the nylon open. Even through the pile of videos on top she could see a corner of Archer's box.

"What's on these tapes?"

"My assignment. It's footage of children and the elderly."

"Children," he said, inspecting a tape and its label. "How do I know you're not lying?"

Cotten wiped her forehead on her sleeve. "You'll just have to take my word for it."

He moved the tapes aside. "Where's your video camera?"

"I'm the reporter," she said. "My cameraman is still in Iraq."

He continued to rummage through the bag. "And this?" he said, lifting Archer's box out of the bag.

"A weight."

"For what?"

"To help hold down and balance my tripod—for my still camera."

"And where is your tripod?"

"I had to leave it behind."

"But you brought this block of wood?"

"It was already in the bag when I grabbed it to leave. I was in a hurry."

He turned the box over, shook it, then placed it back in the bag, and took out her SLR camera.

A rush of relief flooded her.

"Nikon," he said, examining it. "Very nice."

"Yes, it is," she said, growing impatient. "Can I go now?"

"Depends."

"On what?"

"On what happens to this camera."

"That's a seven hundred—"

"Very, very nice," he said, caressing it.

Cotten reached for the camera, but he jerked it away.

"You are anxious to return to America, yes?" he said, removing the lens cap. He looked through the viewfinder. "We have already detained several Americans for questioning. That is our policy." He panned to his left and then stopped. "Do I need to detain you?"

Cotten reluctantly exhaled. "No."

He rotated the Nikon in his hands admiring it, then strung the strap over his head.

Cotten eyed her camera, wanting to rip it off his neck, but decided that under the circumstances she had no choice but to sacrifice it.

Shouts erupted from the direction of the checkpoint. "Fucking fools," he said. He shoved her passport and ID back at her. "Go home, American." He turned and headed toward the disturbance—the Nikon swinging from his neck.

Cotten zipped her bag closed, shoved her identification back in her coat, and walked on.

Beyond the military vehicles was a sea of cars, trucks, vans, and buses lining the shoulders of the highway. People stood on the roofs and hoods, desperately searching for their relatives among the immigrants pouring past. Cotten continued along the highway looking for a taxi or commercial bus.

Suddenly, she heard a loud, shrieking whistle. To her right, a man waved wildly at her from a bus window. It was the Turk from the dig team.

"We go to Ankara, lady," he yelled. "Hurry."

I think I love this man, Cotten thought, sprinting to the bus. Digging into her bag, she retrieved her reserve cash and bought a ticket from the driver. Once aboard, she maneuvered down the crowded aisle and placed her hand on her new friend's shoulder, thanking him as she passed his seat. She squeezed into a narrow spot in the last row of seats. Cotten held her bag close, wondering what it was she had just smuggled out of Iraq. She was anxious to be alone with Archer's box so she could examine it.

In a moment the old bus vibrated and shook, then pulled onto the highway. She took a quick glance out the back window. The tide of refugees had swelled to a flood.

* * *

The long journey across Turkey was uncomfortable. With so many people crammed into the bus, Cotten got a good dose of all the odors the human body could produce. She'd heard once that of all the animals, humans smelled the worst. That was supposed to be an advantage, repelling predators. Now she was sure the story was true. Not only were there the oppressive odors, but the constant joggling of the ride kept her from sleep. When they finally arrived in Ankara, she was starving and felt grimier than she ever had in her life.

After using her credit card to buy the Turk and his friends a meal at a small café near the bus terminal, she gave him a firm handshake before taking a taxi to the Esenboga Airport. There, she booked a flight to Heathrow with a connection to JFK.

As much as she preferred keeping the carryall with her, she decided on checking it so she wouldn't have to explain the wooden box at the Turkish airport security checkpoint. The bag had a better chance of making it through security without incident if she didn't carry it on. All she could do was pray that Archer's box didn't contain explosives or other materials that would set off any alarms.

Cotten sponged off in the airport ladies room but still felt self-conscious when she boarded and sat next to a young woman in a crisp blue oxford cloth shirt and creased pants. The woman made a point of leaning away from Cotten.

Gold and purple twilight stretched across the horizon as she wrapped herself in the airline blanket. Wondering what secret lay within her carryall deep in the plane's cargo hold, she slid the window shade down, closed her eyes, and drifted into a troubled sleep.

* * *

Landing in the U.K., Cotten retrieved her bag from the carousel, quickly checking to make sure the box was still safely inside. A ribbon of arriving passengers made their way into British Immigration. Cotten dug her nails into the palm of her hand as she gripped her bag.

Thankfully, the attendant didn't seem to note her nervousness when he stamped her passport. She moved on to Customs.

"Do you have anything to declare?" the agent asked as she placed the bag on the table.

"No." Her stomach drew into a knot while the man studied her face.

After a pause, he said, "Welcome to the United Kingdom, Ms. Stone," and motioned her on.

Cotten tried to swallow, but her mouth was dry. She smiled at him, gathered the carryall, and moved on. Maybe she could get away with taking the bag onto the New York flight with her rather than checking it. She didn't like it being out of her sight. And it had made it through the first leg home without arousing any safety concerns.

Home. God, it would be good to be home again, she thought, filing through the gate and onto the 747.

It was cloudy, and rain misted on the window as the airplane rose into the sky. She heard the thump of the wheels retracting into their wells. Seven more hours.

As soon as the fasten-seat-belt light went off, Cotten retrieved her carryall from the overhead compartment, took it into one of the restrooms in the back of the 747, and locked the door. She sat on the closed toilet lid and opened the bag. Moving the videotapes aside, she took out the box.

From what she could tell it was made of wood; its color was a dull black—worn and old—a few fresh scratches. She tried to open it but found no lid. Strange, she thought, there didn't appear to be a top or a bottom, no hinges or seams. But Archer had opened it and looked inside. She remembered the intensity of his gaze. She shook the box, but it made no sound. How had he opened something that was as featureless as a solid block of wood? What was so important about this box that he would demand she take it? Why did the Arab try to kill for it? But the thing that haunted her the most were Archer's words. *Geh el crip.*

She finally packed the box back in the bag, returned to her seat, and stowed it in the overhead.

* * *

Arriving at JFK, Cotten quickly passed through Customs and Immigration. As she made her way into the crowded terminal, she stopped at an ATM for cash and then walked through the automatic doors onto the sidewalk. The bitter New York winter slapped her face. This time of year the northeast had no redeeming qualities, she thought. She was glad she had been away for the holidays, away from the snow and the painful end of her relationship with Thornton Graham. Cotten hailed a taxi and climbed into the rear of the cab, the carryall snug in her lap. She gave her midtown apartment building address to the driver before laying her head on the back of the seat.

She kept recalling the disturbing dreams she'd had on the flight. She didn't seem to be able to shake them—dreams filled with the smell of the dank ancient chamber, the deafening blast of the gunshot, the still-warm Arab's blood, Archer's pallid skin and bluing lips, his last effort to raise his head, his breath on her ear as he whispered *Geh el crip*—you are the only one. It was impossible for him to have spoken to her using those words. Impossible. And yet he did.

Through the car's dirty windows she watched the distorted skyline drift into view.

* * *

As soon as she was in her apartment, she left a message on Ted Casselman's answering machine letting him know she had made it back

23

safely. She had called him from Ankara and again from the U.K. But he still insisted on hearing from her the moment she arrived home. Father figure, mentor, friend—he was mad at her for taking such risk and would worry about her until she set foot on U.S. soil.

Fresh from a steaming, thirty-minute shower, Cotten pushed down on the handles of the corkscrew, and the cork popped out of the bottle of chardonnay. She filled her glass. No Absolut tonight. Wine always made her sleepy, and sleep was what she needed most.

Archer's box rested in the center of her kitchen table. She studied it while she sat in the dinette chair cradling the glass of wine between her palms. There were no marks, no joints, and no hinges. If there were seams, they were somehow concealed in the wood grain.

She rubbed her neck. The muscles ached, but the shower had helped ease the tension. The hot water had been delicious, pulsing on her neck and back. Blessedly, the coconut scent of the shampoo helped wash away the odors that seemed to have collected and hung on somewhere in her nose and sinuses. Cotten sipped the chardonnay, then unclipped the barrette and let her damp hair tumble down the back of the chenille bathrobe.

After a few minutes, she got up and wandered into the living room. The pile of accumulated mail lay on the desk where her landlord had left it. "Bills and junk mail," she mumbled, about to rake it all in the desk drawer. There, partially hidden under some even older mail was a silver-framed picture of Thornton Graham. She had shoved it in the drawer the day before she left for Iraq. Becoming involved with him was a mistake. She brushed the envelopes aside and uncovered his face.

Thornton Graham was the SNN news anchor seen across the country during the dinner hour. Handsome, confident, experienced —and married. When she got her first assignment with the network, he had been the one who took special notice of her. Between his charisma, handsome looks, and her admiration for him, she was completely overwhelmed.

Cotten remembered the first time she met Thornton—it was during the Christmas holidays last year. She usually walked to work, but that day she'd taken a cab because she was bringing in office decorations. In order to avoid more than one trip to the taxi, she carried two boxes, slung her satchel over her arm, and gripped a Ziploc bag of Dutch chocolate that she wanted to put in a bowl on her desk. She made it through the front doors with the help of the office-building doorman, and all the way to the elevators. But stepping into the elevator, she bumped the door just enough to make her satchel strap slide down her arm. Someone behind her lifted the strap and put it back on her shoulder. She turned to say thanks, noticing that the hand lingered, and stared into the face of SNN's senior correspondent, Thornton Graham. She managed the thank you, but her voice caught on the word, *you*, coming out garbled. Thornton seemed flattered with her enchantment and flashed his famous smile. She turned, trying to appear nonchalant and not so obviously spellbound—she couldn't help but look at his reflection in the brass elevator doors. But when she did, she was embarrassed to find him watching her. The ride up seemed to take forever. When she got off the elevator, he did, too. Thornton took the boxes and walked her to her office. Before leaving he asked her to join him for lunch later. That was the beginning of what became an almost year-long fiery, physical relationship. Now it was over—over and done.

The wine warmed Cotten as she drained the glass. Her neck muscles relaxed, and she felt the faint buzz of the alcohol. She pushed the stack of letters into the drawer, covering Thornton's face, and strolled back into the kitchen. Glancing at Archer's box she decided that, as a precaution, she needed to put it in a safe place until she figured out what to do with it.

Cotten rinsed her glass. As she dried it, she tilted her head and looked at the teapot sitting on the stove. She had an idea and moved the pot onto the counter, then lifted the range lid.

She took a quick look at the box, then at the space under the lid. Carefully, she placed the box between the heating elements then closed the range lid and heard it click into position. Good a place as any, she thought. She returned the teapot, turned out the lights, and went to bed.

For the first time in years, she dreamed of being a child again, playing on her family's farm. But mostly, she dreamed of her twin sister.

THE TAPE

In the morning, Cotten rummaged through her cosmetics drawer. No mascara. There were several bottles of foundation and an unused blush. Eye shadows, eyeliners, and lipsticks, but no mascara. She'd taken her only tube with her to Iraq and left it in the desert. She examined her face in the mirror. Her wheat-brown eyes appeared neglected. She swept back that maverick wisp of hair that always seemed to stray and gave a last look at her reflection. For an instant, she glimpsed her mother's face in her own. Her fingertips touched the skin beneath her eyes and around her mouth. Memories of the life she'd left behind in Kentucky unsettled her. She'd seen deep lines and dark circles in the faces of the women—women not much older than she was now. Twenty-seven was close to thirty, and thirty was not far from . . .

Her mother had called her fanciful, said she was a dreamer. It was true. And on the wings of those dreams she'd fled a life where women grew old too soon, gave up hope too soon . . . and died too soon.

"I'm sorry, Mamma," she whispered.

Cotten dabbed perfume behind each ear and closed the cosmetics drawer. In the kitchen, she munched on a granola bar and downed a cup of instant coffee. While she ate, she gazed at the stove. It looked normal enough. Just for good measure she pulled a frying pan from the cabinet and placed it on the unit next to the teapot.

Perfect.

She headed along the ten blocks from her apartment to SNN headquarters. It was cold, but Cotten paid little attention. She was anxious to get the answer to some nagging questions. Suddenly, her cell phone vibrated.

"Hello," she said, trying to dodge others on the crowded sidewalk.

"Hey, baby. You're back!"

"Nessi!" Cotten smiled, glad to hear her friend's voice.

"How was it? Looks like things are really heating up over there."

"You won't believe the shit I've been through the last couple of days." She began filling in her friend but deliberately left out the part where Archer had begged her to take the box, had gazed eerily at her as if he knew her, spoke to her in a language that didn't exist for anyone else on the planet but her. Nobody would understand. "Then I had to bribe my way across the Turkish border. I was jammed on a bus for a day with people who smelled like goats. And I think I illegally smuggled some kind of ancient artifact out of the Middle East into the U.S." She caught a glimpse of the *New York Times* headline as she passed a newsstand: MILITARY BUILDUP ACCELERATES. "Other than that, it was uneventful. You miss me?"

"Always." Vanessa Perez said. "I was worried about you. Is your boss pissed?"

"I think he had to double up on his blood pressure medication. I'm heading in to work now. Got a meeting with him at nine thirty, and my edit is at ten."

"What about the *Thorn* in your side?"

"Nessi, lighten up."

"Is he going to be there?"

"I guess. Maybe I'll luck out, and he'll be off on assignment some-where."

"You better start thinking about what you're going to say when you see him."

"I'm over it."

"Yeah, I've heard that before."

Cotten's stomach sank. Nessi *had* heard that before—more than once. She'd always meant it, wanted to believe she was finished with him. But this time had to be different. He was a bad road to travel, painful, and a dead end. She had to convince herself that she had put Thornton behind her—packed that bag and shipped it off to her past.

"You have a shoot today?" Cotten asked.

"South Beach—it's for Hawaiian Tropic—you'll soon see me on billboards flashing a little *T* 'n'*A* in a skimpy bikini."

Cotten laughed. "Knock 'em dead."

"I always do." There was an uneasy pause. Then Vanessa said, "Don't give in to him."

"Give me a little credit." Cotten felt the blast of warm air as she passed through the revolving doors into SNN's headquarters.

"Hey, that's what friends are for." Vanessa half sang the Burt Bacharach lyric. It was their personal mantra.

"It's a good thing you're beautiful, 'cause you sure can't sing," Cotten said with a chuckle.

"I love you, too," Vanessa said, and hung up.

Cotten slipped the cell back in her overcoat pocket and stopped to watch the on-air monitor over the lobby security desk—sound bites from the President's State of the Union address.

She signed in at the security desk and clipped on her identifica-tion badge.

The network's studios, production, audio, duplication, satellite linking and transmission, and engineering took up the first seven floors. Cotten got off on the eighth where SNN had its video edit suites and archives.

"Cotten."

It was Thornton Graham.

She forced a smile and a nod. Shit, why did she have to run into him first thing?

"It's so good to . . . you feeling okay?" he asked. "You don't look—"

"I'm fine. I didn't have any mascara, that's all."

He kissed her cheek, and she smelled his cologne, flooding her head with vivid memories.

"Got a minute?" He motioned toward his office.

"I'm really in a rush."

"Your edit isn't for an hour—I checked."

"I've got to do some research first."

"I've missed you," he said in almost a whisper, touching her arm, moving closer.

There was a heavy silence.

"Thornton . . ." She shook her head, not wanting to look him in the eyes. "Please, it's over."

"No, it's not," he said. "I love you."

"It wasn't love," she whispered. "You know that."

"Cotten, I do love you."

"I've got to go." She headed down the corridor.

"Cotten," he called after her, but she didn't turn around.

She hadn't cried this time—that was a good sign. She'd made the right decision, she thought, and she was going to get through this. If she just didn't have to see him—touch him.

Inside the video archives department, Cotten sat at a computer terminal, entered her security password, and initiated the search function. Then she typed *Archer, Gabriel.* Within seconds, the screen displayed two references. She selected both, chose the retrieve command, and turned to watch through the glass wall. One of the huge carousels filled with videocassettes revolved. A robotic arm zoomed around it, scanning bar codes, then grabbed a cassette, moved laterally to one of the players, and inserted the tape. A video window appeared on Cotten's terminal, and sound came from a small set of speakers mounted on each side of the screen. The images blurred past in high speed as the machine used the timecode on the tape to locate the correct segment. There was a short pause, and then the picture and sound came up.

The first image was an electronic slate: *Ark Search, Archer interview.* A short piece followed from a TV magazine program mentioning Gabriel Archer, whom Cotten learned was a biblical archaeologist and part of the team searching for the remains of Noah's Ark. Nothing else of apparent significance. And nothing to give her a clue how he knew to speak to her in that language. After all, wasn't it just a made-up language—what her mother likened to twin talk?

She stopped the tape and requested the second. This one was longer and featured Archer. The focus was an interview with him at his home in Oxford, England. Although the tape was only a few years old, Archer looked much younger, she thought . . . heavier, healthier, and jubilant. He held a small, round golden plate he had recently discovered on a dig in Jerusalem. Symbols covered the plate, and he claimed it dated to the Crusades. "The kingdom of heaven is like a treasure hidden in a field," Archer said. He quoted scripture many times during the interview. Caressing the plate like it was an infant, he said, "This will lead me to heaven's greatest treasure."

Next came an interview with a staff archaeologist at the Museum of Natural History in New York. The man smiled patronizingly, calling Archer a devotee to his own theories. "Sometimes," he said, "enthusiasm gets the best of the doctor. He's had many extravagant notions." The archaeologist did go on to credit Archer with several noteworthy discoveries, including his work on the search for Noah's Ark, but said his eccentricities diminished his credibility.

There were a few other interviews discussing Archer. One in particular caught Cotten's attention: Dr. John Tyler, a Catholic priest, biblical historian, and archaeologist, spoke kindly of Archer. Tyler had studied under Gabriel Archer and said the elderly archaeologist was dedicated to his work, mentioning that many of his discoveries had shed much needed light on biblical history.

Tyler appeared to be in his mid-thirties, tall with dark hair, and had the rugged face of someone who spent a lot of time outdoors. And he had great eyes, Cotten thought.

She rewound the tape and played Tyler's portion again. He was soft-spoken, but his words were confident, authoritative.

"He has many aspirations," Tyler said of Archer. "I wish him well."

Cotten scribbled down the name of the college where Tyler taught. He was right in New York and could be a good source of information. She thought about what Archer had whispered to her in the crypt and his notability to quote the Bible. Twenty-six, twenty-seven, twenty-eight, Matthew. He had to be referring to a passage in the Bible. She glanced at her watch—about fifteen more minutes before her meeting with Ted Casselman.

Ending the archives search, Cotten headed back down the hall, sticking her head in one of the edit rooms. "Anybody got a Bible?"

"You get religion in the Middle East, Cotten?" the video editor said, looking at her over his shoulder.

"Try the nightstand in a hotel room," an assistant added.

She grinned. "Very funny. Come on, guys. Really, any idea where I can locate a Bible?"

"The religion correspondent," the editor said, and returned to his monitors.

"Right," she said, wondering why she hadn't thought of it. But then, religion was not something she spent a great deal of time thinking about. She checked her watch again as she headed to his office.

"Which version?" the correspondent's secretary asked.

"I don't know; isn't there a standard one?"

The secretary pointed to the door behind her and got up. Cotten followed.

Against one wall was a floor-to-ceiling bookcase. The secretary pulled a King James Version off the shelf. "Just put it back when you're done," she said before leaving.

"Thanks," Cotten said, not looking up. What had Archer said? Matthew? Matthew was in the New Testament, she knew that much. Matthew, Mark, Luke, and John. That was as far as she'd gotten in Sunday school.

"Twenty-six, twenty-seven, twenty eight," she said, flipping through the pages. Running her finger down each page, she stopped at the Gospel of St. Matthew, chapter 26, and read verses 27 and 28 aloud, "And He took the cup, and gave thanks, and gave it to them, saying, Drink ye all of it. For this is my blood of the New Testament, which is shed for many for the remission of sins."

"Jesus," she whispered, then realized the pun. Could all this have something to do with the cup from the Last Supper? Could that be what was in the box sitting under the hood of her Hotpoint stove? Archer said he was looking for heaven's greatest treasure. She blew out a breath at the thought that she could be on top of a huge story.

Pulling the slip of paper from her pocket, she picked up the phone on the desk and called information. After getting the number for the college where Dr. Tyler taught, she dialed it.

"Yes, I'm trying to locate a Reverend Dr. John Tyler. I understand he teaches there." She listened for a moment, and her face dropped. "Well, do you know where he's assigned now?" Another pause and she said, "Let me give you my number."

Cotten hung up, grabbed her things, and rushed to the office of Ted Casselman, SNN's news director. She knocked.

"Come in."

Casselman sat at the head of the conference table, a handful of folders spread before him. Two chairs away from the news director sat Thornton Graham. Thornton smiled warmly as Cotten moved across the room.

Ted Casselman looked up. He was a forty-two-year-old black man, medium build, manicured nails, with some early gray hair that flattered his deep skin tone.

"Well, you're one lucky lady," Casselman said, standing to kiss her on the cheek. "Try pulling a stunt like that again and I'll see to it that the only job you can get is reporting the weather on the local cable channel in Beaver Falls." He glanced at the clock on the wall. "And you're late."

"Forgive me, Ted," she said, putting on her best little-girl smile. "I had to make a quick trip to the archives."

"Oh? I thought you had all your research."

"Just a few loose ends."

"Sit and relax. We're almost done here." Casselman returned to his chair and opened one of the folders. He scanned the top sheet and said to Thornton, "What do you know about Robert Wingate?"

"Basic stuff," Thornton said. "Mostly from his press kit." He let his pencil bounce on its eraser. "He's a wealthy industrialist, new to the

34

political scene, and gaining a sizable following. He's based his platform on family values and high moral character. So far, he seems to have no blemishes—the perfect candidate." Thornton flipped to another page of his ever-present comp book. "Devoted family man and generous with his wealth. One of his pet projects is a national organization that sponsors youth ranches for urban delinquent kids. And it's not only troubled kids he works with. Wingate's been instrumental in getting quite a few chapters of DeMolay going in different areas of the country, especially in Florida, his home state. He's outspoken against child abuse and—"

"Hold on," Casselman interrupted. "What's DeMolay?"

Thornton looked up. "Kids' version of the Freemasons. It's an organization for boys between twelve and twenty-one."

"Anything else?" Casselman asked.

"Can't find a whole lot about him. Wingate popped up on the political scene from out of nowhere. Apparently, he has a substantial money machine behind him."

Ted Casselman scratched his chin. "Let's find out what makes Wingate so perfect. Put together a segment on him for Sunday night."

"I'll get my staff on it right away," Thornton said. He gathered his notes, stood, and came around the conference table to Cotten. "Stop by after your edit if you have a chance."

"I'll see," Cotten said, looking up at him.

"How's the footage look?" Casselman asked her as Thornton left the room.

"It's better than I ever expected. Believe me, Ted, international sanctions and embargos have taken a heavy toll on the Iraqi kids and elderly. It's going to be a gut-wrenching story. But it won't score too many points with the State Department now that they're about to start another war."

"Good, that almost guarantees higher ratings." He stood. "Come on, I'll walk with you to your edit." He put his arm around her shoulders, leading her to the door. "You gave me many a sleepless night, young lady. But you also showed spunk. A scrapper. I like that. Now, I want to see what I got for my extra gray hairs."

"You won't be disappointed, Ted." Cotten liked Casselman and respected him. She regretted making him worry so much about her. And he was the one who could boost her up two rungs at a time on the career ladder.

They entered Edit B. The room was dark except for the soft glow from the wall of monitors and banks of electronic controls.

"I made copies of the script and my notes," she said, handing Casselman and the editor a file folder each. "We can record a scratch track to edit to for now, and get a staff announcer in later." She smiled at the assistant editor. "We're going to need some cuts from the stock music library—lots of drama, dark, powerful stuff. Oh, and some ethnic cuts. Middle Eastern." Then Cotten unloaded the carryall bag. All the videocassettes were numbered, and she stacked them in order.

"Oh, shit," she said. She unstacked the tapes, reading every label again.

"What's wrong?" Casselman looked up from the script.

"I've . . ."

He laid the papers down. "Cotten?"

"You're going to have to start without me," she said.

TYLER

COTTEN THREW OPEN THE door to her apartment and ran to the bedroom. She remembered sitting on her bed last night, unpacking the carryall and taking out the box. That was the only time the missing videocassette could have fallen out. On her hands and knees she lifted the dust ruffle and looked under the bed.

Not there.

She sat up and combed her fingers through her hair, scanning the rest of the worn rug that covered most of her bedroom floor. She hadn't opened the carryall during the bus ride across Turkey, and it was checked from Ankara to London. And on the flight home she'd have seen the tape if it had fallen to the floor of the jet's cramped lavatory. That only left . . .

The crypt.

But she had been certain she'd gathered all her things, all the tapes, yet she had rushed to catch the truck . . . and it was pitch black.

"Just great," Cotten said. Not only were the tapes labeled, she was the principal reporter on every one. And how many times had she said her name and mentioned SNN? It wouldn't take a genius to connect the tape to her, and her to the box.

Maybe the Arab worked alone, just an antiquities thief. Maybe with the chaos of the military activity in the region, no one went looking for him or Archer. Maybe no one had found the tape because the dig site was abandoned.

Maybe.

She sat on the edge of the bed, head in her hands. If someone else wanted that box, they'd go looking for Archer's excavation, realize the artifact wasn't there—and know someone had taken it. Guess who? The girl on the videotape. She might as well have spray painted her name and address in big fat letters on the wall of the chamber.

The phone rang, and Cotten jumped. "Hello," she said. "Yes, that's right. I was trying to get in touch with Dr. John Tyler."

She listened for a moment, then reached in the nightstand and took out a pencil and pad. "I really appreciate you getting back to me." She wrote *St. Thomas College. White Plains, NY.* "Thanks," she said, and hung up.

White Plains was only about an hour north of the city. She'd find Tyler and see what he knew about Archer and his latest excavation.

Cotten went to the kitchen and moved the kettle and frying pan off the stove, lifted the range top, and stared at the box. Did it hold the Cup from the Last Supper—the Holy Grail? And why had Archer told her she was the only one who could stop the sun, the dawn?

Geh el crip. Geh el crip. You are the only one.

The words tolled inside her head as loud as any steeple bells. She had to find out everything about this Gabriel Archer.

* * *

38

The classic Greek architecture of St. Thomas College nestled snugly among oaks and sycamores. The day was cold and crisp, sunlight glaring off swatches of snow on the brown ground. A handful of students moved across the bare winter campus.

Cotten climbed the worn marble steps to the large wooden double doors. A bronze plaque read *Established, January 1922*. Inside, the room had narrow, paned windows that rose from six inches above the floor to the high ceiling. The dark oak planks creaked as she approached the receptionist.

"Can I help you?" the woman asked.

"I'm looking for Dr. John Tyler."

"I don't know if he's here today. It's Founders' Day, and there aren't any classes."

"Would you mind checking?"

"Sure." The woman ran her finger down a laminated list before picking up the phone. "I'll ring his office."

Cotten looked around. Shadows huddled in the corners of the room. The place smelled old and musty. She rubbed her nose thinking she might sneeze. The cushions of the Queen Anne chairs sagged from generations of student bodies. A picture of the pope hung over a faded fabric couch. In the center of the room, behind the receptionist's desk, stood a statue of the Virgin Mary, the winter sun streaming in from the eastern window highlighting her head. Dust motes swirled in the beam as if they had life. Cotten wondered if the statue had been placed there because of the light or if it was a coincidence. Whether by accident or not, the pale glow made the sculpture ethereal.

"There's no answer," the woman said. "I'm sorry."

Cotten took a business card from her purse. "Could you—"

"Oh," the receptionist said, standing. "I completely forgot about the student-faculty football game." She checked the time on her watch. "I believe Dr. Tyler is playing. If you hurry, you might catch him."

She led Cotten outside and pointed in the direction of the athletic field.

Cotten followed the receptionist's directions, crossing the Commons, passing the chapel, and finally winding down a path between the dorms and the gym. She heard the shouts of a small crowd as she approached the football field.

A bleacher, peppered with fifty or so people, bordered a section on the south side of the field. The wooden uprights were old, in the shape of an H instead of the squared-off Y.

Cotten climbed into the stands and sat next to a man with a neatly cropped goatee and mustache. She hugged herself for warmth and asked him, "Do you know which one is Dr. Tyler?"

Wrapped in a blanket, the man lifted his arm from underneath, nodding toward the field. "That's John throwing the pass. You're just in time for the last play." He rose to his feet and yelled, "Go! Go!"

The receiver caught the ball, but was quickly overrun, disappearing under a mound of players. The student team and their fans whooped and hollered in celebration.

The man sighed. "Best team the faculty has put together in a long time, even if we did lose." With the plaid blanket gathered around his shoulders, he stood and crabbed down the bleachers, easing carefully over each row of seats.

Tyler was the first of the faculty to congratulate the students. Cotten couldn't hear what they were saying, but there was a lot of laughter—camaraderie that men always seemed to share in their games. Competition brought out the best in men, she thought . . . and the worst in women.

She climbed down from the stands and approached Tyler. He was tall—perhaps six feet, crowned by thick black hair. There was a slight quirk to the corner of his mouth—as if he knew a secret he was not about to reveal. His tanned skin was a result of exposure at many archaeological digs, she assumed. Even through his sweats, she detected a tautness to his body—a solid look of being in good shape.

"Dr. Tyler?" she said.

He looked up and dropped his hand from a player's shoulder. "Yes?"

His eyes were the deepest blue she'd ever seen, nearly navy except when they caught the sun—even more remarkable in person than on the videotape in the archives.

"My name is Cotten Stone, and I work for SNN. If you have a moment, I'd like to talk to you."

She extended her hand and found his grip polite but firm.

John turned to one of his teammates. "You guys go ahead. Order me a Sam Adams."

"I don't want to interrupt your plans, Dr. Tyler," she said.

"It's fine. They'll be celebrating at O'Grady's all afternoon. More than enough time for me to catch up."

A gust of wind blew Cotten's hair in her face. Her nose tingled from the cold, and she knew it must be red.

"You look like you could use a cup of something hot—coffee maybe?"

"That would be wonderful," she said.

* * *

In his office, John took her coat and hung it on a hook just inside the door.

Cotten sat in an under-stuffed, wood-frame chair. "So, are you always the quarterback?"

"Actually, since it's my first year here, I got thrown into the job. That way, they can blame the new guy if the faculty loses. I'm sure I won't hear the end of it. I warned everyone in advance that their grades could be affected by the outcome, but it didn't seem to help. Now let me get you that cup of coffee. I've only got instant though."

"That'll be fine," she said.

He flashed a smile and moved to a makeshift kitchenette that was partially set off from the rest of the room by a bookcase.

John filled the cups with tap water, then stuck them in the microwave and set the timer. As the microwave thrummed away, he wondered about the pretty young woman sitting in his office. What would bring her looking for him? Why wouldn't she have phoned instead of coming all the way up here?

After he'd fixed the coffee he placed a piping hot cup of Folgers in front of Cotten, then handed her the sugar bowl.

John watched her heap in two heavy-laden spoonfuls, stir, then add another half spoon. She looked nervous, like she was keeping a tight hold on something—like she might explode at any moment. Guarded was a good description.

She looked up and said, "I know, too much sugar. Sugar and Dutch chocolate are my weaknesses."

"Just two vices?" John said. "If only I could be so fortunate." He sat and sipped his coffee, giving her time to grow comfortable.

Cotten glanced around at the shelves that were chock-full of books. "Quite a collection."

"Most belonged to my predecessor. But they do make for interesting reading." He set his cup down and said, "So, Ms. Stone—"

"Please, just Cotten." She picked up one of his business cards. "You even give out your cell phone number? That's pretty trusting and generous." She put the card in her wallet. "And should I call you, Doctor, or Reverend, or Father?"

"How about John?" She appeared to be trying so hard to be proper. Maybe conversing with a priest made her uneasy, he thought. "I have enough students calling me doctor, and I'm currently on a leave-of-absence from the priesthood. So Father is optional."

"I didn't know you could take a leave from your vows."

"Not the vows, just the duties. And, yes, under special circumstances, you can."

"All right . . . John." She flipped her hair off her neck and rolled her eyes. "God, calling you by your first name feels disrespectful. Oh, I shouldn't have said it like that—the God thing. But calling you John is like calling my sixth grade teacher by his first name."

She was stumbling all over her words, and he wished he could help her relax. But he did find the blush in her cheeks and flushing rising up her neck was part of her charm. She had a way about her, a genuineness, if that was a word, that he found pleasing.

"Well, I'm not your sixth grade teacher," he said. "And besides, you'll make me feel like an old man if you don't call me John."

Cotten took a deep breath. "Okay, let me start again. John, I'm doing background for a news feature. The topic is religious legends, things like Noah's Ark, the Holy Grail, that sort of thing."

Her voice sounded less flustered—more professional.

"That's my field," he said. "Biblical history."

"I know. I ran across interviews in our archives that referred to Dr. Gabriel Archer and his expertise in those areas. One of the clips featured you. Since you were so close by, I wanted to talk to you in person. So . . ." Cotten turned palms up. "Here I am."

"I'm glad you came. I knew Archer pretty well at one time. He's quite a character."

"Do you know if he studied languages?"

That seemed an odd question, he thought. "Sure. Greek, Hebrew, Aramaic—a lot of ancient tongues, and of course Latin. Scholars in his field have to have extensive knowledge of those languages."

"Oh, sure," Cotten said. "Of course."

"He loves to get involved with religious myths and legends. And the man can quote scripture with the best of them."

"I saw some evidence of that in the tapes I watched." She cleared her throat and pushed back her hair. "Do you know if he had brothers or sisters? A twin, maybe?"

The conversation was getting even more peculiar, John thought. "I believe Archer was an only child. I never heard him mention brothers or sisters—as a matter of fact I don't recall him ever saying anything about family or his childhood."

Cotten's brows dipped.

"He is passionate about his work, though. His enthusiasm is . . . commendable," John said.

"You sound like you're being kind when you use the word enthusiasm."

"I think his zeal has ended up damaging his credibility."

"How? Seems like that would be a good quality."

John took another sip of his coffee. "Is your background piece specifically on Archer?"

"No, but I thought he was interesting and maybe I could start with some of his quests and accomplishments."

"I see. And you're right. It would seem that his zeal should be an admirable quality."

"But?"

"It's sad, really, because he's a brilliant man. I studied under Archer and worked with him a couple of times in the field."

"Brilliant but eccentric?"

"To the point some might call him an obsessed fanatic. When he discovered an ancient plate in Jerusalem while excavating the tomb of a Crusader, Archer became convinced it would lead him to the Holy Grail. But he wouldn't let anyone else look at it, wouldn't even allow others to authenticate it. I suppose after so much ridicule, he was paranoid that someone might steal his find and claim it, leaving him with nothing but a lifelong work to be scoffed at. It's hard for anyone to take him seriously. He claimed to have deciphered writing on the plate that gave the location of the Grail, but who knows? Most thought he was over the edge, and the plate probably had no value other than being an interesting artifact."

"You don't think he could have really gone on to find the Grail?"

"Hasn't made the headlines, yet," John said. "In my opinion, the Holy Grail is more religious folklore than fact. I like to think of it as a state of mind more than a real object—something in our lives we strive for but may never find."

Cotten frowned. "What is Archer's theory?"

"There are plenty of scenarios—Archer's being one of many. Tradition has it that the Cup from the Last Supper was also used the next day to collect Christ's blood at the Crucifixion. According to numerous stories, Joseph of Arimathea, who was present at the Crucifixion and supplied Christ's burial tomb, was the Cup's first owner. Most historians believe he eventually took the Cup to the Isles of Avalon in Britain—the basis of the Arthurian Legend which most of us are familiar with. But Archer proposes a different scheme. He says Joseph traveled with Saint Paul on the apostle's first mission to Antioch. He took along the Cup as a symbol for newly baptized Christians to venerate. After Paul moved on, Joseph stayed in Antioch. When he died, the Cup disappeared—presumably buried with him.

"From what I've read, Archer then says that the Cup resurfaced around the middle of the third century and was put on display by the

Bishop of Antioch. Then it was lost again—in an earthquake, I think around A.D. 526. Then it was found again some fifty or so years later. All the stories of the Grail have that same element in common—it's found, it's lost, then found again. Adds to the mystery, I guess."

John watched Cotten's expressions, so animated and telltale. He continued. "Archer claimed his research led him to believe that during the last Crusade, a fellow named Geoffrey Bisol took the Cup and fled south. He and a small band of Crusaders were captured near Nineveh in northern Iraq. Bisol maintained that he buried his dead comrades in some of the ancient ruins nearby before making his way to Jerusalem. He didn't have the Cup with him when he arrived in the Holy Land, but swore he knew where it was hidden. Over the years, many groups have extensively excavated the ruins around Nineveh. No one has ever claimed to have found anything that would support Gabriel Archer's theory."

Cotten closed her eyes. She shivered.

"Are you all right?" John asked.

"Just a chill."

SINCLAIR

"Do you renounce Satan?"

"We do."

"And all his works?"

"We do."

The priest recited the vows, then reached into the water in the Baptismal font, scooping up enough to flow over the crown of the baby's head. "I baptize you in the name of the Father . . ."

When the water touched the sleeping infant's skin, she awoke crying.

". . . and of the Son . . ."

Her cries grew louder.

". . . and of the Holy Spirit."

Tears welled in the mother's eyes as she looked down at the infant.

Charles Sinclair stood close by watching the christening of his only granddaughter. His wife clung to his arm. In his early fifties, Sinclair was tall and lean in his tailored double-breasted suit. Thick eyebrows and a generous amount of black hair sprinkled with sterling softened his hard-edged features. His jet eyes peered out from an olive complexion and mirrored a mind that seemed to be working at high speed.

Light poured in through the stained glass windows of historic St. Louis Cathedral in the French Quarter. The cries of Sinclair's granddaughter filled the church.

While the priest continued, Sinclair's mind wandered, and his gaze drifted to the magnificent frescos adorning the arched ceiling. He should have received some word by now, he thought. Concern creased his forehead. A gentle nudge from his wife brought him back.

The priest stood in front of him. "Congratulations, Dr. Sinclair. It's an honor to bring your granddaughter into the Kingdom of God."

"Thank you, Father." Sinclair reached into his suit pocket and removed an envelope containing a check for the priest's services. Then he hugged his daughter and shook hands with his son-in-law. As the rest of the group gathered to pose for pictures, Sinclair glanced toward the back of the church and saw his attorney, Ben Gearhart, slip in and wait in the shadows of the vestibule. "I'll be right back," Sinclair said to his wife.

Joining Gearhart, he strolled out of the cathedral and crossed the street to Jackson Square. They stopped at the foot of the statue of Andrew Jackson. Sinclair asked, "What have you found out?"

"I haven't been able to get in touch with Ahmed, so I sent someone out to see what was going on. I got confirmation earlier this morning that he and Archer are dead. We cleaned it up."

Unlike Sinclair's skin, Gearhart's fair complexion reacted to the cold, dry air blowing across the Square. His cheeks glowed from windburn, and his blue eyes watered. He rubbed his nose with a tissue as he spoke.

"At first I blamed the military activity for the lack of communications, but then I became suspicious," Gearhart said. "I tried to contact him several times but with no luck." He lifted his head to read the taller man's expression.

Sinclair raked a hand through his hair. "How did they die?"

"Ahmed was shot with his own gun."

"And Archer?"

"There was evidence of a struggle, but it appears he died of natural causes. Sounds like he fought with Ahmed, shot him, then keeled over from the ordeal."

"And the artifact?" Sinclair's face tightened.

Gearhart wiped his nose and shook his head.

Sinclair went on. "I take it from your silence that we don't know where the box is, much less have verification of its contents." He walked a few steps ahead, put his hands in his pockets, then turned to face the attorney. "So where is it?" His voice was low, full of control and gravity.

"My contact believes someone else was in the chamber. A videocassette was found near the bodies. It contains news footage shot by a reporter for SNN. A woman named Cotten Stone."

Charles Sinclair saw his family emerging through the cathedral's large wooden doors. His wife waved at him. "Is Stone still in Iraq?"

"We've traced her to New York."

"She could jeopardize everything."

"I realize that. But nothing has shown up in the news. She may not know what it is."

"If she even has it at all." Sinclair looked up at the statue of the seventh president.

"I have someone in New York right now," Gearhart said.

Stepping forward, Sinclair leaned in close to Gearhart. "No more mistakes, my friend." He lowered his head to the wind and walked back to the church.

"Is anything wrong, Charles?" his wife asked when Sinclair returned.

He gave her a light peck on the cheek. "You ride with the children to Broussard's. I'll be right behind."

"Bad news?" she asked.

"Nothing for you to worry about."

Sinclair gave his family a reassuring wave as they walked to the first of two limousines. Then he went back inside the cathedral. The scent of the candles hung heavy, their smoke collecting in the columns of light from the windows.

The old man was there, waiting.

Sinclair walked up the aisle, slid in the pew, and sat next to him.

"How is your granddaughter?"

"She didn't like the cold water," Sinclair said.

"Understandable." The old man, his gray hair the color of ashes, did not look at Sinclair, but stared at the altar. "How are things?" The words were almost whispered.

"There has been a minor setback, but Gearhart is taking care of it."

He looked at Sinclair. "Should I be concerned?"

"No. Not at all."

"Tell me about it. We should have no secrets, no matter how small."

The old man waited as the church became overcome with silence.

Sinclair finally spoke. "A woman reporter—she might have seen something in the crypt. Like I said, Gearhart is on it."

"You know who she is?" the old man asked.

"Her name is Cotten Stone."

The old man rocked back. "Stone," he repeated, then nodded slowly as if coming to an understanding. "You know, Charles, perhaps it is time to give you some additional assistance." He turned to Sinclair. "I have an old friend who can help."

Sinclair fought back a sigh. "It will all be done as you've requested. There's no need to involve anyone else."

The old man patted Sinclair's leg. "Just to be on the safe side. After all, you never know . . ." He turned back toward the front of the church in silence, seeming to signal that the conversation was over.

Sinclair stood and moved to the aisle. Out of habit, he genuflected and made the sign of the cross before walking to the back of the church. Pushing open the door to leave, he turned and stared at the crucifix suspended over the marble altar. Shards of sunlight struck it in an almost surreal way. He could clearly see Christ's head sagging to the side—tired, weary, encircled by an askew crown of thorns.

A gust of cold wind blew through the door, whirling leaves inside and making Sinclair pull his topcoat closer to his neck as he headed toward the waiting limousine.

INTRUDER

COTTEN STONE ENTERED HER apartment, thankful to be out of the
New York winter. She was exhausted, not only from the concerns
brought on by her meeting with John Tyler and the mystery of the
box, but knowing the time spent away from Thornton had not healed
her heart. Seeing him again brought back emotions she had hoped
were cold and dead.

Cotten stripped off her heavy coat and scarf and unloaded her
small bag of groceries. The apartment was chilly, and she turned up
the thermostat, hearing the familiar thump as the gas heater kicked
on.

She rubbed her arms for warmth while thinking about Tyler.
She'd become more and more unnerved in his office, realizing as he
described Archer's theory that she'd been in the crypt, seen the Crusader's bones . . . held the box. Tyler must believe her to be completely
crazy—and ungrateful. She practically ran out of his office after saying she had all the information she needed. How embarrassing. And
John was so polite, even offering to answer more questions.

Thornton crept into her thoughts.

Thornton.

Just letting herself get so deeply involved with him was another in a long line of stupid mistakes. Not only was he married, his face was a household fixture in millions of homes around the country. It would have been hard to pick someone with a higher profile to jump into bed with.

And of course there was the box. Another mistake. She should have left it in the crypt. But wasn't that what she'd done most of her life—run away from problems, decisions, relationships—hoping they would disappear?

They never did.

Before putting the cold cuts in the refrigerator, she made a sandwich, then wandered back into the living room to watch the news. That's when she spotted the blinking light on her answering machine. There were three messages. She sat on the sofa, pressed play, and bit down on the ham sandwich.

Beep.

"Cotten? It's Ted. I got your message that you weren't coming back in today. Are you all right? Why did you leave the edit? What's going on? Call me."

Beep.

"Cotten, it's Ted again. They've just about finished your piece, but there's a tape missing. What should they do? We're running it tomorrow night. If I don't hear from you I'll tell the editor to use some stock cover shots. Call me as soon as you can."

Beep.

"Hi."

Thornton's voice.

Pause.

"I really need to talk to you. I know you think it's over, but it's not. We weren't just having an affair. I love you. And I know you love me. Please, Cotten, we've got to talk."

Pause.

"Can't we just meet for dinner? That's all I want. Just to talk. Call me back. I love you."

The sound of his voice had made her stomach tighten—the same feeling she got so many times when the phone rang and she knew it was Thornton . . . prayed it was Thornton.

The first time they made love it had been raw lust. They'd had lunch on occasion, flirted in the hallways, elevators, and stairwells at work. Then he'd asked her to meet him for a drink one evening. They met in a hotel bar near SNN and within twenty minutes they were tearing each other's clothes off in a hotel room eighteen stories above Broadway. After three clandestine meetings, the first hint of affection finally entered into their lovemaking. But that vanished quickly on Thornton's part, while she still yearned for the gentleness, the sweetness, the love in lovemaking. It became evident he only wanted sex. Nothing more. He denied her accusation, saying it was because they only had those few stolen moments, and she aroused him so much . . . Cotten wanted to believe him, but almost every time, as soon as they finished—he finished—he'd leave, take his limo home to his wife Cheryl while Cotten lay in the rumpled sheets, in the dark, and cried. She'd been a fool to think anything would ever change. A stint in Iraq was supposed to make her forget.

Now it started all over again—his voice brooding and full of sincerity. His words full of promises. How could she detest what she craved? It made no sense. She drank the poison because she loved the taste.

Cotten glanced toward the kitchen. She could see the stove. The box was just one more pebble in her shoe.

Picking up the phone, she dialed Thornton's cell. She almost hoped that maybe he'd be home with his wife and wouldn't pick up.

"Hello," he answered.

"Hi," she said, almost in a whisper.

"Oh, thank God." His voice was urgent. "I've been going out of my mind. I have to see you."

"I don't think that's a good idea."

"Please, Cotten. We need to talk. I've made a decision."

There was a long pause.

"Let me guess. You're going to leave her."

"Yes."

Cotten didn't respond. This wasn't a new tune.

"I know I've said it before. This time I mean it."

"Thornton, don't. I'm emotionally exhausted."

"I know I haven't been fair. Just let me see you. Please. You won't regret it."

I already do, she thought.

Squeezing her eyes tightly shut, she said, "All right," flinching even as the words came out. It was going to be the same old pattern. They'd meet. They'd talk. They'd have sex. It didn't matter what he promised.

"Can you meet me?"

Cotten slumped into the couch cushions. "When?"

"I'm working late, but I'll finish up and get out of here in an hour."

She hung up without answering.

* * *

They had often met at Giovanni's in the past—a small out-of-the-way restaurant about ten blocks from her apartment. It reminded her

55

of the one in *The Godfather* where Michael Corleone committed murder for the first time. Cotten didn't know which of her sins was worse, adultery or stupidity.

When she entered Giovanni's, the head waiter greeted her. "Good evening, Ms. Stone. Mr. Graham is waiting." He led her to a table in the back.

Prints of the old country covered the walls, along with empty Chianti bottles and plastic flowers.

"Cotten," Thornton said, standing and taking her in his arms. "God, I'm glad you came." He tried to kiss her, but she turned away.

"Hello, Thornton." She slipped into the chair across from him.

He took her hands in his and rested them on top of the table. "I was crazy with worry. Ted told me all about your escape from Iraq. You're a lucky lady."

"In some respects."

"So how was it?" Thornton asked. "Did you get the story you wanted?"

"Most of it. It's running tomorrow night."

"I know," Thornton said, squeezing her hands. "I previewed it before leaving work. You did an outstanding job." He paused. "Ted told me you got upset and rushed out of your edit yesterday. He said he tried to call you all day today, but you weren't home. They had to do the edit without you. What happened, sweetheart?"

"Nothing really," she said. "I misplaced a tape and haven't been able to find it yet."

"Important stuff?"

"It was all important," she said, pulling her hands away as the waiter approached.

"Something to drink?" the waiter asked.

"Bring me a big fat Tanqueray and tonic," Thornton said. "Cotten?"

"Absolut on the rocks with a twist, please."

The waiter left, and Thornton leaned back. "I've got to go to the doctor and have my clot time checked tomorrow. Pain in the ass. They can't keep the damn Coumadin levels stable."

She knew he was stalling. "Yes, you've told me that before." Cotten unwrapped her silverware and put the napkin in her lap, fidgeting with it.

"Well, who'd have thought you could get blood clots in your legs just from sitting on a goddamn airplane? Now, with the blood thinner, God forbid, I cut myself shaving—I'll bleed to death."

"Get to the point, Thornton. You're waltzing all around it. Trying to work up a little sympathy first?"

He reached for her hands again, but she kept them just out of range.

"I know what you're going to say, that we've been through this *ad infinitum*," he said. "But this time it's different. I swear."

"Just tell me what you decided."

"I'm going to ask Cheryl for a divorce."

"Why?"

"What do you mean, why? Because I love you. I want to be with you."

"When are you going to tell her?" Cotten prepared for the catch.

"Right away."

She glared at him.

"Very soon. Just as soon as she gets her decorating business on its feet. That way she'll have something to preoccupy her while getting through—"

"Thornton, she's been trying to get that business going for two fucking years." By the end of the sentence, Cotten had raised her voice enough that some heads turned in their direction.

He held his hands up, as if to surrender. "Cotten, please."

"This is the same bullshit you've told me over and over. Nothing's changed, has it? You know as well as I do you can't leave her." Cotten looked up at the cheap, fake flowers. How appropriate, she thought. "I'm so goddamn stupid. I knew what you were doing, and I still came here. I was going to let you sweet-talk me into bed. And while you fucked me and whispered how you couldn't live without me, you'd be checking your watch so you wouldn't get home too late and have to make up some excuse." Cotten rubbed her temples. Her voice dropped. "I can't take this anymore. I never should have come. Go home to Cheryl and leave me alone."

She grabbed her purse, stormed out, and cried her way down the Manhattan sidewalk.

Cotten walked for nearly an hour in the freezing drizzle before flagging a cab. She'd cried until she couldn't anymore. Maybe she'd overreacted and been too harsh. What if he really was trying to leave Cheryl? She was so confused. Maybe she should move out of New York, even go home to Kentucky. That notion quickly dissolved. She had to break this off completely and get over it.

She could live without him, she kept telling herself. There was life after Thornton Graham.

* * *

Cotten sat in her living room and stared at the phone on the table beside her. She knew she would see Thornton at work—there was no way to avoid it. Setting rules up front would be the best thing. She wouldn't talk to him unless it was a matter dealing with her job. She wouldn't answer his calls. And she wouldn't see him alone under any circumstances. Those were the rules—and that's what she would tell him. It was over. The end.

The phone rang, and Cotten answered, but not without first looking at the Caller ID.

"Uncle Gus," she said when she picked up. "How are you?"

"Doing great, little girl. Just checking up on my favorite niece."

That was a joke between them. She was his only niece. She heard him laugh and pictured her uncle's Santa-like frame. Even his hair was snow white like Mr. Kringle's. She loved Gus and wished he would lose weight and stop chain-smoking. She heard the click of his cigarette lighter.

"I haven't talked to you in a while," he said.

"I haven't talked with anyone in the family much since Mama passed away," she said. "But this is a very pleasant surprise."

"It's a shame how younger family members drift apart as the older generations pass on. Not just our family."

"I know. We really should keep in touch."

"And we will. Anything exciting in your life?"

Cotten thought of telling him about the box and Thornton, but she was just too mentally exhausted to do it tonight. "Not really," she said. "And you?"

"Business is booming. I think New Yorkers are becoming more and more paranoid. Makes for the private eye business to go through the ceiling. I've got more cases than I can handle."

"I'm so happy for you," she said. As Cotten talked, her eyes started to wander from table to chair, TV to bookshelves and china cabinet, realizing things were slightly out of place. Suddenly, fear, icier than the Hudson River, coursed through her.

"Uncle Gus, I've got another call," she lied. "I'll talk to you soon."

She didn't wait to hear his goodbye as she gently placed the receiver in its cradle. Taking a much slower, closer inspection of the room, she saw that a small golden horse her mother had given her faced the wrong way on the TV cabinet; the drawer of the end table was not pushed in all the way; the lid to the cedar chest wasn't closed snugly; the books on the shelves rested at odd angles.

Quickly, she checked the other rooms. She didn't have much of value—a few pieces of jewelry, a laptop, a cheap stereo. Nothing was missing.

"Jesus," she said, running back to the kitchen. The box.

The frying pan and teapot sat just as she'd left them. She moved them off the Hotpoint and gripped the stove lid. Pulling up, she heard the clamps give way.

It was still there—the plain, black, featureless box. She eased the stove lid back into place with a click.

Someone had been here, searched her apartment. If they were looking for the box, they hadn't found it, which meant they would be back.

Heart racing, Cotten hurried to her front door, checked the lock, and put the guard chain in place. She leaned against the door and looked around the living room.

In just a few short days *they* had found her.

Picking up the phone again, Cotten started to call the police. But she hesitated, changing her mind. Let's consider this for a moment, she thought. What exactly would she tell the cops? They'd ask questions, and she'd answer.

There was a break-in?

Yes.

Was the burglar still in the apartment when you arrived?

No.

Was anything stolen—missing?

No.

How do you know someone broke in?

Well, some of my things were messed up—out of place.

That's it?

Yes.

Are there signs of forced entry? Was the door jimmied, window broken?

No.

So, if they didn't force their way in, they must have used a key. Who else has a key?

My landlord.

Does he have permission to enter your apartment when you're not at home?

Yes, he collects my mail while I'm away.

Do you trust him?

Yes.

Have you received any crank calls? Any threats?

No.

Can you think of anything in your possession that someone would want to go to this much trouble to steal?

Well, there is the box.

What box?

The box I smuggled into the country illegally from Iraq. You know, one of the Axis of Evil nations we're getting ready to bomb.

What's in the box?

I don't know; I can't open it.

Why?

It doesn't have a lid, hinges, or locks. It's sort of like a solid block of wood.

But you think there's something of value in this featureless box even though you can't open it?

Yes, I think it contains the most treasured relic in the entire Christian world—the single most sought-after item in the past two thousand years—nothing less than the famous, Holy fucking Grail.

Wow, that's impressive. Ms. Stone, are you under a doctor's care or taking any kind of medication? Perhaps you're depressed? Lonely? Having boyfriend problems?

Actually, I had a boyfriend problem just this very evening—

"Shit! Fuck!" Cotten slammed down the receiver. How utterly ridiculous! The police wouldn't stop laughing for a week. She felt the tears forming as she put her face in her hands. The frustration turned to fear. She had to find out what the hell was going on. She had to do something.

Leaning over, she slid her purse out from underneath her coat and pulled the business card from her wallet. Cotten picked up the phone and dialed.

PUZZLE CUBE

AT 1:00 A.M. JOHN TYLER stood gazing out his kitchen window while he waited for Cotten Stone. A full moon turned the frozen lake beyond the apartment complex into a dull gray slab dotted with small pearly patches of snow. The bare maple trees cast bony shadows across the hard ground. It was a Currier and Ives picture. The view made him reflect on how often he thought of himself as a blank canvas. The yet-to-be-created painting was a metaphor for his life. There had to be more, something that would fill this chasm inside. He'd already tried his hand at so many ways to serve God, but none had brought him peace with himself. What was it that God had planned for him? Years of introspection and searching had not answered that question. If God intended for him to live his life as it was now, he would feel satisfied, content, fulfilled.

But he didn't.

John watched the road for headlights. Cotten Stone should arrive any minute if she left right after they had spoken on the phone. And what a strange conversation that had been—her voice urgent as she asked to see him right away, saying that it couldn't wait until morning.

Her apartment had been broken into, but she didn't call the police. She'd explain when she got there.

He stared at the brittle landscape, curious as to what could be so important that she had to see him at this time of night. Something about her behavior kept her on his mind after she'd left his office. She'd seemed afraid—as if she hid something. Cotten had fidgeted, crossed and uncrossed her legs as she spoke, and tripped over her words. Odd behavior for a professional reporter.

A knock made him look away from the window.

For the hundredth time since she boarded the train, Cotten asked herself if she should have waited until the morning. She could have just left her apartment, gone to a hotel, and then called him in the morning. But it was too late for that now. She stood on his doorstep hugging a large leather bag.

"Come in," John said, answering the door.

She stepped past him into his living room.

"Let me take your coat."

She unwound the scarf from her neck. "I know you probably think I'm crazy coming here in the middle of the night like this," she said as John helped her slip out of the coat. She hung on to the bag protectively as she moved about the room, slowly warming up.

"Impressive collection," Cotten said, gazing around.

His shelves were lined with artifacts: pottery shards, drawings, maps, ancient tools, a few brown bones. More shelves filled with books—some old and worn, some new—covered one wall. There were numerous photos of him at archaeological digs; a few in the desert and others in forested mountains. And in a silver frame on the desk was a picture of John alongside other men of the cloth in the company of the pope.

Cotten lifted the photo. "You met the pope?"

"I was in Rome helping a forensic team in relic authentication. Cardinal Antonio Ianucci—he's the Vatican Curator and Director of Art and Antiquities—stopped by to chat and check on our progress. During a break, he gave us a tour of the three Vatican restoration departments—tapestries, paintings, sculptures. As we entered one of the halls, Ianucci said he had a surprise for us. About a half dozen clergy were coming out of a door at the end of the hall. In the middle of the group was the Holy Father. We were stunned. When they got close, they stopped. He blessed us, a camera flashed, then Ianucci ushered us back to our work area. If you consider *that* meeting him, then I did."

"Still, it must have been exciting."

"It was."

Cotten went to the couch and sat silently, twirling a silver bracelet around her wrist. "I guess you're waiting patiently for me to get to the point so you'll know why I rushed here at this ungodly hour."

John pulled up a chair and sat opposite her. "You sounded rattled on the phone. You mentioned a break-in."

"Well, sort of. They got in, but I don't know how. Still, I'm sure somebody was there. I'd been out, and when I came home and looked around, it occurred to me that lots of my things had been moved, shifted, examined.

"Did you call the police?"

Cotten cleared her throat and tossed her hair. "No, I didn't report it. Although I'm positive of what happened, there's no way I can prove it—the police would never have believed me. Nothing was stolen."

John leaned forward and laced his fingers together between his knees.

Before he could speak, Cotten said, "I think whoever broke in was looking for this." She opened the leather bag and removed the box. She held it for a moment, almost unwilling to let it go.

"May I?" he asked, reaching out.

"Sorry," she said, realizing she had not offered it to him.

After rolling it over and studying each side and surface, John asked, "Where did you get it?"

It took several minutes for her to explain how it came into her possession, how she had smuggled it through Customs, how she couldn't open it, and how she had hidden it in her kitchen stove.

"That's quite a story," John said. He rubbed his forehead as if deep in thought. "And I'm sorry to hear Archer is dead. Despite his quirkiness, he was a brilliant man. I liked him."

"Do you have any idea what this thing is?" Cotten looked over at the box in John's lap.

"I think so," he said, examining it again. "I believe it's a medieval puzzle cube. They were very popular among rich Europeans during the Middle Ages. I've only seen a few before—I think I have a book here someplace that has a chapter explaining how to open them."

"What do you think is inside?"

He shook it gently. "Usually, they held a prize or a toy, maybe jewelry or game pieces. I've heard some contained additional puzzle cubes—a box within a box. They were mostly to entertain aristocrats. There were several designs and each type opened in a totally different manner."

Her eyes widened. "Dr. Archer regarded it as something special. He told me two things before he died. The first was a series of numbers and a name—twenty-six, twenty-seven, twenty-eight, Matthew. Then Archer said something about me being the only one who could stop the sun, the dawn."

"That would be quite a trick, wouldn't it?" John smiled. "From what you say, I suppose Archer wasn't thinking clearly. Scrambled thoughts. Delusional."

Cotten balked. No, Archer hadn't been delusional. He knew precisely the words to get her attention. *Geh el crip. You are the only one.* She didn't want to have to get into that or John might really think her out of her mind.

"But the numbers," Cotten said. "I looked them up in the Bible. It's from the Gospel of St. Matthew."

"And He took the Cup . . ." John turned the cube in his hands. "Those words are repeated around the world everyday at Mass. They're the words Jesus used at the Last Supper when He established the sacrament of the Eucharist."

"From what you've told me, Archer was convinced he knew the location of the Cup from the Last Supper. Do you think that's what could be in the box? I mean there must be something of value inside. I don't think someone would be willing to murder for an empty box. And then track me down . . ."

"Are you sure the two events are connected?"

"You think I'm delusional, too?"

"On the contrary." His voice rang sincere, not patronizing. "I didn't mean to sound like I don't believe you. You've had a lot of traumatic things happen. Your reactions are perfectly understandable. By linking the events you are trying to make sense of it."

There were a few moments of silence. John had been kind enough, she thought, but he didn't seem to detect the same significance she did. And he certainly wasn't suspicious that anything as valuable as the Holy Grail rested inside the box. Maybe the break-in and the box weren't related at all. But there was the tape. . . .

"There's one more thing. I think I accidentally left a videotape in the crypt. My face is all over the footage, and the fact that I work for SNN."

"Or you might just as easily have lost it somewhere else. You said you had emptied one of your bags earlier while you were alone in the desert."

"I hope you're right, but I have a sickening feeling I left it in the chamber."

"So someone could have gotten the tape, realized you had been there, and found out where you live."

"Yes." She felt better. He understood she had probable cause for her anxiety. If John could open the box . . . "You mentioned a reference book?"

"It's here somewhere." He rose and went to the bookcases. His eyes moved up one shelf and down the other, finally coming to rest on a tattered cloth-bound book. "This should have something." He pulled down the volume, placed it on the coffee table, and sat beside her.

Cotten saw *Myths and Magic of the Middle Ages* on the cover.

The pages crackled as John leafed through it.

"'Puzzle Cubes and Prize Boxes,'" Cotten said, reading the chapter title. Beneath was a page of text, and as John flipped through the next several pages, she saw drawings and diagrams showing the workings of different box styles.

He studied the diagrams, going back through them repeatedly. Finally, he said, "This one looks right." He took the box and rotated it. Gripping the top and bottom, he pulled in opposite directions. Nothing.

"What do you think?" Cotten asked.

John looked at the diagram again. "I need to figure out which surface is actually the top. Once I do that, it says here that it should open easily."

He shifted the cube a quarter turn and pulled again. Still nothing. It took six rotations and additional reading before a faint click sounded. The top separated, exposing a fine, thin seam.

"I think we've done it," John said.

At the end of the first crusade Jerusalem had been retaken by the Christians. The Prieuré de Sion, a group of monks whose objective was to return the thrones of Europe to the descendants of the Merovingian bloodline, a bloodline they believed was established through a union between Jesus and Mary Magdalene, created a military arm of warrior monks to protect Jerusalem and those who traveled there.

From a simple quest, the new organization grew, made up of the elite and powerful of Europe having positions of authority in politics, religion, and economics. Free from taxes and accountable only to the pope, over the centuries, it became one of the world's wealthiest and most influential organizations. It was called the Knights of the Temple of Jerusalem or the Knights Templar.

CROIX PATÉE

John set the box on the table before carefully sliding the top sideways. It opened and swung down revealing a tiny set of hinges on the inside that kept the top attached.

Cotten saw that the inside was filled with a white linen-like cloth wrapped around an object. "Look at that," she said, pointing at the corner of the material's top fold. Woven into one corner was a cross and a five-petal rose, and on the opposite corner were embroidered two knights riding the same horse—the words *Sigillvm Militvm Xpisti* stitched in a circle around them. Although slightly faded with age, the cross was still red, the rose pink, and the words golden.

"One second," John said. From a drawer in a rolltop desk he withdrew a pair of white cotton gloves. Slipping them on, he cautiously removed the contents of the box and unwrapped the cloth.

Cotten bit on her bottom lip when the material fell away revealing a chalice. It was about six inches tall and four inches in diameter at the rim of the bowl. The surface was a dull gray metal. A simple line of tiny pewter-colored beads ran around the base, while a necklace of miniature grapevines curled around the throat.

"It's in remarkable shape," he said, "if it's really two thousand years old." His gloved finger rubbed a small imperfection on the back side of the Cup. "Other than this little nick, I'd guess it has been well cared for." John turned the chalice around. "IHS," he said as he touched the engraving on the side.

"Is it the Grail?" she asked.

"I don't know." He gently pressed into a thick, dark substance coating the inside. "Probably beeswax."

"It's so . . . plain," she said. "I guess I expected something a little flashier."

"You've seen too many Indiana Jones movies."

"You're awfully calm to be holding what could be the Holy Grail."

"I've been burned in the past by a few clever fakes of other artifacts."

"Well, this is my first, so bear with me while I get excited." She grinned, and he returned a smile. Cotten pointed at the engraving. "What's IHS?"

"It's the emblem—like a monogram—for Jesus' name. The early Christians used the three letters during Roman times to identify each other. It's also the first three letters of His name in Greek. And in Latin, some say it stands for *In Hoc Signo Vinces*, or In This Sign You Shall Conquer. My guess is the engraving was added much later, perhaps while it was in Antioch."

"So you believe Archer was right?"

John held the relic up so the light shone on it from different angles. "I wish I could say for sure. I'll admit that Archer's theory seems to ring true." He ran his fingers over the needlework on the cloth.

"Are the words significant? And the cross, the rose—the knights? What do they mean?"

The red cross had four equal arms that flared at the ends. "Croix Patée," he said. Then he touched the golden threads forming the words *Sigillvm Militvm Xpisti*. "Seal of the Army of Christ. The dog rose was their symbol—rosa carina. It stood for the virgin and the virgin birth, chosen because the dog rose doesn't need to be cross-pollinated to produce its fruit, the rose hip."

"Talk to me," Cotten said. "What does it mean?"

"Near the end of the Seventh Crusade a group of religious zealots, known as the Knights Templar, was formed. They wore the Cross Patée—the Templar's Cross—emblazoned on their white habits, and their seal was two knights riding the same horse, a symbol of their vow of poverty. Their mission was to protect the treasures of the great temple of Jerusalem. It is suspected that in reality, they plundered the wealth of the temple and hid it away. Instead of being impoverished, they became exceedingly wealthy as well as powerful, answering only to the Church. Some of the Templars claimed to be of divine lineage, descendants of a proposed union between Jesus and Mary Magdalene. They also proclaimed themselves as *Guardians of the Grail*."

John held up the chalice. "If this is truly the Cup from the Last Supper, it would be the most prized relic in the Church—in all of Christendom."

"Why the wax?" Cotten asked.

"I would assume to protect the inside from being touched or contaminated. If it held the blood of Christ, it would be considered quite sacred."

As Cotten stared at the Cup, Archer's dying words still spooked her. "What about the message that I'm the *only one* who can stop the sun, the dawn? How would that tie in?"

He shook his head. "No idea."

She shifted. "It really bothers me, John. If I'm the only one to do whatever Archer was talking about, then I'm the only one they're looking for."

"Who?"

"Whoever broke into my apartment. I've got a bad feeling about the whole thing. You weren't there when the Arab pulled the gun and tried to kill Archer. He wasn't just stealing some old trinket box. He was driven—I saw it in his eyes. It was creepy. Archer believed he had the Grail, and whoever tried to kill him was convinced of it, too. Even *you* said if it's genuine, it would be the most valuable relic in the world. It's a logical conclusion that whoever searched my apartment was looking for it."

"Maybe you're right."

Cotten put both hands to her mouth and spoke into them as if guarding the words so they didn't escape her lips too quickly. "I could have been hiding the biggest religious story of the century underneath the lid of my stove."

"Are you Catholic?" John asked.

"No." Her expression turned from wonderment to puzzlement.

"Christian?"

Her fingers intertwined in her lap. "I'm not sure I know how to answer that."

"Embarrassed to tell me because I'm a priest?"

"No, I really *don't* know how to answer. I used to go to church, believe in religion, God, all that."

John looked at her as if trying to read her thoughts.

"I was born in Kentucky, an only child—my twin sister died at birth. My father was a farmer; we were poor. When I was six there was a terrible drought, and we lost everything. The bank foreclosed, and my father committed suicide. Mama always said she thought there was something more, something else troubling my father. He'd been despondent for quite a while, even before the drought, but nobody knew why. He wrote a note blaming God for ruining our lives. At the time, I agreed with him. Before the drought, we were a churchgoing family.

"After my father died, my mother and I moved to a small house, and she went to work in a textile mill—we barely got by for years."

"Well then, you do believe. In order to blame God, you have to believe He exists."

"That's how I felt back then. When I got older, I realized the saying on the bumper sticker is right—shit happens. It was just a frigging drought." She wiggled her fingers in the air. "Nothing supernatural, no divine hand descending from the heavens to smite the Stone family. My father needed to blame something, someone. He hung it on God. I let go of that a long time ago—never went back to church."

"I'm sorry about your father and what happened to your family."

"Why did you ask me about my religion?"

"I just wondered what this," he motioned to the Cup, "means to you."

"Actually, a great deal—but probably not what you think. If this is the real thing, it means the biggest story of my career. It could be my ticket to a senior correspondent's position at the network."

He stared at her in silence.

"We all look at things differently, John. Like my father and I—he blamed God; I blamed a lack of one. This relic could be your salvation. And it could be mine, too. But in a different way." Cotten leaned back her head, eyes closed, then looked at him again. "I'm sorry, but you and I just don't have the same beliefs."

He held up his hand. "That's not a problem. Hey, my closest friend is a Jewish rabbi. We grew up together. He's one of those friends you don't see much, but know you can count on. But talk about differing views. We're the real odd couple. You can imagine some of the discussions we've had over the years."

"Look," she said, "besides the career move, the sooner I write this story, the sooner I can stop looking over my shoulder. Once I tell the world about the Grail, the focus will be on it, not me. I'll be just another byline." She moved to the edge of the couch, aware that he watched her. "So how do we prove it's the real deal?"

"Well, the metalwork is fairly easy to match to a known style and time period. The wood and the hinge of the box can also be dated and matched to others like it—so can the cloth. And the beeswax can be pinned down with radiocarbon dating."

"What's next?"

"I'd like to take it to Rome. The dating technology at the Vatican is some of the best in the world."

"Why the Vatican? I mean I realize that's your thing, but what about right here in our own backyard? Doesn't Brown, or NYU, or Columbia have an archaeology department?"

"Sure. But the Vatican has been in the authentication business for centuries. Who would you rather interview for your report—Professor John Doe of a local university or Cardinal Ianucci, the curator of the largest collection of religious relics and artifacts in the world?"

"Okay, you've made your point." Cotten smiled shyly. "Do my aspirations to snag the big story make me greedy?"

"That's what reporters do," he said. "Reporting your story with St. Peter's Basilica in the background would be impressive."

"Or standing next to a Michelangelo while interviewing that cardinal you mentioned would look good on my demo reel." She shook her head. "You must think I'm shameless."

"No, I think you take your job seriously, and you work hard at it to be the best. There's nothing wrong with that. I envy you."

Cotten found his remark curious. "Really?"

"I don't think it's common for most people to live their passions. Some are lucky, like you. I can see the fire in your eyes. You can't wait to jump on this story. That's what fills you up. My grandfather was fortunate that way. He was an archaeologist, too, and when I was a kid he filled my head with tales of ancient civilizations. Talk about fire in somebody's eyes. You couldn't help but listen to him and become excited. Those wondrous stories stayed with me. It's what made me go on after my ordination for a degree in Medieval and Byzantine Studies and later in Early Christian Studies."

"I hate to admit it, but I didn't know priests did other stuff. You know, other than priestly things."

John laughed. "I've done that, too. I was an assistant pastor in a small parish for a short while."

"You didn't like it?"

"Barbara Walters has nothing on you," he said. "You're going to get the whole story."

"Hope so. I find it interesting. So did you like being shepherd of your small flock?"

"As a matter of fact, I did."

"But?"

"But, Ms. Walters, it didn't fill me up is the best way I can put it. I've always wanted to serve God. That's never been a question. What's the *best* way is another story. Maybe it was all my grandfather's stories of the windswept plains of Africa or the ancient tombs below the streets of Middle Eastern cities. Who knows? I took a leave of absence from the priesthood to live some of those tales, see if it put fire in my eyes." John folded is arms. "Now you know my life story."

She looked into his navy blue eyes. They were gorgeous with or without fire. But Cotten felt as if she had intruded, been too much the reporter, especially since it was she who had come to him for help in the middle of the night. "I feel like I should apologize, first for keeping you up and secondly for prying. I didn't mean it that way."

"I know you didn't. If I'd been offended, I wouldn't have spoken so freely. It was my choice."

They sat in silence for a moment, then John said, "How about a snack? I've got some rhubarb pie."

"Sounds great. I'll help." She followed him into the kitchen.

"How soon can we leave?" she asked.

"What?" He opened a cabinet. "Plates are in there."

"For Rome. How soon can we leave?"

"Well, I suppose today if I can make the arrangements."

Cotten found two small plates and set them on the counter. "Yes, today. Can you set it up?"

John pulled the pie from the refrigerator and looked at his watch. "It's still early. I have a friend with some clout. Felipe Montiagro, he's the Vatican Apostolic Nuncio."

"I'm not familiar . . ."

"Apostolic Nuncio. Vatican City State is a sovereign country. The nuncio is the equivalent of an ambassador. Archbishop Montiagro is the Vatican ambassador to the U.S. and works out of the Vatican embassy in Washington. We go way back. Let me give him time to get into his office; then I'll start with a call to him."

He cut two pieces of the pie, slid each onto the plates, and put them on the kitchen table. Grabbing two forks from the drawer, he said, "Soup's on."

They sat across from each other—Cotten watching him put a bite of pie in his mouth and chew. When his eyes met hers, she looked down at her pie and cut a piece with her fork.

"And I need to call a cab," she said after tasting. "I've got to go home and pack."

"It's two in the morning. You're more than welcome to stay in the guestroom. Besides, if there is a connection between the box and the break-in, your apartment may not be the best place to go."

John was right. Maybe she shouldn't return to her apartment at all. She could buy a nylon duffle bag and essentials at the airport—she still had her passport in her purse. And she would treat herself to a shopping spree in Rome once the relic was safely in the hands of the Vatican. "If I spend the night, won't your neighbors gossip?"

"Most of them are students, and they haven't even come in for the night." With a lighthearted smile, John added, "Besides, a lot of them are in my classes, and they want a passing grade."

They both laughed and finished up their pie slices. John stacked the dishes in the dishwasher and they returned to the living room.

"Did you bake the pie?" she asked.

"No, it was a gift."

"A lady friend?" Cotten asked, immediately wishing she hadn't.

John grinned. "Kind of."

"Really? I mean, can you—I didn't know a priest—even on leave—"

John laughed aloud. "My lady friend is seventy-eight years old, has acute arthritis, suffers from cataracts, and still finds time to bake me a pie every Thursday. This week was rhubarb."

Damn, she thought. Why had she asked that? *P-r-i-e-s-t, Cotten. Don't you get it?*

"Let's put this away for the night," John said as he wrapped the relic in the Templar cloth and placed it back in the box. He put it inside Cotten's bag. "Come on, I'll get you settled in."

He led her down the hall to the guestroom. It was plain and sparsely furnished—a single bed topped with a thick comforter, and a nightstand with a tiffany-style lamp, along with a small dresser and mirror. A simple crucifix hung on the wall at the head of the bed. It looked like he had made no investment in this place for it to become his home, she thought. He must not have decided that this is where he wanted to stay or what he wanted to do. He still hadn't found his passion.

"Nothing fancy, I'm afraid," John said.

"It'll do just fine."

"Bathroom is next door on the right. Anything else you need?"

She shook her head. "Can't think of anything."

He set the bag on the bed before saying goodnight.

John closed the door, and she heard the wood floor creak as he walked away.

Cotten gazed in the mirror. Her hair was all about, makeup long faded, eyes dull with exhaustion. "What must he think of me?"

She undressed, peeling away all the layers, then retrieved the blouse, but thought better of it. It would be too rumpled to wear in the morning if she slept in it. So, panties only it was. The room was warm enough, and the comforter looked cozy.

As she pulled back the covers, a tap on the bedroom door startled her. "Just a minute." Quickly, she slipped on her blouse and held it closed. Cracking open the door with her free hand, she peered around it through the small gap.

"I have some pajamas for you," he said. "They might be too big, but you can roll up the sleeves."

She reached through the door. "Oh, thanks," she said. As she pulled them through the narrow opening, they caught on the door handle, snapped from her hand, and fell to the floor. Cotten quickly bent over to gather them up.

John had squatted to help her. When he looked up, she heard him suck in his breath. She realized her blouse had fallen open. Frantically she fumbled to close it while he handed her the pajamas.

"Sorry," he said.

Cotten edged behind the door again, clutching the nightclothes to her chest, only her face peering around. God, she had just flashed him . . . flashed a priest for God's sake.

"See you in the morning," he said, stepping away.

* * *

"You've got to trust me on this, Ted." Cotten spoke into the in-flight telephone. "I'm sitting next to Dr. John Tyler. He's an expert, and he's examined the relic. He's ninety-nine percent certain it's authentic."

She turned to John who gave a hesitant shrug.

They were over the Atlantic on a direct Delta Airlines flight to Rome's Leonardo da Vinci International Airport.

"Get the marketing department ready to promote the biggest religious story since the Shroud of Turin," she said. "But don't leak what it's actually about. Not yet. Not until we've turned it over to the Vatican."

"I'll call our Rome bureau chief," Ted Casselman said. "I want you to keep in constant contact with him—update him on everything. He'll arrange for a production crew, editing, and anything else you need. Once you've got your piece, uplink immediately."

"I'm the principal, right?"

"Yes."

"The Rome bureau is there to support me, right?"

"Yes."

Cotten slammed back in the seat. "I love you, Ted."

"Yeah, I know. But just once, I'd like to think *I'm* in charge of assigning stories."

"You won't regret this."

"Right." There was a pause. "Isn't that what you told me from Baghdad?"

"This is the break I'm looking for and the story you need to boost those sagging ratings."

"Be careful, Cotten." Ted Casselman hung up.

She pushed the telephone into its holder on the back of the seat in front of her and turned to John. "What?"

"Ninety-nine percent certain?"

"Where's your faith?"

"I've got plenty of faith. Scientific proof is something else."

She reached over and patted his hand. "You worry too much."

There are several royal and noble European families that are believed to be of the Merovingian bloodline, the divine lineage. They are: Hapsburg-Lorraine, Plantard, Montpezat, Luxembourg, Montesauiou, some branches of the Stuarts, and the Sinclairs.

BREEDING

"AND WHO IS THAT?" the *Time* science correspondent asked, pointing to a framed photograph on the desk.

"My new granddaughter," Charles Sinclair said. "She was christened only last week in St. Louis Cathedral."

"She's beautiful. You must be very proud, Dr. Sinclair."

"I am."

"And I see you like ocean racers." The correspondent motioned to a collection of photos along a side wall. "Those are impressive boats. Do you drive them?"

"No, no. BioGentec sponsors a number of high-speed racers. Smaller versions are a hobby of mine, though. I have a few go-fast boats. I take then out sometimes on poker runs."

"How does that work?"

"We usually start at Friends Restaurant in Madisonville, then onto The Dock in Slidell, then we race the twenty miles across Lake Pontchartrain. We hit a few spots there, then back across the lake to Friends. At every stop we have a drink and draw a card from the deck. At the end of the day, the best five-card poker hand wins the pot."

"Do you always win, Dr. Sinclair?" the correspondent said, smiling.

"Always."

Both men laughed.

"And other hobbies?" asked the correspondent.

"I own a few thoroughbreds."

"And are they winners, too?"

"But of course. No triple crown yet, but we've fared well at Evangeline, Saratoga, Aqueduct, Bel—"

"You have a fancy for racing and competition."

"I suppose I have a penchant for speed, not necessarily the competition. But there's more to it than that. I admire and appreciate the craftsmanship, the perfection in the construction of a racing vessel. The performance reflects the attention to minute detail."

"And the horses?"

Sinclair leaned back and steepled his fingers beneath his chin. The faintest beginnings of an arrogant smile etched his face. "The breeding."

"Apropos," the correspondent said as he scribbled a note. He looked up at Sinclair. "Getting back to your comment that cloning is nothing new?"

"Human clones walk among us everyday. You've probably met quite a few. They're called identical twins—babies born from a single egg in their mother's womb that splits into two."

"How do you answer your critics who say that you're trying to play God by attempting to clone a human?" The correspondent made another note on his pad. "Even a Nobel laureate like you must think about the ethics issues."

"I'm just a scientist trying to save lives. I discover by research, by carrying out experiments. Nothing more should be read into it." Sinclair glanced at the antique mantel clock over his library fireplace. He didn't want to get any deeper into the ethical minefield. Through the French doors leading to the brick patio of his plantation estate, he saw the Mississippi beyond the ancient magnolias. Dark clouds gathered across the river.

"Some social justice advocates oppose cloning," the correspondent said. "They fear a widening gap between the haves and have-nots if affluent parents decide to genetically enhance their children."

"That might be a by-product of our research one day. Just like anything else, you have to weigh the benefits. We're pioneers venturing into new frontiers," Sinclair said. "Therapeutic cloning gives us the ability to get perfectly matched tissue for the patient, whether they have Parkinson's disease, diabetes, spinal cord injury—so the patient will not reject those cells. That's what we do at BioGentec. We don't debate ethics, we don't play God—we simply work to save lives."

"But you must realize—"

The phone rang on Sinclair's desk. He held his hand up. "Excuse me a moment." Picking up the receiver, he said, "Yes?"

"They're on a plane to Rome," Ben Gearhart said on the other end. "The priest is helping her take it to the Vatican."

Sinclair smiled. "That's very good news." He replaced the receiver and looked back at the correspondent. "You were saying?"

THE CARDINAL

"Your Eminence, Father Tyler and the SNN reporter are on their way up," Cardinal Antonio Ianucci's aide announced. "They've just passed through security."

"Thank you." The cardinal gazed out his second story office window. Adjacent to the Vatican Museums, his office overlooked the inner courtyard of the Belvedere Palace. He remembered a diplomat once telling him that in America an office this big would be called a formal ballroom. A frescoed ceiling met walls covered with medieval tapestries—a Persian rug the size of a swimming pool accented a portion of the fifteenth century wooden floor. Two-hundred-year-old brocade and damask couches and chairs were placed strategically around the room, their hand-carved legs rich in gold leaf.

The cardinal returned to his desk to study the flat screen monitor. At 68, he moved with ease, dedicating over an hour each morning to a strict regimen of exercise. Born in Italy to a British mother and Italian father, he grew up fluent in both languages. Even as a youngster he was fascinated with the trappings and traditions of the Catholic

Church and the priesthood. Early in life he set his goal, heading toward it as if traveling through a tunnel—no sidetracks, no distractions, no deviations. He knew he had been called, and he wanted to serve God in the most powerful way he could.

With degrees in theology and cannon law, Ianucci had taught at the Urbanian University in Rome prior to attending the Vatican's diplomatic college. He spent over a decade serving with the Secretariat of State after being made a bishop in 1980. In 1997, he was elevated to cardinal, and in 2000 the pope appointed him Vatican Curator. Among the elite inner core of the Vatican, he was considered a leading candidate for successor to the papacy—the goal at the end of the tunnel—God's supreme servant.

Ianucci was familiar with John Tyler, having met him on a number of occasions, but he read the priest's bio to refresh his memory. It stated that Tyler was currently on a leave-of-absence. The cardinal wondered why he had requested the leave, something so rarely sought or granted.

When Archbishop Montiagro had called him about Tyler and the discovery of a relic that might possibly be of unprecedented importance, Ianucci rearranged his schedule to accommodate a meeting. As with any new discovery, he was excited. "Unprecedented importance," he whispered. "I could use some of that."

Montiagro had made it clear that Tyler insisted on bringing along a member of the press. That puzzled the cardinal. Ianucci hadn't gotten the impression that the priest was glory hungry. He might have to remind Tyler of the Vatican protocol when it came to the press—a protocol that did not put American reporters at the top of the list. Besides, Ianucci had his own list—select members of the world press—ones he knew and trusted to quote him verbatim. The Vatican was a sovereign nation in which serving God was the focal point of every movement, every thought, and every deed. Not the place for American reporters whose objectives were usually either sensationalism or exploitation.

The cardinal closed the file and put the computer into sleep mode.

"Eminence, your guests are here," the aide announced after knocking and opening the massive door.

"Show them in." He stood and came around his desk. "Ah, John," he said as the two visitors approached. Extending his right hand palm down, he said, "It's good to see you again."

"Your Eminence." John accepted the cardinal's hand, genuflected, and lightly kissed the sapphire-stoned ring of his office. "Thank you for taking the time to see us. I'd like to present Cotten Stone, a correspondent for the Satellite News Network. Ms. Stone came into possession of the artifact while on assignment in the Middle East. She'll be covering the news of its authentication for her network."

"I'm pleased to meet you, Ms. Stone. I hope you will take pity on an old man and speak of me only in glowing terms when you file your report."

"I'm sure there would be no other way, Eminence," Cotten said, shaking the cardinal's hand.

Ianucci studied her—composed, self-assured, he thought. Still, he'd be delicate in his suggestions of how he would like to handle the situation. "Please, both of you sit and tell me what you have." Returning to his chair, he nodded to John.

"Are you familiar with Dr. Gabriel Archer?" John asked.

"Oh, yes," Ianucci said, tapping his finger on the desktop. "I read only this morning that his Turkish team had reported his death— heart attack, I believe." The cardinal made the sign of the cross. "May he rest in the peace of the Lord."

John continued. "Then you are aware of his excavation in Iraq?"

"I am. He accumulated an astonishing body of work throughout his career—the end must have been frustrating for him with his obsession with finding the Grail."

"His frustration may have paid off," John said. "Ms. Stone was with him when he died. I'll let her tell you."

One of the cardinal's eyebrows arched and there was a quick flutter, like a bird's wing inside his chest. "Please."

She told her story, ending with how she sought John's help in the opening of the puzzle cube and the discovery of the Cup inside.

The cardinal twirled his thumbs. "You say another man was killed in a struggle with Archer—an Arab?"

"Well, I assumed he was Arab. The clothes, appearance, and his accent," Cotten said.

"Strange, the article didn't mention anything other than Archer having a heart attack. Hmm."

Cotten looked at John, but didn't say anything.

Ianucci wondered what was on the reporter's mind. He waited a moment before speaking again, giving her an opportunity to talk. When she failed to do so, he said, "Let us suppose the man who tried to steal the relic from Archer was only an antiquities thief."

"If it weren't for the break-in of my apartment, Eminence, I would agree," Cotten said. "But there's too much of a coincidence. That's why I'm anxious to place it in the hands of an organization like yours that can assure its safety."

"You brought the relic with you?"

"Yes." Cotten opened her bag and produced the box.

Ianucci's pulse quickened.

She handed it to John. With precise movements, he slid open the lid, letting it drop back on its hinges. He placed it carefully on the desk.

"Our old friends, the Templars," Ianucci said, peering at the cross, the rose, and the seal woven into the cloth. Tiny beads of perspiration dampened his scalp beneath his red zucchetto.

"I had the same reaction, Eminence," John said. John produced a pair of white gloves from his pocket. He gently removed and unwrapped the Cup, setting it beside the box.

Hairs on the back of Ianucci's neck prickled, and a surge of nerve impulses raced down his arms. Gabriel Archer was no fool. If he believed this to be the Holy Grail, there was a strong likelihood that the Cup from the Last Supper sat only inches away.

Ianucci opened a desk drawer and retrieved his own pair of gloves. Slipping them on, he picked up the chalice and examined it—exploring the engraved monogram, the small band of beads, and the grapevines winding around the neck. The exhilaration was difficult to contain. He pointed to the dark substance coating the inside. "Beeswax?"

"I think so," John said.

"An appropriate method of preservation for that time period." The cardinal inspected the Cup from all angles, finally setting it down again. He leaned back and cocked his head, first to one side and then the other as he continued to study the relic. "The style and metalwork seem concurrent with others I've seen of that era. The engraving was probably much later."

"Agreed," John said.

"Radiocarbon dating the wax should be fairly straightforward." The fluttering in his chest made him cough. He pressed his fingers to his carotid, checking the irregular beat, unable to take his eyes from the chalice. His heart regained its rhythm. "We have a number of vessels with which to do a side-by-side comparison." Ianucci looked up.

"All right. Let's deliver it to our experts and see what they find." He stood. "Where are you staying?"

"*Nova Domus*," John said, coming to his feet.

Cotten rose and turned to John. "Is that all?"

"For today, Ms. Stone," Ianucci answered.

"But SNN is ready to—"

The cardinal smiled, holding up his hand. "You must be patient."

"Do you think it's authentic? What's your best guess?" she asked.

John gently took Cotten's arm. "It has to go through a lengthy process—there won't be any guessing."

Cotten edged her arm away. "I realize that it will take time." She turned to Ianucci. "Your Eminence, I took John's advice and agreed to bring the relic here. But there are many other organizations qualified to authenticate it in return for guaranteeing me the exclusive." She took a slight step forward toward the desk. "If I could have your word, the Cup is yours."

The significance of the relic far outweighed who reported the story first, the cardinal reasoned. He would grant her a fleeting moment of fame. Then she would be on a plane fading into obscurity while he continued his journey toward his ultimate goal. The Grail story would give him additional notoriety, helping him gain prominence among his colleagues. A prominence that mattered the next time the College of Cardinals gathered in the Sistine Chapel in secret conclave and cast their ballots for the man who would become the next bishop of Rome, Holy Father, successor to Saint Peter, Vicar of Christ.

"You have made your point, Ms. Stone. I will alert you as soon as I have word. Until then, take time to enjoy the sights of Rome while our people perform their work. I am sure Father Tyler will be happy to act as your tour guide." Cardinal Ianucci nodded, clearly dismissing them.

They thanked Ianucci and walked across the ancient wooden floor. As the echo of the fourteen-foot-high doors closed behind them, Ianucci moved to the window overlooking the palace courtyard, waiting until his pulse slowed. Only then did he allow himself to look back at the Cup on his desk.

* * *

At twilight, John and Cotten took the cardinal's suggestion to take in some of Rome's famous highlights.

As they walked, Cotten couldn't help but rehash what Ianucci had said. "Someone got rid of the Arab's body so there would be nothing suspicious," she said, walking alongside John. "Don't you see, it's a cover-up? The cardinal said there was nothing in the news about the dead Arab—just Archer's death due to a heart attack."

"It is strange there was no mention of the Arab."

"I'll tell you what, when this story breaks, I'm leaving that part out. I don't want them to come looking for me again." Cotten glanced up and stopped dead. "Oh, my God." The lights striking and splaying off the Coliseum's travertine and stone gave it an overwhelming sense of grandeur.

"Amazing, isn't it? It's quite astounding at night," John said as they approached the Coliseum.

Cotten's eyes fixed on the structure that was the symbol throughout the world of the Eternal City—the emblem of Rome's greatness. "I've seen pictures and movies, but—"

She waved her arms toward the Coliseum. "This is why. This is what kept tugging at me as I grew up in Kentucky. This is why I do what I do, John. There is so much to see. I want to see it all." The timbre of her voice dropped. "And I don't think I'll ever see enough." She turned in a circle, feeling as if she couldn't take it all in. It wasn't just the splendor, it was the whole package—the stunning beauty, the wonder of the structural design, the history. "I'm babbling," she said. "Sorry. You talk. Tell me about the Romans, about the gladiators, the architecture. Were Christians really thrown to the lions, here?"

"Debatable," John answered.

She moved close to him. "Tell me everything. I want to hear all the details."

"At one time it was the most beautiful amphitheater in the world. An ecclesiastical writer—Bede—once wrote that 'while the Coliseum stands, Rome shall stand, but when the Coliseum falls, Rome shall fall and when Rome falls, the world will end.'"

She sensed his eyes on her as she moved in front of him. She felt the tough outer shell she tried so hard to hide behind, crack, just enough that he was catching a glimpse of what lay inside. For some reason she no longer wanted to keep that armor intact. She was more fanciful and idyllic than she liked to admit, but with John she didn't sense the need to hide that part of her. It was refreshing to be Cotten Stone, girl from Kentucky, vulnerable, sometimes childlike. Always being in control, being strong, pretending that she could handle anything, was exhausting. She enjoyed allowing the delicacy of being a woman come through, not having to be the hard-edged reporter. The last time she'd felt this free, this true to herself, was before her father died. Everything changed the day he killed himself. Cotten, a little girl with a name as soft as the clouds, turned to stone. How often she thought about the irony of it. *Cotten Stone.*

Suddenly, she faced John, grabbing his hands. "How could anyone see this and not be moved?"

94

Cotten looked down at their hands. "Oops—not appropriate. I keep forgetting."

When she loosened her grip, John held on a moment. "It's okay. There's nothing inappropriate for two friends to show affection."

Taking several steps backward, she bent at the waist, and laughed. "John, you know what would be a riot? It would be just my luck to fall in love with a priest. Fits my M.O. One more way to avoid rejection. I mean, look at my last debacle. Thornton Graham and I were lovers. Did you know that?"

"Not exactly."

"He's married and way out of my league. He couldn't reject or hurt me because I couldn't really have him in the first place. See what I mean?" She leaned her head back and glared at the sky. "Does that make sense?"

"You're too hard on yourself—a beautiful, bright, resourceful woman. Look at what you've been through. Nothing short of extraordinary, from the Iraqi desert to the halls of the Vatican. Why on earth are you afraid someone might reject you?"

She laughed again, but tears huddled near her lower lashes. "You know just the right things to say. If you weren't a . . . well, I'd hug you."

John put his arms around her. "Priests hug people all the time," he said. "Don't ever let the things that happen in life make you lose the sense of who you really are and what you're made of."

How he eased her, she thought as John let go of her.

"You know you can apply that same advice to yourself."

He slipped his hand inside the collar of his shirt and lifted a crucifix on a chain. "This belonged to my grandfather. It represents what's important to me—serving God. It's not that I have doubts; I just can't find the right niche. What is it that God has planned for me?" He laughed softly. "Am I a shepherd or Indiana Jones? I know that He'll show me the way. He'll lead me to where I am to be." He laughed again. "Sometimes I think He has a sense of humor and fetish for riddles." John put the cross back inside his shirt.

"Maybe you just need to be patient. Like you said, He'll show you the way. But do you really have to be a priest in order to serve God? I mean there's got to be lots of ways ordinary people—" She stopped herself. "Well, you know better than I do."

A lazy smile spread across his face.

She wondered if he was looking at her as she looked at him. How much, right now, in the glittering reflections of the Coliseum, in the tender fading twilight, in the soft breeze, in this perfect moment, she wanted to thread her arms through his—just to be held by someone who wanted nothing from her.

"What are you staring at?" John asked. "Do I have something on my face?"

"No, I'm sorry. This is such an incredible moment, and I'm so overwhelmed."

She came to stand next to him, and John touched the small of her back to guide her on. She began to walk beside him, and then his hand was gone.

How solid John was in his faith, Cotten thought. She couldn't imagine having so much trust in the idea that God would divinely move her along a path to her destiny. Like John's hand against her back, God's hand had fallen away from her early on. After all, God had better things to do. She'd scratched and clawed and dug her way to where she was. On her own. God had nothing to do with it.

THE EVENING NEWS

"And now, *Close Up*, our special segment on stories and events that significantly impact our lives." Thornton Graham read from the teleprompter as he stood on the SNN weekend news set in front of a blue wall. Chroma-keyed electronically behind him was a stylistic composite graphic of the Vatican, the faces of Cotten Stone and Dr. Gabriel Archer, and various religious symbols including a simple chalice.

"As reported earlier in the newscast," Thornton said, "the Vatican announced today the discovery of Christianity's most sought-after relic—the mystical Holy Grail. In an SNN exclusive report, correspondent Cotten Stone not only brought you the story, but was at the heart of it. A few weeks ago, while returning from assignment in Baghdad, Stone found herself abandoned in the Iraqi desert. Seeking safe passage to the Turkish border, she stumbled across an excavation of an ancient tomb headed up by this man, noted archaeologist, Dr. Gabriel Archer."

Archer's face filled the graphic behind Thornton.

"Before Dr. Archer succumbed to a fatal heart attack, he gave Stone a box he had recovered from the tomb and asked her to keep it safe. After returning home, Stone sought out the help of noted historian, archaeologist, and Catholic priest, Dr. John Tyler, who was able to open the box."

The graphic dissolved to a picture of John and Cotten standing beside the *Pieta*.

"Inside was this."

Dissolve to a photo of the chalice.

"This Cup is now believed to be the one used by Jesus Christ at the Last Supper—the same one tradition says was used to collect His blood at the Crucifixion. Down through the centuries it has been known simply as the Holy Grail."

Dissolve to Cotten and Cardinal Ianucci.

"Vatican Curator, Cardinal Antonio Ianucci, revealed during Stone's report that the preliminary examination of the relic suggests it is authentic."

The video changed to a full screen sound bite from the interview. Cotten sat opposite the cardinal in an ornate library deep inside the papal palace.

"We considered many factors," Ianucci said, "including metalwork, the patina, craftsmanship, historical descriptions for comparison, and the radiocarbon dating of what we have now determined is beeswax—the protective layer coating the inside of the Cup."

Close-up overhead shot looking inside of Cup.

"Do you think you would have been this certain if you had not obtained the additional artifact from Dr. Archer's estate in England?" Cotten asked.

"The markings on that artifact—the plate Dr. Archer discovered in Jerusalem—added many of the missing pieces to the puzzle," the cardinal said. "Again, that also has been examined and determined to be authentic. After deciphering its markings, we traced the Grail's journey with great accuracy from its first owner, Joseph of Arimathea, who traveled with the Apostle Paul, all the way through its final resting place near the Assyrian ruins in Nineveh, Northern Iraq. Although there are breaks in the lineage, other documents from our archives filled in most of the gaps. The evidence is quite convincing."

Cotten asked, "What are the Vatican's plans for the relic?"

"It is truly a gift from God—a key piece of Christ's life and our religious faith, and it belongs to the people. We intend to make it available to view and venerate. It will be displayed on special holidays like Good Friday and eventually taken on tour."

Back to Thornton.

"But perhaps the most astounding part of this story is not the Cup itself, but what may lie inside. In a surprising last-minute revelation, Cardinal Ianucci told Stone that by using the latest in solid matter, 3D imaging technology, a microscopic layer of residue was discovered beneath the protective beeswax, residue that some have already speculated could be actual traces of Christ's blood. As expected, this startling announcement has sent shockwaves through the worldwide Christian community generating discussion and debate."

Thornton turned to a headshot camera.

"So, with all the news of war and unrest across the globe filling our headlines each day, it's nice to bring you a story that has a happy ending—one that bolsters the faith of Christians everywhere and offers all of us something to ponder as we go about our lives. I'd like to end by saying that we at SNN are proud of Cotten Stone and her work to bring this important story to you. She's just one more reason you can always trust the Satellite News Network for the news that makes the difference."

Full shot of Thornton with Close Up segment logo behind him.

"If you'd like more information on the Holy Grail, its history, and recent discovery, log onto our website at satellitenews-dot-org, and join us each night for the SNN Evening News. I'm Thornton Graham. See you next time."

"Yes!" Cotten screamed, jumping into the air, her arms thrust over her head. The monitors went black as the taped replay of the newscast ended.

Applause erupted throughout the conference room packed with SNN staff. Shouts of congratulations and excitement filled the air.

"Good job," Ted Casselman said, standing next to Cotten.

She threw her arms around his neck. "Thanks, Ted." Then she turned to Thornton who had also been standing beside her while the tape played. "And thank you, Thornton." She gave him a peck on the cheek before stepping back.

"You did a great job, kid," he said. "We're all glad you're home safe and sound."

"All right, people," Ted Casselman said finally. "There's other news out there. Let's go report it."

As the staffers filed out, Casselman pulled a number of message slips from his pocket. "Seems a few people want to talk to you."

"What do you mean?" Cotten said.

"*Leno, Letterman, Oprah, Nightline, The Today Show, People* magazine, *Larry King, GMA*." He leafed through each one. "Not to mention a ton of religious organizations."

"The only way you can top this is to cover the Second Coming," Thornton said. "You're a genuine celebrity."

"What should I do?" Cotten asked, taking the message slips.

"That's your call," Casselman said. "But it couldn't hurt showing your face on a few of those talk shows—good for you and the network."

"I'm just glad it's over," she said. "To be honest, I hope I never see that Cup again."

"Never say never," Thornton said. "Maybe we can talk later?" When she didn't respond, he turned and followed the last of the staff out.

She watched him pass through the door, his gait so familiar—long, even strides.

"I can't wait to see the ratings," Casselman said, drawing her out of her thoughts. "But before you hit me up for a raise . . ."

"Can we talk, Ted?" She motioned to two chairs.

"Sure."

When they were seated, she said, "I need some time off." She looked into his eyes. "This has been almost more than I can handle."

"Understandable."

"Can you spare me for a week?"

"Maybe." His face gave away that he was only toying.

"Really, Ted. I need to crash."

"Your fifteen minutes worn you out?"

"It's not the fifteen minutes. I like the attention. It's everything that led up to it, starting from the minute the driver dumped me in the desert. I'm drained—I need to regroup. Just a week, Ted. I want to go to Miami. My roommate from college—I told you about Vanessa—the model. I'll stay with her, soak up some sun, and get all this behind me."

"I'll make you a deal." He paused for a moment, tapping the ends of his forefingers together. "The Robert Wingate thing—you remember, the guy who is going to throw in his hat for the presidential race?"

"I thought Thornton was covering it?"

"He is. But Wingate is giving a get-acquainted dinner for the media in Miami, his hometown, next Saturday. Thornton will be heading to Washington on special assignment—can't be in two places. We need to be on top of Wingate when he announces his candidacy. If you'll cover the dinner, I'll pay for your week on the beach."

"I only have to attend the dinner? Just the one evening?"

"That's it. And you can take your friend along. Just do two things: observe and see if you can chat with Wingate, get a feel for him, maybe set up an interview. Then document your thoughts and impressions, and send them back to Thornton."

"It's a deal." She extended her hand, and they shook. "Thanks."

"Get with Thornton and let him fill you in on what he's got so far."

"Right," she said, reluctantly. She'd dealt with Thornton pretty well until now, she thought. No more outbursts. No more crying.

"Cotten, I know all about you and Thornton. Just do your job and don't worry. I'll keep him out of your hair."

She threaded her hair behind her ears. "I'll be fine," she said, wondering whom she was really convincing. "You're the best, Ted."

"Yeah, I know. Now, return some of those calls and see how many interviews you can get in before you leave. Remember, you're a celeb. Milk it."

As she walked from the conference room, she realized that through all the excitement and celebrating she found herself thinking more and more of John Tyler. Especially when she saw the picture of them together on the newscast. She wondered if he had returned from Rome yet. It would be nice to talk to him.

Back at her desk, Cotten dialed John's number, but got his answering machine. Maybe I shouldn't call anyway, she thought. She hung up before the message beep.

She lifted the receiver again and dialed Vanessa's cell.

"Hello," the voice on the other end answered.

"Nessi!"

"Oh, my God!" Vanessa Perez shouted into the phone.

"Calm down, girl."

"Are you kidding? You're a certified star. I saw you all over the evening news. I can't believe it. I'm telling all my friends I know you."

"Will you please calm down."

"Okay, okay."

"I want to swing down for a visit. Are you going to be home next week or are you off to some exotic—"

"I'm free for the weekend, but I've got a shoot coming up in Nassau at the first of the week. But it's only a two-dayer. You can hang out, and then I'll be back."

"Sounds great. Then I'm coming down, if it's all right."

"It's perfect. Excellent timing. There's going to be a huge festival—kind of like a mixture of *Calle Ocho* and Fantasy Fest. They're calling it Miami Phantasm Jubilee—a half million people dancing in the streets partying their brains out."

Cotten waved at two staffers who came by to congratulate her as she said, "Sounds like just what I need. I'll fly in Friday night. Saturday evening I've got to attend a political dinner. I can get two passes if you want to be my date—very high-end stuff. After the dinner, I'm free."

"I guess I can be good long enough to get through some highbrow dinner."

"I'll rent a car and come straight to your apartment. What's that club on SoBe you told me about?

"Tantra's—it's wild, Cotten. Think you're ready?"

"More than you know. Love you." Cotten hung up. She missed her friend and desperately needed a change of scene. A good mix of relaxing and partying might help her stop thinking about Thornton . . . or John Tyler.

Cotten looked at the stack of message slips on her desk. She slowly went through the pile before deciding on three. "Here goes," she said, picking up the phone.

THE SECRET GARDEN

COTTEN DROVE HER RENTAL car down the long, tree-lined entrance to Vizcaya, James Deering's palatial villa on the shores of Miami's Biscayne Bay. The Italian Renaissance-style mansion, built in 1916 on a 160-acre estate, contained Deering's collection of art and furnishings reflecting 400 years of European history. Over the decades, Vizcaya had hosted popes, presidents, and kings. Tonight, it would be the majestic backdrop for a man wanting to run for President of the United States.

"This place is incredible," Vanessa Perez said, sitting in the passenger's seat. She finger-combed her long black hair. "I've done a dozen photo shoots here, but I still get goose bumps."

Millions of tiny lights lit the gardens and villa giving Cotten the impression of a star-filled wonderland. Every twig and branch twinkled in the soft breeze from the bay.

"It's magnificent," Cotten said. The lights, the fountains, the breeze, all reminded her of Rome and the evening at the Coliseum.

White-shirted valets opened the car doors. Cotten and Vanessa got out and made their way up the regal steps of Vizcaya's west facade—a grand entrance between two stone towers connected by a low wall with old world Italian grillwork.

They entered the reception room and picked up their name tags. The hum of voices and rustling of formal attire filled the air.

In her tight little black dress and spike heels, Vanessa was a sexual magnet, Cotten thought, as men glanced in their direction.

One man stepped in front of them. "You look absolutely elegant, as always," he said to Vanessa.

His suit—Cotten guessed it cost more than she made in a month—hugged his tall, slim frame.

"Thanks, Felipe." Vanessa shot him the same smile that had graced the cover of so many magazines. "I want you to meet my best friend, Cotten Stone from SNN. Cotten, this is Felipe Dubois, the editor of *Deco Dining*."

"Of course, Ms. Stone," Dubois said, a look of sudden recognition on his face. "I saw you on *Oprah*. What an experience you had."

"Meeting Oprah or finding the Holy Grail?" Cotten said, shaking his hand.

"Both, of course," Dubois said, laughing heartily. "Do you believe it's real, the Grail, I mean?"

"I'm no expert, but the evidence seems convincing. At least that's what the Vatican says."

"Vanessa, where have you been hiding this gorgeous creature?" he asked. "She should be right there on the cover of *Vogue* next to you." His hand moved with a flourish, and he spoke with a drawl at the end of his words, as if they were taffy and he had to pull them slowly from his tongue.

"I've tried many times to get her to come over to my way of thinking." Vanessa winked at Cotten.

"Behave," Cotten said. "If you'll excuse me, I'm going to mingle. Nice to meet you, Felipe. Nessi, I'll see you at our table. The number is on your ticket."

As she walked away, she glanced back to see a half-dozen men surround Vanessa Perez, vying for her attention. Cotten found it amusing that most of them never realized they had no chance.

The mansion was arranged around a central courtyard in the style of a sixteenth century Italian villa. She wandered across the crowded courtyard, through a number of high-ceiling rooms, and finally emerged on a grand stone veranda running the length of the villa and overlooking the bay. A smooth jazz trio played at one end while guests chatted, sipped champagne, and munched on smoked salmon and stone crabs.

As she wove her way through the attendees, a nagging headache reminded her of the previous night. She and Vanessa had started the evening with a spicy dinner and giant margaritas at Tequila Blue before moving on to Tantra's. From the moment they walked in, Cotten felt the sensuality of the place—fresh cut grass floor under her feet, the scent of jasmine, the waterfalls, people smoking glass hookahs of Middle Eastern tobacco, the long mahogany and copper bar, the New Age music. Vanessa said the club was the hotspot for South Beach's beautiful people, and true to her word, they passed Janet Jackson and her bodyguards just leaving. After hours of dancing, downing Cuervo 1800 shots and flutes of champagne, more dancing, more shots, and propositions by as many females as males, Cotten finally called it quits. Taking a cab back to Vanessa's beach apartment, she left her friend with two Dolphins cheerleaders trying to become fire-eaters with a box of matches and a bottle of 151.

The soft jazz, combined with the fresh breeze coming in off the bay and across the Vizcaya balcony, soothed her headache. Cotten stood by the railing, looking down at the expansive ground-level patio covered with dinner tables and a dais for the honored guests. A small group gathered to the side around a tall man in a pinstripe suit. He had an obvious flair for attracting attention and seemed to enjoy it. His mannerisms and body language suggested plenty of self-confidence. He was either a uniquely charismatic individual or had been well coached, or both. He already looked presidential, she thought. She stood intrigued as she watched Robert Wingate, the *perfect* candidate.

When the dinner seating began, Cotten joined Vanessa.

The menu was lavish, including crispy whole red snapper with coconut rice and spicy red curry sauce.

"This is delicious," Vanessa said, sipping her white wine. "Wingate must be made out of money."

"It would seem so," Cotten said, wondering just how deep his pockets went. His speech would start soon, and she looked forward to hearing if his voice matched the rest of his commanding presence.

They chatted with others at their table, most of the talk centering around questions about the Grail. Every now and again, Cotten glanced at Wingate. As the dessert of caramel rice pudding topped with fresh mango and currants was brought to each guest, she noticed someone, whom she assumed was an aide, approach him. The man whispered into the candidate's ear. Wingate's perpetual smile faded.

Glancing over his shoulder, Wingate looked in the direction of Vizcaya's classical gardens—acres of paths and fountains that wound among a maze of rare, exotic flowers and plants. Standing, he made what appeared to be apologies to those at his table and moved toward the gardens.

Ted Casselman had asked Cotten to observe, and that's what she intended to do. "Be right back," she whispered to Vanessa as she stood and headed through the sea of tables toward the gardens. Following Wingate on a parallel course, keeping the candidate over her left shoulder about a hundred feet away, she entered the spider-webbed paths that weaved among fountains, pools, and cascades. Although the gardens were lit, much of it was torchlight throwing flickering patches of light at her feet and reflecting off the sculptures and decorative urns along the path. Passing through a double grotto, Cotten entered the high-walled Secret Garden, a private place where Deering family members were known to retreat from the formality of the main house. It was the same garden where in 1987, millions of television viewers around the world watched as Pope John Paul II and President Ronald Reagan met during the Pontiff's first visit to America.

Catching glimpses of Wingate, Cotten was able to keep up with him. Delicate lighting hidden among the surrounding hedges and vines gave the scene a van Gogh, *Night With Stars*, appearance.

As Cotten watched from the shadows, Wingate stopped at a small circle of limestone benches surrounding a Florentine fountain with stone fish jumping and spraying streams from their mouths. He came face-to-face with a man dressed in street clothes, not the formal attire of the evening. The man handed Wingate what Cotten thought was a business card. The candidate held it up to catch the light and read it. They spoke for a few moments—Cotten getting the impression through their gestures and body language that the discussion was heated. Over the white noise of the fountain, she thought she caught a fragment of an argument. At one point, Wingate stabbed his finger toward the man's face, then pitched the card at him like a Frisbee. It whirled on the air for a moment before cart-wheeling to the ground.

Wingate turned and moved hastily down the path, back toward the villa. The stranger watched Wingate leave, waiting a few minutes before leaving.

Once the crunching of his steps along the gravel path faded, Cotten snatched up the business card. She stole a quick look at it, then fell in behind the unknown man, keeping her distance. He moved briskly to the central courtyard, the reception area, out through the mansion's front entrance, and into a waiting limousine.

Cotten stood on the steps until the black limousine's taillights vanished before she headed back to the dinner.

"Are you all right?" Vanessa asked as Cotten slipped into the seat beside her. "I was getting worried."

"I'm fine." Cotten dropped the card into her small sequined handbag. "Just making some business contacts. Did I miss anything?"

"Only Chris Matthews from MSNBC. Very cool guy. He actually stopped and said hello. Other than that, just a couple of boring politicians giving some speeches." Vanessa nodded toward the stage and podium. "Your guy disappeared for a while, but he's back and about to make his case."

Cotten watched Robert Wingate thank the state senator who introduced him.

"Good evening, my friends of the press," Wingate said after stepping up to the microphone. "I can't tell you how happy I am to be here on such a glorious night in South Florida."

* * *

"This is SNN correspondent, Cotten Stone," the aide said.

Cotten and Vanessa had waited in the reception line for about ten minutes when their turn came to meet Robert Wingate.

"It's a pleasure, Ms. Stone." Wingate extended his hand. "Congratulations on your exclusive coverage of that amazing Grail story. It's not often that a reporter gets to make the news and then report it. Great job."

"Thank you."

"I caught some of your appearances on the talk shows, too. You've become quite a celebrity."

"It's been fun to share what happened with so many." Cotten turned to her right. "I'd like you to meet—"

"Another celebrity," Wingate said, shaking hands with Vanessa. "It's impossible to stand in a grocery checkout line these days without seeing you on a magazine cover, Ms. Perez."

"Somehow, I can't imagine you standing in a checkout line," Vanessa said.

"You might be surprised to find I'm just an ordinary guy." Wingate met her smile with an equally enchanting one. "Are you Cuban?"

"My parents were born in Cuba. I'm a Miami-Jackson Memorial Hospital-born American." Vanessa's chin rose slightly.

Cotten flinched. Wingate had picked on Vanessa's pet peeve—being proud of her Cuban heritage but not liking people to assume she was anything but American.

"Then we're both native-born Floridians—rare birds in these parts," Wingate said.

Before Cotten stepped away, she said, "Could I schedule an interview with you, Mr. Wingate?"

"I can't think of anything I would enjoy more," he answered. "Give me a call."

Then as if changing TV channels, he turned to the next person in the reception line and said, "And how are you tonight?"

The candidate's aide motioned for Cotten and Vanessa to move on.

"He's definitely charming," Vanessa said.

"Just another politician," Cotten said. But something had upset him in the Secret Garden. Had she discovered a crack in his perfectly polished veneer?

"Can we go have some fun now?" Vanessa asked, pretending to tug at Cotten's arm.

"I'm ready."

PRIESTESS

COTTEN FELT THE THUNDERING bass like a fist on her chest. Strobes flashed in a continuous storm of color. She was immersed in a sea of swirling motion, pounding Latin music, and tightly packed bodies. For the last two hours, she and Vanessa had moved from club to club along *Calle Ocho* in the Little Havana section of Miami. Every street, ally, room, and corner overflowed with Miami Phantasm Jubilee partygoers. Now her head spun from too many exotic drinks, and her legs wobbled. Sweat soaked her dress, its filmy fabric clinging like cellophane. She felt queasy and needed to get some fresh air and use the bathroom.

She grabbed Vanessa's arm, pulling her close. "I've got to use the ladies room," she shouted.

Nodding that she understood, Vanessa kept on dancing.

In the back of the room, Cotten found a hallway with women waiting in a long line.

"Shit," Cotten said. She looked at a girl next to her, hoping she spoke English. "Is this the only bathroom?"

The girl stared at her questioningly.

Relying on her high school Spanish, Cotten asked again, "*Otros baños?*"

"*Afuera,*" the woman said.

Cotten shrugged.

The woman's wide mouth slackened, and she put a knuckle to her lips as if thinking. Finally, she pointed over the heads of those in line and said, "Outside."

Cotten worked her way around the dance floor to the entrance. Once she had pushed through to the sidewalk, she was immediately caught up in the crowd. Blaring music from a live band on a stage in the middle of the street made it impossible to ask for directions.

She moved through the crowd for about a block, then turned down a side street. A teenage couple, wound together in a mad embrace, leaned against a wall. She hated to disturb them, but she really needed to find a bathroom.

"Excuse me," she said. "Can you tell me where I can find a restroom?"

The boy looked around, clearly annoyed at the interruption.

"Bathrooms?" Cotten asked. Her voice softer with an apology riding on it.

"*Sí,*" the girl said. "There is a little restaurant down there," she said, looking further down the street.

"Thanks." Cotten passed several closed stores before she got to the sandwich shop, its front window filled with pictures of Cuban sandwiches and hoagie-style ham and cheese called *media noches*. The inside was filled with people either eating at small Formica tables or waiting in line to place an order.

"*Baño?*" she asked a black woman wearing an apron bearing the shop's name, *Badia's Café*.

But the woman either ignored her or didn't understand.

Where was the frigging bathroom for God's sake?

Bathrooms had to be in the rear of the place, she thought. Making her way to the back of the shop, Cotten saw two unmarked doors. She pushed open the first and entered a storeroom filled with boxes of cooking supplies. There was an additional door beyond the shelves. She found it already open a few inches, and she pushed on it.

What she saw stunned her—a small room shimmering with candles through a thick smoky haze. A handful of people knelt on the bare concrete floor, chanting. At the other end of the room stood a table covered with wooden, African-art-style statuettes along with many of Jesus and the Virgin Mary. Circles, arrows, and strange symbols that Cotten didn't recognize covered the wall.

She found herself mesmerized by the scene. Stepping into the room, she quietly watched as an old woman, some kind of priestess, Cotten assumed, stood before the group. The old woman had rutted ebony skin stretched tightly over her face and wore a long white dress with her head wrapped in a white scarf—the end falling down over her shoulder. A large yellow flower rested over her left ear. Her eyes were closed, her head bowed in what appeared to be deep prayer or meditation.

No one seemed to notice Cotten, nor acknowledge her presence as the incantations continued. From a corner of the room came the jingle of a tambourine—its player tapping in rhythm to the prayers.

Was it Voodoo? Cotten wondered. Santeria? Black Magic? There was such a mix of cultures in Miami—this could be any number of Caribbean religions. Although she found it fascinating, she suddenly remembered how much she needed to locate a bathroom.

As she started to leave, the chanting stopped abruptly and the old woman looked up at her.

"I didn't mean to interrupt," Cotten said, taking a step backward.

The worshipers stood and moved aside, clearing a path to the front.

The priestess approached, raising her bony hand until her finger pointed at Cotten.

Cotten froze, transfixed. With the smoke of hundreds of candles encircling them, the priestess stepped so close that their bodies almost touched.

The rattle of the tambourine started its tinny music. Like the sound of buzzing insects, the congregation resumed chanting, their gaze fixed on Cotten and the priestess.

Cotten's eyes burned from the smoke as the priestess leaned forward, her lips touching Cotten's ear. She strained to hear the old woman over the noise. "What?" she said, working at understanding the frail voice buried in the thick island accent.

The woman whispered again, but his time not in English. "*Geh el crip ds adgt quasb—*"

Cotten's eyes grew wide and her head jerked up, her hand covering her mouth. She stared in disbelief as the woman returned to stand beside the altar. "What did you say?"

SOUTH BEACH

THE OLD PRIESTESS DIDN'T answer Cotten. Instead, she closed her eyes and seemed to return to her meditation.

"Oh, my God, this can't be," Cotten whispered, backing through the door.

Cotten pushed her way past the sandwich shop customers until she was again in the side street. Holding back a scream, she ran toward *Calle Ocho* and the sound of the blaring street band.

Like swimming against the current, she forced her way through the mass of dancing bodies and partygoers along the sidewalk until she was in front of the club. The whole scene seemed to swallow her up as she tried to remember where they had parked her rental car. Then she heard a familiar voice.

"Cotten?" Vanessa emerged from under the club's awning and ran to her friend's side. "What is it, baby? Are you all right?"

Cotten stared at Vanessa as if she were a stranger. Her world spun.

"What's wrong?" Vanessa asked.

"Get me out of here, Nessi, please. Get me out of here."

* * *

Cotten squinted into the bright sunrise as she stood with her feet in the surf behind Vanessa's South Beach apartment. Sunbeams glistened off the water like iridescent jewel filaments. The nip in the morning air felt good. She aimlessly chewed on a thumbnail cuticle while staring through dark sunglasses at a container ship on the horizon. From a quick glance in the mirror earlier, she knew that her eyes were puffy and red from crying.

"See this shell," Vanessa said, picking up a half an angel wing seashell and casually examining it. "You'll only find single ones washed up on the beach. Know why?"

"No. But you're going to tell me, aren't you?"

Vanessa grinned. "Angel wings don't have any ligaments that hold them together. They burrow down tightly in the sand and count on the sand and these little adductor muscles to keep them closed."

"How do you know stuff like that?" Cotten asked.

"I dated a marine biologist."

"I remember her. Didn't she go to work for Sea World in Orlando?"

Vanessa nodded.

"Nessi, about last night. I told you what the old woman said—it was the same thing Archer said when he gave me the box—about me being the only one who could stop the something or other." Cotten pressed her hand to her trembling lips and fought back tears. "It wasn't *what* they both said, Nessi, it was how."

"Like a threat?"

"No," Cotten said. "Remember me telling you that I had a twin sister who died at birth?"

Vanessa thought for a second. "Yes, you called her Motnees."

"Right. And remember how I said when I was little I could see her and talk to her in our secret made-up language."

"But you said she wasn't real—just an imaginary playmate."

"I said I made her up because I didn't want you to laugh at me. But I *did* believe she was real, very real."

"Cotten, she died. So you had to have made up all that stuff." Vanessa gathered her hair to the side. "And what's that got to do with the old woman last night? Or the guy in Iraq?"

Cotten removed her dark glasses and looked deep into her friend's eyes. "The old woman and Archer spoke in the same language Motnees and I used. Nobody knows that language. Nobody! I'm surprised after all this time it even came back to me."

Vanessa's mouth opened slightly as if she was going to say something, but before she could, Cotten said, "Let's say Motnees really was a figment of my imagination. Let's also say I made up our twin talk and pretended to talk to her—just kids' stuff, okay? How would anyone else know that?"

Replacing the dark glasses over her eyes, Cotten turned back toward the ocean. They didn't speak for a while as they stood in the sand gazing out over the water.

Finally, Vanessa said, "I've got to tell you that's the creepiest thing I've ever heard." She tossed the angel wing into the water.

"What can it possibly mean?" Cotten watched a few minnows in their endless search for food circle the spot where the shell splashed.

"Are you absolutely sure they were the same words the guy said in the tomb?"

"There's no mistake. *Geh el crip*. It means, you are the only one. That's what Archer said. First he said I had to stop the sun or the dawn, or something like that. Then he said, '*Geh el crip*.' You are the only one. Last night, the priestess said '*Geh el crip ds adgt quasb*.' *You*

119

are the only one who can stop it. No, stronger than stop. More like destroy."

"Destroy?"

"First she whispered in English. It was hard to hear her, but it was what Archer said. I'm the only one to stop the sun and something else. I didn't hear the end clearly. Her voice trailed off. But then she spoke in twin talk. She said, 'You are the only one who can destroy it.'"

"Cotten, you've got to admit, that whole talking to your dead sister thing is pretty creepy."

Cotten glared at her.

"Sorry." Vanessa put her arm around Cotten's shoulder as they turned and started walking. "Okay, let's think this through. Two different people on separate occasions tell you that you're the *only one* who can stop something—stop the sun from coming up or stop the dawn. And they also both happen to speak some made-up language you used to communicate with your deceased twin sister when you were just a little girl. Let's forget the weirdness of it all for a moment." Vanessa nodded toward the horizon. "There's the sun, and it's dawn. How could you possibly stop that from happening? It makes no sense in any language."

"I need to talk to someone."

"Your priest friend?"

"I tried to call him again, but all I got was his machine. He may not even be back from Rome. I don't know what else to do."

Vanessa dropped her arm. "Cotten, don't bite my head off, but what if you just think that's what you heard? You said her voice was really frail and you had to strain to understand her."

Cotten's expression softened, and she sighed. "I guess I did have a lot to drink." Still, she hadn't told Vanessa or anyone the whole story about her twin—why Motnees didn't come to her anymore—why they no longer spoke.

Cotten walked along the surf line, Vanessa beside her. A few sandpipers darted across their path picking at the beach for hidden morsels.

"I'm flying to Nassau in the morning for a series of shoots," Vanessa said. "So the place is yours for a couple of days. Just kick back, relax, and forget about what happened. Chill. Read a trashy novel, soak up some sun, flirt with the guys on the beach—some are actually straight. Hell, get laid."

Cotten chuckled. Thornton was the only one she'd had sex with in the last year. She had never been able to get into the casual sex scene. She looked back at the sunrise. "The whole thing is nonsensical. The sun . . . the frigging dawn." Cotten scuffed the shallow water. "Screw it."

"That-a-girl." Vanessa took Cotten by the hand. "Let's get some breakfast."

* * *

Cotten stood on the balcony watching Vanessa cross the parking lot to her car. The model turned and waved before getting into her M3 convertible and pulling out onto A1A. Cotten glanced toward the beach that was quickly filling with sun worshipers before she went back into the apartment. She remembered the first day of college when she'd met her roommate, the strikingly beautiful Latin girl from Miami—Cotten a journalism major, Vanessa, drama.

Three things Cotten discovered about Vanessa that first year were her sense of loyalty to friends, her generous heart, and her wonderful ability to laugh when things were the bleakest. After all the years, those were still what she loved most about her. When Vanessa confessed her sexual preference, it hadn't mattered to Cotten. They vowed that it never would get in the way of their friendship. They were closer than sisters throughout college—trusting, confiding, and counseling each other through broken loves, paralyzing finals, and countless bouts of self-doubt.

Cotten fell back on the bed. Good God, how did the girl keep up the pace? It was Sunday morning after a Saturday night all-nighter. Cotten was exhausted and hung over, and Nessi was off to work looking like a zillion bucks. And Vanessa would be all put together tomorrow, too, when she hopped on a plane to the Bahamas. She was non-stop.

Cotten groaned, hugged a pillow to her chest, and yawned. She lay there another ten minutes, images of Iraq, the children's eyes, Thornton's eyes, John's eyes, the candles and their reflection in the old woman's eyes, circling in her head. "Get over it," she said, turning on her side. She tried to sleep, but couldn't. Finally she got up.

Pulling her planner from her carryall, she flipped to the address tabs before picking up the phone and dialing. Three rings later, there was an answer.

"Ruby Investigations."

"Hi, Uncle Gus."

"Well, well," Gus Ruby said. "I'm surprised my favorite niece still speaks to us lowly peons after hobnobbing with the pope and all."

"First of all, Uncle Gus, I didn't hobnob with the pope—he was busy doing pope stuff. And second, I would never consider you a lowly peon. You're one of the highest ranking peons I know."

"Now, I feel better."

"Hey, why are you answering your home phone with *Ruby Investigations*?"

"I gave up on the shitty answering service so I switched my call forwarding on the weekends to this line. I get a lot of business on Saturdays and Sundays, thanks to Friday and Saturday nights. Tell me, so how is it being renowned throughout the land?"

"When I see my picture on *The National Enquirer* cover next to the "Blind Baby Raised By Worms" story, I'll know I've really made it."

Gus Ruby's deep barrel laugh rocked the phone line. "You've got a great sense of humor, little girl."

There was a lengthy pause before Cotten said, "I know you're real busy these days, but I need a favor if you can swing it."

"What's up?"

"Robert Wingate. Ever heard of him?"

"A blurb on *60 Minutes* and some other news magazine. New candidate, right?"

"You'll hear more about him soon, I'm sure. No one knows much about Wingate other than he's a wealthy businessman who's decided to give politics a whirl. He sort of sprang up one day. Like everybody else, we're going to do a feature on him. But I need that little extra twist you always seem to uncover. Can you do an in-depth background check—finance, business, social, the works? Maybe even follow him around for a while and see what gets him off? You got anyone to spare? The network will cover fees and expenses like always."

"Where's he going to be?"

"Right now he's in Miami—his hometown. I'm down here, too."

"Miami? It's snowing like a mother here. Shit, I'll come down and do it myself—anything to get out of this meat locker. How long you gonna be there?"

"The rest of the week."

"Are you staying at your roommate's place again?"

"Yeah, Vanessa's."

"My God, that woman's as hot as a Saturday Night Special that's been fired six times."

"Uncle Gus, did I ever tell you Vanessa is gay?"

"When I was your age, little girl, I was a sexual Tyrannosaurus. I could turn her around in one night."

"Should I remind you of what happened to the dinosaurs?"

The phone line quaked again with Gus Ruby's roaring laughter. "Well, you tell her I'm on my way, and she better be ready."

"I'll warn her."

When the laughter finally stopped, Gus said, "Okay, I'll start digging on this Wingate thing. Let's plan on meeting later in the week. I should have some preliminary material by then. I'll call."

"That sounds perfect. I love you, and I'll see you—oh, wait, there's one more thing." Cotten reached for her small sequined handbag and pulled out the business card.

* * *

The chirping sound came from her beach bag. Cotten lay on a large towel, the South Florida sun warming her bikini-clad body. She put down her paperback then retrieved her cell phone.

"Hello."

"Hey. I'm in Washington." Thornton's voice was low as if he weren't alone and didn't want anyone to hear. "When are you coming back?"

"Never."

"Cotten, we need to talk."

"We are talking."

"I could take a flight to Miami and be there tonight."

"No."

"Why not?"

"For the same reasons I gave you the last hundred times. Thornton, unless you've got some other business to discuss, I have to go."

"What's so urgent that you have to hang up?"

"I'm trying to figure out how to stop the sun from rising."

"What?"

"It's a long story." She took a deep breath. "Really, I've got to go. Give Cheryl my love."

"Don't hang up. Not yet. Okay, official business from now on."

Cotten lifted her finger from the *end* button on the phone. "Go ahead," she finally said. She was a professional—she could do this—just business. And she did want to run the Wingate thing past Thornton, anyway. He had a sixth sense for news.

"Ted told me you covered the Wingate dinner. How'd it go?"

"Interesting. The guy is slick and very rich. He rented one of the most expensive party venues in Miami and had it catered first class."

"What did he have to say?"

"The speech was all about family values, protecting children, high moral fiber—the usual blah, blah, blah."

"That's it?"

"I requested an interview but haven't followed up on it yet."

"Sounds like a wasted trip."

"I'm not down here just for Wingate, Thornton. I'm on vacation." She switched ears. "There is one thing. Just before he gave his speech, he left for a secret meeting with some guy who wasn't a guest at the dinner. I think the guy was just a courier delivering a message. He talked to Wingate and handed him a card. The perfect candidate lost his temper. He got really angry, jabbed his finger in the guy's face, and hurled the card back at him."

"Do you know who he was?"

"No, but I managed to get the card after they left. Nothing on it but a name and a scribbled message that says call immediately."

"What's the name?"

"Ben Gearhart."

CRANDON PARK

THE DISTINCTIVE RAP BEAT of Eminem pounded through the palms and sea grapes from a boom box as two teenage boys sat on a concrete picnic table sipping canned drinks. Their heads bobbed to the Miami radio station.

Gus Ruby shifted his gaze to them and lifted the binoculars. Too young to be drinking beer, he thought. Skipping school, no doubt. He watched through the windshield of his rented Grand Marquis behind a stand of coconut palms. There were a dozen other cars in the lot at Crandon Park on Key Biscayne, four miles across the Rickenbacker Causeway from Miami. A constant breeze blew from the ocean a few hundred yards away carrying the sound of the surf mixed with the music.

The humidity attacked his huge frame, and Ruby's body sweated profusely. He wiped his forehead with a paper towel he tore from a roll he kept on the seat next to him, already missing the cold of upstate New York. He knew once again why he had never migrated to South Florida—his body mass couldn't survive the humidity, even in January. The summer would be intolerable.

Ruby had used Velcro to mount a tiny digital video camcorder on the dash, and he glanced from time to time at the small monitor sitting on the passenger-side floorboard. He'd already recorded about ten minutes of Robert Wingate—baseball cap pulled low, dark glasses, and windbreaker with upturned collar—sitting alone at a picnic table twenty yards away from the two teens. Beside him on the table was a black briefcase. Wingate stared at the turquoise water of the Atlantic.

Ruby had followed Wingate from the time the candidate left his Star Island estate and drove his 911 Turbo across the MacArthur Causeway, south on Biscayne Boulevard, and finally across the Rickenbacker to Key Biscayne. With twenty-three years of Interpol behind him and another ten running his own private security firm, Gus Ruby was a master when it came to such covert endeavors. Although he needed a large car to fit his bulky frame, his rentals were always white. He actually didn't like the color white, it annoyed him, but it was the invisible color in investigative work. And he'd chosen a Grand Marquis with dark tinted windows because South Florida swarmed with them—a favorite among retirees.

As he was about to light up a Camel, Ruby noticed one of the teens turn off the music, hop off the table, and walk toward Wingate. The other boy followed.

Punks, he thought. Their waistbands sagged below their underwear, and at least three pounds of gold-plated, gold-filled, gold-colored jewelry hung from their necks down the front of their *wife-beater* muscle shirts. Ruby hated the cocky dress and mannerisms. The boy in the lead wore a black bandanna around his forehead contrasting his pasty skin and scraggly whiskers. Not even old enough to grow a decent beard, he thought. The other kid sported dreadlocks, cola-colored skin, and extra thick brows and lips. Both walked with a swagger.

Ruby's Glock sat on the seat beside him. Wingate hadn't qualified for Secret Service protection yet since he had not officially announced his candidacy. A guy like Wingate, alone and driving a $120,000 sports car, was an open invitation for trouble.

The boys stopped in front of Wingate, and Ruby moved the gun into his lap, just in case. He'd allow a theft, even a mugging—neither was worth giving away his cover. But he couldn't let anything more serious happen to Wingate.

Ruby held the binoculars firmly to his eyes and turned on the power switch to the directional mic. A small ear bud connected to a sound amplifier cord he'd threaded out the door and up the antenna—the tiny microphone attached at the top.

"What do you want?" Wingate asked.

"You got somethin' for us?" Bandanna said.

"Like what?"

"Like a donation to the Boys Club," Dreadlocks said, jabbing the air with his fingers, gangsta-rap fashion. His tightly woven ropes of hair swung back and forth.

Wingate held the briefcase out to him. "Do I get a receipt? For tax purposes, of course."

"Open it," Dreadlocks said, handing the case to Bandanna.

Ruby heard the locks click.

"What the fuck is this?" Bandanna said, throwing the briefcase at Wingate as pieces of plain, white paper, dollar-bill-size, flew out and floated through the air.

"Fuck you, man," Dreadlocks said, bouncing in a squat, shaking the briefcase, the remainder of the cut-up paper spilling on the ground.

A caustic smile creased Wingate's face. "Tell your boss I'm not making any *donation* to his *club*. Especially to someone who doesn't have the balls to come here himself. He sends children to do his dirty work."

Dreadlocks stood and poked his finger close to Wingate's nose. "You gonna fucking regret this, asshole. He ain't playin' games wit you."

"You're right," Wingate said. "No games. And tell him I said get fucked." He slipped off the table, turned his back on the boys, and walked toward the parking lot.

Ruby reached for the Glock, waiting to see if either of the teens pulled a weapon.

"Fuck you!" Dreadlocks called.

"Yeah, fuck you!" Bandanna kicked the case.

Gus Ruby arched a brow. More than one person would be interested in this tape.

* * *

Gus Ruby paused the video playback, freezing the image of Robert Wingate walking to his Porsche.

Cotten stood and went to the window overlooking the beach from Vanessa's apartment. "He's being blackmailed," she said, her back to her uncle. "But for what?" She watched a formation of pelicans glide on patrol over the beach.

"Here's a guy who wants to run for president, and he's being shaken down by amateur thugs. This has scandal written all over it." Gus Ruby leaned into the couch. A flame jumped from his Zippo as he lit a Camel.

130

Cotten took a sip of her Absolut—ice clinked. "Maybe he figured acting tough would scare them off." Then she turned back to Ruby. "What did the boys do after Wingate left?"

"One made a cell phone call." He fast-forwarded the tape. "Here."

Cotten returned to the couch to watch.

Bandanna said into the phone, "He tried to fuck us over." There was a pause. "The case was full of blank paper."

Dreadlocks said to Bandanna, "Ask him if we still get paid."

"We still get paid?" Bandanna listened, then nodded to Dreadlocks. "What next?"

A jumbo jet approaching Miami International drowned out the answer. Bandanna ended the call, hopped off the table, and grabbed the boom box. The two shuffled out of frame, and the screen went to snow.

"Mr. Wingate has a secret," Cotten said, finishing the vodka.

*　*　*

Cotten figured she would test the water with a phone call before confronting Wingate in person.

"Hi, this is Cotten Stone with SNN. May I speak to Mr. Wingate?"

"Mr. Wingate doesn't take calls from the press at his private residence." The female voice had not identified herself.

"I apologize for calling Mr. Wingate at home, but I had a few important questions for him. I met him at Vizcaya the other night, and he told me I should call."

There was a long pause before the woman said, "One moment, please."

Cotten waited—hearing muffled voices on the other end. Then she heard the telltale clicks of someone picking up a receiver and another hanging up.

"Ms. Stone. So nice of you to call." Wingate sounded sociable and pleased. "I hope you enjoyed our little shindig last Saturday. I think Vizcaya is absolutely astounding, don't you agree?"

"It's beautiful. I want to thank you for having us. Everything was delicious. And thank you for taking my call."

"What can I do for the woman who found the most valuable religious relic in the world?"

"I'd like to sit down with you and conduct an in-depth interview. I'm sure our SNN viewers would love to know where you stand on all the key issues we face during the coming election year. Since you haven't given any other network or publication that honor yet, I'd like to be the first."

"And I'd like to give it to you. My press secretary handles all those arrangements—it's something I don't get involved with. If you want, I'll let him know you'll be calling and to be sure to schedule you in."

"One of the topics I'd like to cover is your recent trip to Crandon Park."

Silence.

"I'm afraid I don't know what you're referring to," Wingate said, finally.

"Yesterday, two thirty? Two punks, a briefcase full of blank paper?"

"You must be mistaken, Ms. Stone. I was in a policy meeting all afternoon."

"It sure looks like you on the video. Sounds like you, too."

"What are you doing, following me? Videotaping me? Who the hell do you think you are?"

His voice had changed from the pleasant, confident one she'd heard at the beginning of the conversation, suddenly taking on a razor edge.

"Who's blackmailing you, Mr. Wingate?"

"What?"

"Then you deny it?"

"Yes. What is this all about?"

"Just looking for the truth. The American people have had enough scandals. They want to know up front what the candidates are all about. They yearn for an honest politician, even if he isn't squeaky clean; they just want somebody to be straightforward from the get-go, no cover ups, no more of the false watch-my-lips denials. You know what I hear Americans saying? They say, 'I don't care if you smoked dope in college, I don't care if you had an extramarital affair, as long as you lay it on the table for me and don't lie to me.' This could work to your advantage. Maybe you'd like to do the exclusive and come clean."

"I don't think so, Ms. Stone. Talk about blackmail, who's blackmailing who now? Ratings, that's all you're interested in. You don't care if you screw up somebody's life to get a story. You're nothing but a greedy piranha."

"You have a reputation for being press friendly. Look, if I've found out about this, someone else will, also. You might as well nip it right now. I can give you the media platform to do it. A preemptive strike of sorts."

"There's no reason for me to go on the defensive. I haven't done anything to defend."

She heard seething in his voice, though he made the attempt to sound unaffected. "I believe others will see it differently. They'll see tarnish on their rising star. I won't blow the whistle if you agree to the exclusive. Otherwise, I'll have to go with what I've got."

"I've tried to be nice, but I think you've crossed the line. Tell your SNN buddies that you have managed to blackball the network. Got it? Any questions?"

"Just one."

"What?"

"Who's Ben Gearhart?"

Click.

NO STRINGS

"WHAT DO YOU THINK?" Cotten asked Thornton Graham as the video of Wingate at Crandon Park went to black. They sat in the conference room at SNN headquarters in New York.

"I think you exposed a raw nerve—especially when you hit him with that Gearhart reference. Wingate's reaction is definitely a red flag. Keep on his ass."

"Me? This is your story."

"I'm buried with the Iraqi situation—Ted said I may be broadcasting from the region by the end of the week. I'll give you everything I've got on Wingate and suggest to Ted that you take over."

"You think I'm ready?" Cotten said.

"You just came off a whopper. Now keep the momentum going with that beautiful face in front of the camera. That's the key."

He brushed her bottom lip with his thumb, but she found herself not reacting to his touch like she would have a month or even a few weeks ago. "Are you trying to make yourself feel better?" she asked. "Tossing poor little Cotten a crumb to keep her happy?"

"Do you consider yourself a first-rate reporter?"

"Yes."

"Well, I think we both are. The way I see it, we can help each other."

"I'll tell you what I don't want. If this story breaks big and I'm on it, I don't want to see you in the wings with that *I'm a martyr* expression plastered on your face. The one that says what a magnificent sacrifice the big guy made for the poor little upstart female reporter."

"That's not my intent, Cotten. Look, I'm telling you I'm overburdened, and you're already on top of this. But if you're going to be so goddamn stubborn, then I'll ask Ted to give it to somebody else."

Cotten folded her arms. "Are you sure that's all there is to it? No strings?"

Thornton plowed his fingers through his hair. "Jesus, why do you always overanalyze? Sometimes you just need to jump on the horse and enjoy the ride. For God's sake, can't you let me do something nice for you without kicking me in the balls?" He leaned in close. "No strings—cross my heart. So do you want it or not?"

"I want it," she said, trying hard to believe him.

* * *

Cotten sat in her apartment staring at the evening news on TV—Thornton looked good, as always, as he reported the latest developments from the multilateral military buildup in the Middle East. She needed to call Gus and let him know she was the lead reporter on the Wingate investigation now. As she reached for the phone, it rang, startling her.

"Hello."

"Cotten, it's John. I'm just back from Rome."

She settled into the corner of the couch and pulled a throw pillow onto her lap. "It's good to hear your voice. How was your flight?"

"I'm trying to adjust to the time difference."

The small talk made her uneasy. She wanted to say she missed him, but reconsidered. "It usually takes a couple of days to get over the jetlag," she said.

"Cotten . . ."

"Yes?"

"I was thinking maybe we could get together—catch up on things."

"I'd love that. I have some interesting things to tell you." She closed her eyes and was suddenly back in Little Havana, the old woman whispering in her ear.

"Really? What?"

"I'd rather not talk about it on the phone." She wished John were here now.

"Are you all right?" he asked.

"John, I know the Cup is thousands of miles away and out of my life, but something happened a few days ago—I'm still a little shaken."

"How about lunch tomorrow? I could come into the city and meet you."

"Yes—wait." She thought for a moment. "I can't. I have a working lunch scheduled with my news director."

There was a pause. "Well then, first chance we get . . ."

"Yes, first chance."

"So . . . you take care."

"You, too."

She started to hang up but squeezed her eyes shut hoping he hadn't put the phone down yet. "Still there?" she asked.

"Yes."

"What about tonight? I mean, I know it's short notice, but—"

"Tonight would be great. I'll catch the train and be there in a few hours."

Neither said anything for a moment. Cotten leaned her head back on the couch, staring at the ceiling.

"Where would you like to go?" he asked.

"It doesn't matter. You pick the place."

"Give me your address."

She told him the directions.

"I'll be there soon," he said before hanging up.

Cotten flung herself lengthwise on the sofa and pulled the throw pillow over her face. She was afraid she was falling in love with a priest.

* * *

"Want to come in first and have a drink?" Cotten asked. "Priests do drink?"

"Very funny," John said, smiling as she let him in.

"That won't make it too much like a date, will it—if we have a drink before going to dinner?"

"A drink would be perfect," he said, taking off his overcoat.

Cotten headed for the kitchen. "Sit, relax, and I'll tell you your choices." She reached in the cabinet and pulled out a bottle of Mike's Hard Lemonade, a half-empty fifth of Captain Morgan's Rum, and a rectangular bottle of Ballantine scotch—calling out each as she placed them on the counter. "And I've got some Absolut," she said opening the freezer. "What would you like?"

"The Ballantine is fine—with water and ice."

"My dad liked scotch on holidays." She poured the whiskey into a heavy tumbler and added some bottled water. "Most of the time he just drank beer, but special occasions brought out the scotch."

She poured herself an Absolut over ice.

"There you go," she said, handing him the drink. Sitting in the chair opposite the couch, she leaned forward and pushed a coaster across the coffee table toward him. It was nice seeing him in street clothes—a beige button-down shirt and a silk tie—its background was shiny champagne with small earth-colored geometric designs. A brown sport jacket matched his trousers. He could have stepped right out of *GQ* and into her apartment.

He sipped his drink. "You look great."

"I was just thinking the same about you. Rome must agree with you."

"I made a reservation at the Tavern on the Green," he said.

"Perfect. This *is* Dutch Treat."

"No, no. Not this time. I'm taking you to dinner."

"Then the next one is on me."

"We'll see." He took another sip. "You said on the phone that you were still apprehensive about the Grail. Why?"

Cotten lifted the glass of vodka to her lips. She loved it right out of the freezer—it turned from icy to warm and velvety on the way down. "I was in Miami on a working vacation. My girlfriend and I went out one night to a Cuban street festival. It's a bit of a long story, but somehow I wound up alone in a weird religious ceremony or ritual—Voodoo, Santeria—something of that sort. Before I could leave, this old woman, the priestess conducting the ritual, said the same words to me that Archer did in the tomb in Iraq." Just thinking about it made the hair at the nape of her neck prickle.

He leaned back as if in thought. "That is bizarre."

"How could either of them . . . what does it mean?"

John shook his head. "I really don't know. Other than an amazing coincidence, it doesn't make a lot of sense." He tugged an earlobe.

"This whole thing started when Archer gave me the Grail and said I was the only one to stop the dawn, and now some freakin' black magic woman has said the very same words." She took a big sip of the Swedish vodka.

"At least you aren't still holding the Cup. It's half a world away—that should give you some reassurance."

Cotten twirled her hair into a thick cord as she spoke. "It should . . . but it doesn't. Somehow I get the feeling that *it's* not over yet. And I don't even know what *it* is."

"I don't blame you for being upset. One would think there's a message here, but I'm at a total loss at what it could be."

She gave up a smile. "At least you didn't ask me if I was sure about what the woman said. Yes, I'd been drinking, but, John, I heard her loud and clear. Yes, there was a lot of noise, but I didn't make it up—didn't imagine it. You believe me, don't you?"

He placed his half-finished drink onto the table. "Tell you what. Let's catch a cab and you tell me more about what happened on the way to dinner. Maybe something will click."

Cotten smoothed her skirt over her knees. She was going to have to reveal everything about Motnees—things she had never told anyone, not even her mother. "John," she finally made herself say, "there's something else I have to tell you."

TWIN TALK

John finished his scotch as Cotten continued.

"I hope you have an open mind," she started, "because if you even remotely suspect I'm crazy, this will clinch it." She drained her Absolut. "Okay, here we go." Blowing out a breath, she said, "I was born a twin—an identical twin. Fortunately, I was healthy, but my sister was not so lucky. She had a heart defect and died right after we were born. As I got older, one of my earliest memories was of an imaginary playmate—a girl. She was invisible to everyone, but as real to me as you are right now. At night, especially when I was afraid, she'd come through my window and hover in a corner of my bedroom near the ceiling, and I'd feel safe. Other times she'd come and we would talk until I finally fell asleep. We played together nearly everyday. I tried to explain to my parents that she was real, but my mother ignored it— my father humored me, sometimes pretending as if he really believed me. But no one took me seriously. She told me she was my twin. I called her Motnees, though that wasn't my twin's given name. It was just part of our make-believe world."

Cotten watched John's face. Seeing what appeared to be sincere interest, she continued.

"Motnees and I had a language all our own. It wasn't something that I spent time thinking about—it was just there from the start—like a second language that I was born with. My mother thought it was gibberish and jokingly called it twin talk since I insisted Motness was my sister. Actually, she was shocked I even knew that I had a twin. She swore she had never told me. She believed I was too little to understand. I've read articles about twin talk—idioglossia is the scientific term. It really exists. It's the language twins sometimes invent to communicate with each other even before they speak the language of those around them. Have you heard of that?"

"Sure. It's pretty well documented."

"When I was about four years old, I got sick. It started with an earache, and my mother gave me aspirin for the pain. But it was more than an earache; it was the flu. I got better, but two weeks later I became violently ill. When the doctor examined me, he found that my liver and spleen were enlarged. He asked Mama if she had given me aspirin when I had the flu. When she said yes, he suspected Reyes Syndrome. He had her take me straight to the hospital—pediatric ICU.

"We later learned that every minute matters with Reyes—you go downhill pretty fast. So when we got to the hospital they drew blood, got an IV in me, and put me in a private room. In a couple of hours we got the news that it wasn't Reyes. I got well enough to go home, but over the next several months there were disturbing symptoms. My spleen stayed enlarged, and tests indicated I was still sick, but the doctors didn't know with what.

"One afternoon I rode my trike to the mailbox with my mother. While she collected our mail from the box, I pedaled out into the road. A pickup swerved to miss me. Mama heard the tires squeal, grabbed me up, and popped me on the thigh. It scared her and she told me to never, ever go into the road again. That night, when she dressed me for bed, she saw red blood blisters on my leg—blood right at the surface of the skin—in the shape of her hand.

"Next morning she took me back to the doctor, and he asked her how hard she'd hit me. Mama said hard enough for me to remember not to go in the street again, but not hard enough to leave those marks. He examined me, and my mother was certain he was looking to see if I had been abused, but of course I hadn't. Then, a week or so later, Mama had me in the tub, and this time she saw blood blisters from under my armpits stretching to my back. She called Daddy in to take a look. He told her how we'd been playing that afternoon and he had picked me up under the arms and swung me in circles. The blisters were from his hands. Daddy was so distraught at the thought he might have hurt me that he cried."

Cotten cleared her throat, choking up at the stirred memory.

"Next day it was back in town to see the doctor. He sent us into Bowling Green to specialists who decided there was a possibility of lymphoma or leukemia. They scheduled me for a lymph node biopsy and bone marrow biopsy. Luckily, I was too young to understand how serious it was. The night before the surgery I remember a terrible storm. As my mother slept in a chair next to my hospital bed, Motnees appeared. She whispered to me that everything would be all right—that my sickness would go away. She also said it was the last time she'd come to see me.

"The next day I had the biopsies, and when the reports came in the results showed no signs of any disease. None. I was a perfectly healthy little girl."

"That's a beautiful story," John said.

There was one last thing she had to tell him. She scored her bottom lip. "All of my symptoms disappeared—gone, zip, zilch, nada.

Doctors had no explanation. But I knew what had happened. Motnees had taken away the sickness. I never saw her again."

Cotten paused. Now she had to drop the bomb. She sat up straight. "This may be the hardest part for you to believe, John. The language Motnees and I spoke is the same one that Archer and the old priestess used when they both told me that I am the only one."

* * *

When they were seated in the Terrace Room at the Tavern on the Green, John said, "Maybe the language you and your sister used is what's referred to as the language of heaven. There are plenty of references to it. It's called Enochian. Some say it's the tongue of the angels. That would make sense if Motnees is an angel."

"You already know I don't buy into that heaven-hell thing. But maybe sometimes the spirits or souls of those who die come back and hang around for a while. Or maybe my sister, being identical, coming from the same egg, was just another part of me. Or maybe I was the fanciful kid my mother said I was, and Motnees was only in my imagination." She caught her breath and came back to the same question. "But disregarding all that, John, how did Archer and the old priestess know how to speak to me in that special twin talk? How did I even remember it?"

"I don't know."

"You don't think I'm crazy?"

He smiled at her. "I wouldn't go that far."

"Well, thanks a lot," she said, a little bit of a bite in her voice. "On the brink, but not completely over the edge?"

"Cotten, I think you're intelligent and well grounded—definitely anything but crazy. You're the one with doubts. Let go. Believe in yourself."

She lowered her eyes. "Sometimes that can be very hard."

John sat back. "Everyday, things happen around us that we can't explain. Some call those events miracles and visions, and some explain them away with fate or luck—take your pick. But you don't have to convince me that your twin sister could be an angel. Angels are my stock-in-trade. They're on my team." John paused and smiled at her.

"Your team, not mine," she said.

"And that's where you're wrong. Stop being so stubborn, so resistant. Cotten, if God is trying to deliver a message to you through Gabriel Archer or the old woman in Miami, or a Chinese fortune cookie for that matter, just give in. Let it happen. Do you honestly believe things occur for no reason? Do you think you and I are sitting here together tonight because of chance? To me, that would be frightening beyond belief. There is purpose even when it seems like madness—there is a grand plan to what sometimes appears as chaos. And we have a part to play in that plan. God will reveal everything when he feels it's the right time. Okay?"

Cotten turned toward the window. "You'll excuse me if I don't have as strong a conviction as you."

"Fine. I accept that. So does God. Just don't be so hostile."

"You're the expert." She wanted to trust in John's judgment, his faith, but there was also the growing fear that things were moving beyond her control. Was God really trying to give her a message or was she *majorly* screwed up? She looked back at John and forced the dark thoughts into the shadows where they belonged. "Let's talk about something else."

They chatted about several world issues including politics in the Middle East and what it had been like for her while she was there.

* * *

John decided to lighten the conversation.

"Want a quick history lesson on the Tavern on the Green?" he asked.

"Sure," Cotten said.

"Look all around you. Now, try to imagine the original building in 1870. It was a sheepfold. At one time it housed two hundred South Down sheep that grazed across the street in Central Park." He watched her face in the light of the Waterford Crystal chandeliers. Here was this beautiful woman who most assuredly had her own guardian angel, and she didn't even think she believed in them. But he knew that deep inside she had to—turning away from God was only a wall to keep her from hurting anymore. Behind that wall was someone who was closer to God than anyone he had ever met. He was discussing sheep with someone who had actually *talked* to an angel, spoken the language of heaven. And whether she understood the significance or not, she had delivered to the world the greatest religious symbol of all time—the Cup of Christ. He was in total awe of her but couldn't express his feelings without embarrassing her.

"You wouldn't know now that it was ever a sheepfold," Cotten said.

The waiter came, and John ordered a bottle of Pinot Grigio.

"Tell me about Rome," she said. "Have they proven it's the Grail?"

John slipped his linen napkin in his lap. "That can't ever be proved beyond a doubt. It's educated conjecture. The metal work, the detail on the vessel, Archer's plate and its translation, the cloth and seal, everything adds up—but it'll never be one hundred percent."

"What about the stuff inside, the residue beneath the wax? Is it blood? Christ's blood?"

John folded his hands on the table. "Without removing the wax and taking a sample, we'll never know. Could be blood, could be any-thing. I pressed them to analyze it, but they refused."

146

"Why? Wouldn't they want to know?"

"In order to find out, some of the blood would have to be sacrificed. In the eyes of the Vatican, that would be tantamount to sacrilege."

"Oh, for God's sake—excuse me—but does the Catholic Church still live in the Dark Ages?"

"I made that same argument—not with those exact words, of course—that God provided us with the knowledge, and I believe He intends for us to use it. Think of the impact on Christianity if they announced it was human blood, male, type O negative—the universal donor. What else would you expect of Christ's blood? *His* blood. There has to be a reason why someone sealed and protected whatever is in the Cup. And to see the DNA! Would there be genetic markers? Could we scientifically trace Christ's lineage? The ramifications are phenomenal."

"And they still refused?" Cotten said.

"If there's even the slightest chance that it is Christ's blood preserved inside the Grail, then it's all that exists of His earthly body. There is no more. Destroying even a few molecules is unthinkable. The Church most often takes the conservative stand on an issue until proven otherwise. That's why science and religion are so often at odds."

Cotten sighed. "Like stem cell research or birth control. It's not just Catholics. Fundamentalists fight the evolution battle every day." She paused for a moment. "I thought there was some kind of light you could shine on blood to make it show up even if someone had tried to clean it off. I see it all the time on crime shows. Wouldn't that work?"

"It would if you didn't have to spray or swab the evidence with Luminol first. Doing that would mean removing the wax and exposing the residue. They won't go for it."

The waiter presented the wine. John tasted it—crisp with a light fruit spiciness. He approved.

"Look," Cotten said, peering out of the glass pavilion at the view. "It's spectacular."

"Do you know your eyes literally glitter when you take in something beautiful—like when we were at the Coliseum, your face brightened."

"Maybe growing up wanting so badly to see the world made me that way. Everyone called me a dreamer, including my mother. The only one who supported me was my father. He told me I was destined for great things. I couldn't wait to venture into the world. Once I graduated and got my first job, I was excited about finally being able to go places and take my mother with me. And you know what, she had no interest. She believed if it wasn't within a fifty-mile radius, it wasn't worth seeing. I never understood that mentality. She missed so much."

"Some people are content to stay right where they are, forever."

"What about the curiosity to see an ocean or a desert? How can anyone live an entire life inside a fifty-mile circle?"

John smiled. "In many ways, Cotten, we all have a fifty-mile circle that keeps us confined. Mine's a bit smaller—it's called a Roman collar."

The Knights Templar became one of the wealthiest and most powerful organizations in the Western world. It was a spectacular rise to power that had hardly been seen before or since. Their wealth grew, and their descendants retained control over most of their holdings even to the present.

GUARDIANS OF THE GRAIL

CHARLES SINCLAIR SAT BEHIND the massive ebony table in the private teleconference center at his plantation estate. He looked at the seven blank plasma monitors arranged along the wall in the dark, wood-paneled room.

Beside him, Ben Gearhart reached for the control panel built into the table. "We're ready to start bringing them online."

Gearhart flipped the first switch and plasma monitor number one flashed to life. From Vaduz, the face of the Chancellor of Liechtenstein appeared.

"Good afternoon, Charles."

"Hello, Hans." Sinclair said, before making a few notes on a legal pad.

Gearhart flipped the next switch, and the second screen flickered on revealing the CEO of the International Bank of Zurich.

Moving down the line of switches, Gearhart caused a new face to appear on each monitor. They included a former deputy commander of the Soviet Army and current chairman of the Department of Defense for the Russian Federation; a cabinet minister to Her Majesty's government; the chief justice of the French Supreme Court; the German minister of finance in Berlin; and the president and founder of GlobalStar in Vienna, Europe's largest telecommunications network.

"Can all of you see and hear me clearly?" Sinclair asked.

There were nods along with verbal confirmations from the seven faces filling the video screens. "Then let us begin." Turning his attention to the Chancellor, he said, "Hans?"

"Thank you, Charles. I'm proud to report, gentlemen, that of the twenty-seven hundred members of the Council on Foreign Relations, we now influence slightly over ninety percent. These members are networking their people into the U.S. State Department while building relationships with our partner one-world government groups in Canada, Britain, and Japan. This is, of course, a key ingredient to our success because the CFR is committed to the elimination of national boundaries."

"Excellent progress," Sinclair said as the other Guardians reacted.

The British cabinet minister said, "The other two groups committed to our cause—the Trilateral Commission and Europe's Bilderberg Group—are both almost totally under our influence. As you know, the Trilateral Commission focuses on financial and political matters while the Bilderbergers are concerned with military and strategic issues. Since some of you or your associates are members of those groups, I don't have to tell you about our sweeping accomplishments."

"Let me comment for a moment, gentlemen, on some developments with the World Bank and the International Monetary Fund," the Zurich banker said. "A large number of Third World countries defaulting on their huge loans owed to Western banks are now vulnerable to pressure to cooperate with the World Bank and its terms. This is because Trilateral bankers—our bankers—are now in a position to dictate new terms. There's no other place to go for loans—they have no choice but to use our money. We're seeing this in action every day. We're also seeing progress in moving to a cashless society with credit and debit card use growing substantially."

"You're right," Sinclair said. "The processing of cashless transactions and electronic fund transfer is becoming one of our major sources of revenue, especially in the U.S. We predict a sixty percent market share by the end of the year. Our next step is to put into circulation bar-coded currency.

"The bar code technology being developed with some of our strategic partners has been perfected for biomedical purposes as well. The new nanobarcodes, the ones made with gold and silver, are so minute that several hundred thousand of them can fit in a single centimeter. You can see the implications—we will use these nanobarcodes to track our citizens."

"What is the public response to the introduction of your presidential candidate?" the president of GlobalStar asked.

"As you know," Sinclair said, "we have been grooming Robert Wingate for quite some time, and we feel from the initial response that he will do fine."

The Russian general spoke. "My intelligence tells me there are personal problems with Wingate that might jeopardize his chances."

"I am aware of that. We're taking appropriate action to resolve these minor issues," Sinclair said. "We see no reason for changing our timeline or any of our benchmarks."

"What of the woman who found the Cup?" the French Chief Justice asked. "Is she a threat?"

"We are keeping our finger on that, also," Sinclair answered. "We will keep watch."

"And when do you go to the Vatican, Charles?" the president of GlobalStar asked.

"I will be leaving at the end of the week."

"What makes you think you can persuade the cardinal to do what we require?" the GlobalStar president asked.

"His Eminence wants only one thing in life, and I am the only one who can deliver it to him. At least that is what he will believe." A smile spread across Sinclair's face. "Cardinal Inaucci's weaknesses are his devout faith and his rationale that he is to be rewarded for such devotion."

"I hope you are right," the GlobalStar president said.

Sinclair rose. "Gentlemen, for centuries, it has been the goal of the Guardians to unite nations into a worldwide empire. The dream of returning to a time not unlike ancient Rome where citizens could travel in safety over thousands of miles while speaking one language, being governed by one set of laws, and supported with a common currency, is about to become reality. We will accomplish this because we are on the threshold of the Second Coming of Jesus Christ. As prophesied, He will return again like a thief in the night—and no one will know the hour or the day. Well, I say to you that we know the day—we will pick the hour. He will lead us into a new age—an age where all will believe in what He says."

Sinclair extended his arms. "And he will say exactly what we tell him."

"The enormous possibilities of scientific and technological progress, as well as the phenomenon of globalization, which increasingly extends to new fields, demands that we always be open to dialogue with every person, with every social event, with the intention of giving each one a reason for the hope we bear in our heart."

—Pope John Paul II—receiving forty-four new cardinals during the consistory, February 21, 2001

BLASPHEMY

"Your Eminence, thank you for agreeing to see me on such short notice." Charles Sinclair stood in the middle of the cardinal's office, hand outstretched.

"How could I say otherwise to a man of your stature?" Cardinal Ianucci came around his desk to greet the Nobel laureate. "It is both an honor and a privilege to be in the presence of such an esteemed scientist, even if we don't see eye to eye on all the aspects of your research." He smiled warmly to soften the comment. In fact, Sinclair had been the topic of many heated theoretical and ethical discussions in the halls of the Vatican. The specter of human cloning was one of the most controversial issues facing papal dogma.

"You are most kind, indeed." Sinclair shook the cardinal's hand—in his other hand he held a small, silver, titanium travel case.

"Please." Ianucci motioned to an intricately embroidered chair—its legs ending in lions' claws that appeared to grip the sprawling Oriental rug. Once the cardinal returned to sit behind his desk, he said, "How was your trip?"

"Splendid. The duck l'orange was memorable."

"In-flight gourmet dining is rare these days. The only time I get good airline food is when I fly with the Holy Father." He chuckled. Wanting to get past the small talk, he asked, "What can the Holy See do for you, Dr. Sinclair?"

"Perhaps it's what I can do for you, Your Eminence."

"And what would that be?"

"Can you assure me that we will not be interrupted for the next hour?"

Ianucci glanced at his schedule log before picking up the phone and instructing that he not be disturbed. "You have my undivided attention, Dr. Sinclair. But a half hour is the best I can do."

"Then that's all I can ask." Sinclair leaned back, put the case in his lap, and rested his hands on top of it. "Do you believe the Bible is truly the word of God?"

The cardinal covered his mouth and coughed shallowly. "But of course, Dr. Sinclair," he said, sounding a bit indignant.

"Then you believe it contains God's revelation about our ultimate destiny."

"I do."

Sinclair smiled. "One quarter of the Bible is prophecy, and we must not ignore or reject any of it. Remember what the Apostle Paul said in Acts about the Jews: that because they did not listen to the voices of the Prophets, they actually fulfilled the prophecy by condemning Jesus."

The cardinal leaned forward. "Dr. Sinclair, do you think I rose to this station without knowing what is in the Bible?"

"Certainly not. And please don't take offense. But I must prepare you for what I am going to say. I want you to recall the book of Revelation where it says 'He stands at the door and knocks. If any man hear my voice and open the door, I will come in to him.' Eminence, I believe that today, God knocks at our door. We mustn't turn a deaf ear to the prophecies."

"I'm finding your Bible study lesson tedious, Dr. Sinclair."

"Please bear with me, Eminence. My point will be made clear soon."

The cardinal nodded, reluctantly—he had a full schedule today and grew impatient with Sinclair's patronizing ramblings.

"Can you describe for me how you envision the Second Coming?" Sinclair asked.

Ianucci tapped a finger on his thigh. *Where was Sinclair going with this?* "Interesting question. That seems to be a popular topic these days with so many books being written on the subject—apocalyptic fiction, they call it. Well, in the classical sense we're taught that Christ will return in a triumphant conquest of good over evil, gathering to His bosom those who have been faithful, and sweeping them into everlasting joy and peace. A good model for Renaissance painters, Dr. Sinclair, but probably not reality."

"Exactly."

"The fact is that no one knows for sure when or how Christ will return. The prophecy is right there in the Bible, but there are dozens of interpretations. We do agree, however, that many signs of His return are present. Of course time is relative. How soon He will come again is parlayed about by all who study the scriptures. Does that sufficiently answer your question?"

Smugness set in Sinclair's eyes. Ianucci cocked his head wondering what brought on such an expression, and why the doctor was delaying his response.

Finally, Sinclair spoke. "Eminence, I not only know *when* Christ will return, but *how*."

Ianucci pushed forward. "You mean you have a theory?"

"Not a theory. I know."

"Dr. Sinclair, many men down through the ages spent their lives dedicated to studying and investigating the written word for that single purpose."

Again, that faint smile creased surface lines in Sinclair's face, but he said nothing. It made Ianucci shift in the chair. "You believe you can predict when the Savior will come again, and you have traveled all this way to share that knowledge with me?" the cardinal asked.

"I must, Your Eminence, because without you, it will not take place."

Ianucci leaned back, interlocking his fingers over his stomach. He wondered if the famous scientist had joined the likes of some doomsday cult. The line between genius and insanity . . . He would humor Sinclair for a few more moments before politely ushering him on his way. "I'm listening."

"Most who preach the Word of the Lord look at the prophecies as proof of the approaching Apocalypse. But they wrongly fixate on the fire and brimstone in Revelation. We must think of it as God's promise that He will send His Son again to earth so mankind will finally have peace on earth—heaven on earth. Who's to say in what manner Christ will return to Earth? What if it's in a way no one has thought of—a means that mirrors the times, the technology? I believe you and I have been selected—chosen by God to make it happen.

"I recently had a vision, Eminence. I was awakened in the middle of the night by a brilliant white light. At first I was frightened, but soon, a sense of peace overwhelmed me. I heard a voice—one as clear as my own is now. The voice quoted scripture. 'The wolf also shall dwell with the lamb, the leopard shall lie down with the young goat, the calf and the young lion and the fatling together; and a little child shall lead them . . .' Are not science and religion often in opposition— the wolf and the lamb? Yet prophecy is that we will lie down together, fuse with a common objective. And like our two disciplines, the world will follow, the calf, the lion, the fatling. Peace is to come. And heed these words especially, *a little child shall lead them*. It is those words that made God's plan so unmistakable to me. It clarified what my purpose is on Earth—and yours as well. Since that night, my whole life has changed."

"And what is your purpose—and mine?"

"God has given me great talents, Eminence, just as he has bestowed so many upon you. My knowledge of genetics has allowed me to perfect a method of reproducing a human by using DNA. And God has blessed *you* with being a great spiritual leader to shepherd Christ's church and prepare it for the Final Judgment. He has led us, guided us, brought us to this day. Every decision we have made in our lives has been governed by this hallowed inevitability. We have the means and the power to fulfill our destinies."

"I don't think I follow you. What inevitability? What do genetics and cloning have to do with God's plan for us all?"

"God has delivered to you the Cup from the Last Supper—the Cup that caught Christ's blood at Calvary. Sheltered for centuries in a dark, arid tomb, it is the only remnant of Jesus Christ left on Earth. Beneath the protective layer of beeswax inside the Cup is the blood of Christ—blood holding the secret of His DNA. It is a gift from God— a means to an end. And the end is by His doing—His divine plan. Jehovah delivered the Cup to you, to the spiritual leader He has chosen over all others. And He has delivered it at this time, a time when the technology is perfected. Jesus Christ, the son of God, the Messiah, is coming back. And we have been chosen to do God's work."

"You are suggesting that I somehow turn over the Cup of Christ to you so that you can clone—?" Ianucci made a fist and pounded it on his desk, then rose to his feet. "This is blasphemy! Out! Get out!"

"I'm not surprised by your reaction, Your Eminence. These are not concepts we ponder often. It is certainly foreign in nature to a man like you. All I ask is you think about what I've said. And while you do, consider the moments in history when an unusual or controversial concept was proposed and immediately labeled blasphemy, only years or even centuries later proven true." Sinclair took a folded piece of paper from his pocket and laid it on the cardinal's desk. "Just think about it. Pray about it. God is waiting for you."

"Go," Ianucci said, his voice low, drawing out the word with disgust.

Sinclair nodded as he stood. With the travel case in hand he turned and left.

Ianucci sat. For many moments, he stared at the folded paper before picking it up and opening it. After reading the note, he balled it in his fist. Trying to wipe what had happened from his mind, he scanned his calendar and made a phone call to check on the progress of the restoration of a newly acquired Raphael.

But he couldn't clear his head, couldn't concentrate on anything except Sinclair's words. When he finished the call, instead of hanging up the receiver, he held onto it and pressed the button with his finger. He sat motionless, as if time had arrested. A few moments later he released the button and dialed his aide.

"Cancel my appointments," he said. "I will be out for the rest of the day."

Ianucci left his office and closed the door. So deep in thought, though he passed several others, he did not acknowledge them.

My God, what if Sinclair was right. What if Christ is to return again just in the manner he said?

Inside his quarters, Ianucci fell to his knees at his bedside, propping his elbows on the mattress, dropping the crushed paper on the spread. He prayed for God to direct him, tell him how it was to be.

The rest of the day passed as he shifted between praying and reading scripture. At sunset he stood at his window and watched the sky turn from gold to scarlet and purple. Had God indeed taken his hand during his earliest years and led him to this very moment in time? He had always known God favored him—always known he was destined to rise to the top, to lead the Church. Every cell in his body was indoctrinated with that belief. He had never dared to consider it might even be more than that. Perhaps he was destined not to lead the Church, but the whole of mankind. Could it really be that the Almighty entrusted him with the Second Coming?

Ianucci's tears fell onto his folded hands. He wept until his body trembled and exhaustion weakened him. Sure that he could hear a chorus of angels, he stared at the crucifix on the wall.

The cardinal sat on the edge of the bed and uncrumpled the paper Sinclair gave him, reading the hotel name and room number again.

Then he reached for the phone.

THE SIGN

THE CARDINAL CHECKED HIS watch. He'd told Sinclair to come at 11:00 AM. It was ten after. He drummed his fingers on the desktop. Perhaps he shouldn't have called the geneticist. But he had to hear more—at least part of him did. On one hand, he steadfastly denied any validity to Sinclair's logic. Certainly it was as close to blasphemy as you could get in today's modern, open way of thinking. But somewhere in the recesses of his mind, Ianucci kept asking himself the same questions. What if this was the ultimate test of his faith? What if human cloning was the method by which Christ would return—the wolf will dwell with the lamb, the Church and science lying down together? The young lion and the fatling together. And how would the cardinal be judged if he ignored the direct word of God? In other words, what if Sinclair was right?

The ring of the phone startled Ianucci. He picked it up and listened, then said, "Send him in."

As the door opened, the cardinal sat up straight and smoothed the fabric of his cassock over his stomach. "Good morning, Dr. Sinclair." He motioned to the chair in front of him.

"Eminence," Sinclair said, nodding. As he had done yesterday, he put the travel case in his lap after sitting. "I am pleased you have decided to consider all I have to tell you."

"Do not misinterpret my invitation. I have not changed my mind, but I feel that I want to hear the basis for your premise. If nothing else, I will have the opportunity to discredit it."

"Your wisdom further validates why God has chosen you to do this very special task."

"I am not interested in your flattery, Doctor. If I recall, we had begun a discussion of how the Messiah will come again."

"Exactly. His Second Coming will not be what has been traditionally envisioned. Of course, John, Matthew, Ezekial—all those who wrote about Christ's return to Earth couldn't have possibly described it with clarity. How could they have explained even simple objects such as a telephone or an airplane, much less DNA? Jesus is coming back to a modern world, our world, to reign supreme. No one has been able to determine how or when because the event was described by men who lived thousands of years ago. But with this vision that I had, it all became so clear.

"The Second Coming is at hand, and you and I have been chosen to make it happen. Matthew twenty-four—when asked when He would come again, Jesus indicated a time when nation would rise against nation, there would be famines, earthquakes, and pestilence. He called those things the beginning of birth pains. Is this not what we are witnessing across the globe—earthquakes, volcanoes, floods, unusual weather patterns that have catastrophic effects?

"Apocalypse, chapter six, verse eight, St. John's vision of the pale horse—are we not discovering new diseases springing up around the world on a continuous basis—diseases resistant to anything man does to stop them?

"Apocalypse, chapter six, verse five—famine. Over a billion people face starvation this year. Is that not astounding in a world that has seen a man walk on the moon?

"The scriptures teach us that the single generation that witnesses the rebirth of Israel will also witness the promised return of the Messiah. And we have seen the false prophets that precede his return—the Jim Joneses and David Koreshs leading their followers into mass suicides. We now have the weapons and the technology to completely annihilate all life on earth. Would that not explain the prophecies of attacks from the air, the poisoning of a third of the planet, the death of billions? God's precise plan that was outlined thousands of years ago is unfolding.

"The time is now. His divine hand has brought the two of us together—you as a Prince of the Church, and I, an unworthy servant to whom God has given the gift of knowledge so His will may be done, that His son will live again. We must have the courage to do what He asks—to be instruments of the Father."

Sinclair stared intently at Ianucci. "Do you have the courage to take up this task, Eminence?"

Ianucci's thoughts flapped through his head like batwings—trying to make sense of what Sinclair said, scrolling through all the biblical text that had been brought up, and more—Isaiah, Daniel, Luke, Zechariah—for confirmation. What Sinclair said sounded logical. But it went against everything the cardinal had ever believed and had been taught. Maybe the man was deranged. Yes, that was it. Sinclair was demented—obsessed with his own power—driven by his super ego.

"You're insane," Ianucci said, standing to pace.

Sinclair remained calm and soft-spoken. "No, Eminence. I'm not only perfectly sane, I'm inspired. Just consider it for a moment. Why do you think the Cup was delivered to you personally? Why now?

Even the Talmud speaks of the birth pangs of the Messiah . . . irresponsible government, wars, poverty, the breakup of families, and great scientific advances—a time of miracles. Is it not a time of miracles when from a minute drop of the very blood He shed for us, with our help, He will live again? In the days of the Blessed Virgin, who could have imagined the miracle of the Virgin Birth? Don't you see? This is The Miracle."

"You are wrong. This is wrong," the cardinal said, rubbing his chest, feeling as if a vise had clamped over his ribs. "Stop. I want to hear no more."

"How do you know I'm wrong? The world is not flat, Eminence. Christ said 'Blessed are those who have not seen and yet believe.' He has chosen you. How can you refuse?"

Ianucci turned his back to Sinclair, looking out the window into the courtyard below. "A clone of Jesus, even if it were possible, would simply be a replica, not . . . Christ, not our Redeemer. Perhaps you can clone a man, but how do you give a replica the soul of our Savior?" The cardinal faced his visitor and watched the geneticist's eyes soften.

"I can't," Sinclair said.

The words hung in the air as if he wanted Ianucci to think about the question.

"You're right," Sinclair finally said. "*It* will be a replica only . . . until the Holy Spirit enters it. Just as the Holy Spirit entered the Virgin Mary so she could conceive and give birth. If you believe that was possible, you cannot deny this. And you will be his mentor. The child will be your charge. Think of it. You are the one God has selected. You cannot refuse."

"Mentor the Christ child?" Ianucci could not get enough air into his lungs, and for an instant his heart lost its rhythm and fluttered randomly. He coughed, and with the length of his forefinger the cardinal swabbed the perspiration from his upper lip. "But the Cup was buried in the desert for centuries. There's no way the DNA could be preserved."

Sinclair maintained that constant vague smile as he continued. "Not true—for two reasons. First, from a scientific point of view, although the blood cells would have broken down over the millennia, the nuclear material present in the white blood cells would have remained intact in the form of chromosomes. The chromosomes could be preserved because the Cup contained wine from the Last Supper prior to catching the blood. The presence of alcohol would have acted as a preservative preventing the bacterial-induced degradation of the nuclear material. I can extract the nuclei and insert them into a human egg. After the sperm and egg nuclei fuse, the process is arrested, and the diploid nucleus is removed and replaced with a diploid nucleus extracted from the material in the Grail. This is similar to the way Dolly the sheep was created. The engineered zygote is allowed to divide a number of times in a lab culture before being implanted into a surrogate mother."

Ianucci held up his hand, shaking his head. "That means nothing to me, Dr. Sinclair. Nothing. You might as well be speaking Martian." He walked back to his chair and sat.

"Then perhaps this will. The DNA has been preserved because it is Christ's blood—divine blood. This is the work of the Father, and by His hand it is preserved. It is truly a time of miracles, Eminence."

The full impact of Sinclair's reasoning shook the cardinal. Deep inside his core, something that felt like a large pane of glass cleaved, fractured, shattered. It just could be that Sinclair was not mad, but perfectly sane . . . exactly right. He calculated how it made sense. Ianucci's words came with difficulty. "It has already been decided that the wax will not be removed—no research will be done on the so-called residue beneath. It is out of my hands. Tampering with the relic in any way would be discovered immediately."

Sinclair took the titanium travel case and sat it on the cardinal's desk. "I have a solution."

Ianucci stared at the case. He said a quick, silent prayer for strength. He needed more, something that would kill the last fragment of doubt. "Dr. Sinclair, I think you have an amazing imagination, but it will take more than your theories to convince me that either you or I, or anyone on this Earth for that matter has been chosen to help bring about the Second Coming."

"With all that I've presented you, Eminence, what more of a sign would you need?"

The synapses in Ianucci's brain fired like sparks from a green wood fire. "One that would be unquestionable," he said. "One that I could not ignore."

The phone on the cardinal's desk rang. "Excuse me," Ianucci said to Sinclair before picking it up. "I asked not to be interrupted." He listened for about thirty seconds before placing the receiver back on its cradle. A glacial chill surged through him, and he wrung his hands to still the tremors. Ianucci sank deep into his chair. Looking up, he saw Sinclair staring at him.

"Are you all right, Eminence?"

"The Holy Father . . ." Ianucci voice quaked.

"What?"

"The Holy Father is dead."

THE SEED

IT WAS MIDNIGHT AS the black limousine sped west along Interstate 10 away from New Orleans International, its interior shielded from view by dark tinted windows. Charles Sinclair sank into the plush leather, relieved to be home from Rome. He felt exhilarated, having done his job convincingly.

"You look content, Charles," the old man said. "I take it things went well."

Sinclair had slipped into the limo so quickly he hadn't noticed the old man sitting in the darkness opposite him. His eyes slowly adjusted.

"Things went very well," Sinclair said. "The cardinal's intense faith made him the ideal choice. That along with his ego."

He and the old man had not spoken since the christening in St. Louis Cathedral. Sinclair was still amazed at how, without hesitation, he had placed his entire future in the old man's hands.

It had started when Sinclair was struggling to find elusive answers to persistent roadblocks in his research. The old man came to him and presented solutions that quickly proved correct, ultimately leading to international recognition and notoriety. Funding, grants, and lavish fees for lecture tours made Sinclair one of the wealthiest scientists in the world. Universities fought to have his name associated with their institutions. Corporations pressed him to join their boards, openly admitting that they sought the prestige of his fame. He quickly took on the mantel of celebrity—his counsel sought from every corner of the globe.

"Have you shared your progress with your fellow Guardians?" the old man asked.

"They are pleased. We're close to reaching our goals—nothing stands in our way."

"Except the woman."

"You mean the reporter? But I assumed once the Cup passed out of her possession, she was no longer a threat."

"Do you think it a coincidence that Archer gave her the relic and now she stirs the winds around Wingate?"

Heat surged through Sinclair's body—the old man's words cut like a stiletto.

"She was chosen. Everything is by design, Charles."

"What are you talking about? She's just a news reporter—a rookie at that. She stumbled across a story, reported it, gained some notoriety, and moved on. Besides, every reporter is nosing around Wingate." Sinclair's palms turned clammy—his underarms dampened. "What do you mean by she was chosen?"

"How can I say this so you will understand? It is a complicated matter, on a magnitude that is difficult for you to comprehend." He was quiet a few moments, looking out at the passing city as if searching for the right words. "Some years ago, a former associate betrayed me—*contracted* with my adversary. He was weak, unable to cope with . . . *life*. So pathetic, he died by his own hand. As part of that contract he proffered his seed, his daughter. She is the reporter."

Sinclair's gut twisted. *Adversary? Contract? Proffered his seed?* The air turned to syrup making him work at breathing. They'd never discussed who the old man was—intentional on Sinclair's part. If he didn't ask, he wouldn't have to know. And if he didn't know, he could sleep at night. But with these latest revelations, there would be no more claiming ignorance—no more pretending the old man was just a brilliant consultant. Sinclair was about to cross a line. He had tasted the rewards that the old man delivered—the fame, wealth, power—knowing they couldn't compare to what was coming in the New World he was helping create. Now he must make a choice. He remembered the question the *Time* science correspondent had asked—do you always win?

There could be no turning back.

"Then Stone is guided by the hand of God?" Sinclair asked.

"Yes," the old man said. "Our only advantage is that she has not yet discovered her true nature. The last time we spoke, I offered to have an old friend help with this matter. I have been in touch with him several times since then. He said he contacted you, but you declined his offer to assist."

"I told him we did not need his help at the moment."

"But you do, Charles. And he is the one who can give it to you. He can get you information vital to keeping this matter from getting out of control."

Sinclair needed straightforward information, not more of the old man's riddles. "But Stone seems so weak, confused. Vulnerable."

"Do not underestimate her. Those things which you might see as weaknesses in her are strengths. You must distract her, slow her down until the project is complete."

Until a few moments ago, Cotten Stone was a non-issue—nothing more to worry about. Now Sinclair faced a whole new set of challenges. But before he could address them, he had to ask a question that had constantly eaten at him from the beginning—the question of the Cup itself.

"There is still no scientific confirmation that the relic is genuine or that the residue inside is actually blood," Sinclair said. "The Vatican refused to test it. So far, it's just conjecture on your part."

"You still have reservations? Such little faith. Have I ever misled you? Told you anything that proved untrue?"

"But we are basing everything on your word alone. Are you positive that the relic is authentic?"

"Charles, I know it is hard for you to grasp the scope of what you are dealing with. Trust me, the Cup *is* authentic, and what is inside *is* the blood of Jesus Christ."

"How can you be so sure?"

"Because I was there when they nailed Him to the cross." The old man smiled at Sinclair. "I am the one who sealed the Cup."

THE SECRET ARCHIVES

THE CARDINAL'S FOOTSTEPS BARELY made a sound along the dark corridor below the Tower of the Winds. On each side, hidden in shadow, were bookshelves that if set end-to-end would reach over seven miles. Like a twilight apparition, the red-cloaked figure gripping the handle of a silver travel case entered the Hall of the Parchments. Around him were gathered thousands of historic documents that he knew, sadly, were turning purple from a violet-colored fungus that conservators had been unable to control.

At 2:00 AM, the passageways through the Secret Archives were deserted—to save energy, a minimum of lamps barely lit the way. From one small island of light to another, he felt the illusion of being in an underground world.

The cardinal passed the shelves that housed the transcripts of the conclaves for papal elections dating from the fifteenth century. Anticipation quivered in his stomach. Would his name be among them someday?

He'd been caught off guard by both Sinclair's visit and by the pope's death. For days he had had difficulty sleeping, and he lacked an appetite—much unlike him. He'd prayed for guidance. At last, in a dream, he believed God *had* come to him, shown him a vision of himself standing on the papal balcony wearing the triple tiara of the papacy, holding the hand of a small boy, and the people below falling on their knees in praise. Tonight he took the first steps on the Lord's chosen path. Tears streamed down his cheeks, overwhelmed that God had chosen him above all others.

Near the end of the corridor, a large carved walnut door stood closed. As Vatican Curator, Cardinal Ianucci was the only person other than the prefect to possess its key. He inserted it into the lock. With a faint click, the bolt gave way, and the door opened.

Ianucci entered the oldest part of the Secret Archives where the most ancient and precious items were kept. Huge cabinets bearing the coat of arms of Paul V, the Borghese pope who set up the Archives in the seventeenth century, lined the vault. Priceless collections of handwritten letters and documents dating back to the eleven hundreds were stored there, including letters of the Kahn of Mongolia; notes to the pope from Michelangelo; Henry VIII's petition seeking the annulment of his marriage to Catherine of Aragon; the last letter of Mary Stuart written a few days before she fell under the axe of Elizabeth; a letter from a Ming empress written in 1655 on silk asking that more Jesuit missionaries be sent to China; and the original dogma of the Immaculate Conception bound in pale blue velvet, its ink over time turning a warm yellow so that it appeared written in gold.

Digitizing them seemed so clinical and sterile to Ianucci. Gooseflesh broke out on his arms. He treasured these beautifully marred-with-age documents, their musty parchment smell being a perfume to his senses. But he understood the need for technology. The iron in Michelangelo's ink had turned corrosive and ate away at the great master's letters, leaving them full of minute slashes. The purple fungus that seemed to have slipped into every nook almost overnight proved unstoppable. Decomposition of these great works was defeating the conservators, forcing the Church to embrace technology. The Church, which so often wallowed in the past, raised its muddied head and slowly moved into the new world. The wolf and the lamb . . .

Sinclair was right, the cardinal thought. This was a different world —one of miraculous technology. Of course God had provided the knowledge—so, of course, He meant it to be used.

Passing through the vault, Ianucci descended a wide spiral stairway to a sublevel. At the bottom, a second vault door stood closed. Beside it was an electronic alarm keypad. Pressing in his code, the cardinal waited until the large internal bolts shifted open, and the heavy door swung forward.

He entered a chamber about the size of a high school gymnasium. Narrow aisles formed a labyrinth between the network of high shelves and cabinets. Passing by some of the most precious relics of the Church, including pieces of the True Cross and tiny bone fragments of the apostles, he stopped at a large black safe, its front bearing the symbol, IHS. Below the monogram was a combination wheel lock. He placed the travel case on the floor, then turned the wheel lock first clockwise, then counterclockwise, then again clockwise until he heard a soft click. Ianucci opened the door, touched a sensor, and the inside of the safe illuminated. A variety of boxes, envelopes, and other containers filled two of three shelves. On the top self sat the medieval puzzle cube.

The cardinal's hands trembled as he slipped on a pair of cotton gloves before reaching for the cube. Setting it on top of the safe, he repeated the motions John Tyler had shown him to open the box and carefully removed the cloth-wrapped chalice. His ears filled with the sound of his coursing blood—his chest pounding with every thump.

Cardinal Ianucci crossed himself, asking God to make him worthy to touch the Cup of Christ.

He opened the titanium travel case and removed the replica of the Grail, carefully jacketing it in the Templar cloth before putting it in the cube. Then he placed the Cup in the foam cutout insulation inside the travel case, closed the lid, and sat it on the floor just outside the door of the safe. After returning the cube to its resting place, the cardinal checked over the interior of the safe while removing his gloves, stuffing them in his pocket. Everything was in place. With his sleeved elbow he touched the sensor, and the vault was instantly in darkness. Slowly, he shut the safe door and spun the combination lock.

Ianucci dabbed the dribble of perspiration at his hairline with the back of his hand, then bent to pick up the case.

"Eminence?"

The voice came from behind him. He stiffened. "Yes," he said, without turning around.

"What are you doing?"

CALL WAITING

COTTEN STRETCHED ACROSS THE unmade bed, folding one arm behind her head, her other hand holding the phone receiver to her ear.

"Are you going to have to go to Rome?" she asked John.

"No. I don't think so, since I just got back. And there really isn't anything for me to do."

"When will they elect the new pope?"

"The conclave has to begin no less than fifteen days after the pope's death. That gives all the cardinals who are eligible to vote time to travel to Rome. It also gives them time to get organized, both for logistics and politics, and of course to have the funeral. My guess is about a week."

"Will they come up with a list first, like nominations? What are the qualifications, anyway?"

"Technically, any Catholic male can be elected."

Cotten adjusted her head to rest better in the crook of her arm. "That's it? Any man who's a Catholic? I thought he had to come up through the ranks—had to be a priest, then a bishop, then a cardinal or something."

"Nope. Any Catholic man is eligible. Of course, once elected, he'd have to accept the job. In reality, it's a death sentence. Once you're pope, there's no retiring or resigning or taking time off. You're it for life."

"Let me get this straight. Mikey Fitzgerald, the barkeep at the Rathskeller, who is Catholic, not necessarily a good practicing Catholic, could be the next pope?"

"You got it, but Mikey's a long shot. Put your money on one of the senior cardinals—someone like our friend Antonio Ianucci would be a likely choice, but there are half a dozen who have a good chance."

A beep sounded on the phone. "Hold on a minute," Cotten said. "I've got a call coming in."

She hit the flash button. "Hello."

"Cotten, it's me," Thornton Graham said.

"I'm on the other line."

"Can you call them back? This is costing me a sweet penny."

Cotten grunted an annoyed sigh. "All right." She didn't want to hang up on John, but Thornton was calling from Rome. She supposed it was the right thing to do. Again she switched lines. "John, it's Thornton. He's covering the pope's death, and he's calling long distance. I'm sorry, I need to take his call."

"Sure. I'll talk to you soon."

She clicked over to Thornton. "Okay. I'm back. I hope this is important."

"I miss you. And it's not the geographical distance. It's the distance that you've put between us. I don't want to—"

Cotten rolled to her side. "Stop. Please."

"How can I? What do you think, I can just flush a handle and everything I've felt for you will disappear down the toilet?"

"Good choice of words, Thornton." Cotten's eyes closed. Funny, this time she was worried about hurting him, not him hurting her. "I did it. You can, too. It's time to move on. I think it's probably better if we only speak about work-related things. I thought we already got that straight."

"I slummed in some dive of a bar tonight and sat there thinking about nothing but you. Five, six Grand Marniers later I got the courage to call."

"I'm not going to listen to this, Thornton."

"I just needed to hear your voice." He breathed out a long, mournful breath. "Do you know I haven't had sex since the last time with you? What does that tell you?"

Cotten sat up. "That you're horny and you're calling for phone sex. It's not your heart that's aching, Thornton, it's your dick."

"Come on, Cotten. Missing the feel of your warmth isn't an insult. I've been sitting here with people all around me, and all I can hear in my head are your little whimpers, your—"

She glanced at the clock. Nine o'clock. "It must be about three in the morning. You need to go to bed. Too much Grand Marnier. You'll kick yourself in the morning."

"No, I won't."

"Trust me. Close your mouth, go back to your room, and crawl under the covers. I'll make it easy for you. From now on, I'm not going to answer your calls at home anymore. And don't leave me messages on the answer phone. I'll know it's you from the Caller ID, and I'll delete them without listening. If you need to talk to me about work, call me at the office. Goodnight, Thornton. See you when you get back."

"I won't give up."

"Goodbye, Thornton."

THE CODE

THE LAST RAYS OF the sun illuminated the chalky trail of the small charter jet streaking toward New Orleans. The solitary passenger, Cardinal Antonio Ianucci, dressed in a black suit and Roman collar, sat in the wide leather swivel chair watching Bogalusa and Picayune pass beneath. Ahead, the fading sunset reflected off the dark waters of Lake Pontchartrain.

After the long flight from Rome, the jet had refueled in New York where two U.S. Customs and Immigration officers boarded. The cardinal presented them with his diplomatic passport—a leftover from his years of service with the Vatican Secretariat of State.

He declared nothing.

Shortly after takeoff he had enjoyed a dinner of grilled calamari, Sicilian style, followed by veal scaloppini with wild mushrooms along with half a bottle of Revello Barolo.

"Your Eminence, can I bring you anything else?" the young female attendant asked just before the pilot announced their final descent.

"No, thank you." The cardinal was content, his belly full and his insides warm with wine.

Ianucci rested his head on the back of the seat and thought of his encounter two nights previous with the prefect in the Secret Archives. The cardinal had explained that he was leaving the next day to visit relatives in America. He would be bringing them gifts—rosaries and religious medals that had actually touched the Holy Grail. It was enough to convince the prefect that the midnight visit to the Archives was innocent. Clever, he thought.

Afterward, the cardinal had returned to his Vatican apartment, fallen on his knees, and prayed to God to forgive him for lying, but knowing it was necessary to fulfill divine providence, to accomplish God's will.

The pontiff's fatal heart attack caused enough disturbance in the Vatican that Ianucci found it easy to slip away, telling his staff he would return to Rome within a few days.

But the upheaval at the Vatican paled to the turmoil inside him. He kept replaying Sinclair's arguments in his mind and reciting the logic of the scriptures. And the death of the Holy Father . . . that had to be the hand of God delivering a sign to him.

He pried his fingers between his throat and collar, feeling the need for air. His palms and soles iced, but were wet with perspiration. He was doing the right thing, he reassured himself. The Cup had been delivered to him—God's hand at work. With the Heavenly Father's blessing, he accepted the task of leading the Church, preparing the flock for the Second Coming, and . . .

He blinked back tears. God would entrust him to mentor the child.

Ianucci looked down at the city lights spreading across the darkness like the wave of profound faith that spread through him. This had to be right.

The signs were all there.

With a thump, the jet touched down and taxied to a private aviation terminal. As the whine of the turbines wound down, Ianucci took the titanium travel case from the storage cabinet. He blessed the crew before disembarking.

Charles Sinclair emerged from the waiting limousine and walked toward him, his hand outstretched. "Your Eminence, welcome to New Orleans. I hope you had a good flight."

"Yes, very pleasant."

"It only gets better from here." He motioned toward the travel case. "May I?"

Ianucci's fingers tightened around the handle as one last spurt of doubt sputtered in his brain.

"Your Eminence?"

The cardinal looked at Sinclair. "If you don't mind, I'd rather hold on to it a bit longer."

"I completely understand," Sinclair said, and the two men walked to the limousine.

In another few minutes the black stretch limo sped across the tarmac onto the airport access road and blended into the rush of city traffic.

* * *

Giant, deep green magnolias lined the entrance drive to Sinclair's plantation estate on the banks of the Mississippi. Ianucci watched the lights from the sprawling mansion appear through the shadows of the trees, first as a distant twinkling and finally a flood of brilliance.

"I thought we would be going directly to the BioGentec facility," the cardinal said.

"I've prepared a long time for this day, Eminence. Everything we need can be done right here. It keeps our work private. I'm certain you will be impressed with our lab. The specifications bore our task in mind."

The limo pulled up to the main house, and the cardinal waited until the driver opened the car door. Getting out, he looked up at the three-storied, columned mansion, cascades of light from the floodlights washing over the surface. *White, all white, how perfect the color. Pure. Unsoiled. Innocent. Immaculate.*

"Beautiful, Dr. Sinclair," Ianucci said, standing on the brick driveway. He found his hand clutching at his chest, the other gripping the handle of the titanium travel case. So this was the place the child would be *born*. His eyes drifted over the estate and up to the sky—a clear sky, every star shining. Yes, he stood on sacred ground.

Although he couldn't see it, the cardinal felt the heaviness of the river nearby. In the distance, a tugboat's horn sounded. The world went on, not knowing what was about to happen here. *As a thief in the night.*

"Your bags will be brought to your room," Sinclair said as they entered the grand foyer. The marble floors led to a staircase beneath a massive crystal chandelier. "Would you like to freshen up from your trip?"

"I'm fine, Doctor—and very anxious to proceed."

"But you must be tired. We could wait until morning. And to be honest, Your Eminence, the lab is somewhat boring—just a jumbled collection of tubs, wires, electronic monitoring devices . . ."

"No, no. I do not believe I could sleep. Besides, in some respects, I feel I'm about to enter the new Bethlehem—the modern-day manger so to speak. I must see it."

Sinclair gestured. "Then right this way." He led the way past entrances to rooms that included a library, a video conference center, and his personal office, and then into a barren hallway. At the end of the corridor was a metal door resembling the entrance to a bank vault. Installed in the wall by the door was a combination keypad mounted beside what looked like the bowl of a metallic soupspoon resting on a protrusion extending a few inches.

Sinclair placed his index finger face down in the spoon-like device. Instantly, a digital readout above the spoon scrolled the LED message: *Dr. Charles Sinclair. Identity confirmed.*

"You use your fingerprint as security?" Ianucci asked.

Sinclair gave the cardinal a condescending smile. "We go way beyond fingerprints here, Eminence." He pressed a series of numbers into the keypad and the display changed to *Learning New User.* "Please place your index finger on the scanner as I just did, and I'll explain."

The cardinal did as he was told. He looked up at Sinclair. "It has a tickling sensation."

"That it does, Eminence. We now have a sample of your DNA— the most reliable source of human identification known to man. A minute layer of epidermis has been sanded off your finger—so minute that you only detected a tickle. Within seconds, the skin cells were analyzed and your complete DNA profile is now stored in our databank. Even if you altered your fingerprint pattern, which I'm sure you would not do, Eminence, we could still positively identify you. Our new BioGentec DNA security system is one hundred percent accurate.

Sinclair gave the cardinal another patronizing smile and tapped the screen, making Ianucci look at it.

Enter code.

"What we're about to do here demands intense safeguards," Sinclair said. "As accurate as DNA identification is, the system requires a second security check—an entry code. Without it, the system prohibits entry even with DNA identification."

Ianucci lightly rubbed his thumb against his index fingertip while he watched. "What is the code?"

Sinclair reached for the keypad and pressed the six-digit combination. "One I think you would find most appropriate."

STATIC

Cotten held the tv remote in her lap while she watched the news she'd taped. Three days ago John had called her early in the morning before she got out of bed and told her the Grail had been stolen. She was stunned. After hanging up, she immediately called Ted who told her Thornton was already on it and would be reporting from Rome on the evening news. She felt unsettled all that day, nervous, apprehensive, looking over her shoulder. For her, hearing that the Grail had been stolen was like a stalker victim learning the perpetrator had escaped from prison. She taped Thornton's report, knowing she would want to watch it again.

And so she did, tonight.

"As preparations for the pontiff's funeral are being finalized, it was announced today that a theft of unprecedented proportions has occurred at the Vatican." Thornton Graham stood in the international press area of St. Peter's Square and read from the teleprompter.

"Scientists in the antiquities authentication department have confirmed that what is considered the most prized religious relic in the world, the Holy Grail, has been stolen. Although details are sketchy,

SNN has learned that the relic, recently discovered and brought to the Vatican by one of our own correspondents, is missing, and has been replaced with a counterfeit.

"The artifact had been brought out of its safekeeping for a brief photo session for *National Geographic*. It was at that time that the fraud was discovered.

"A source inside the Vatican, who requested anonymity, told us that although the replica was obviously the work of a master craftsman, during close inspection it was determined to be a fake. When the authentic Cup was first examined, a small nick was observed on the back, the opposite side of the engraving. During the photo shoot for *National Geographic*, the prefect realized the object being photographed had no nick. The magazine session ended abruptly.

"All the news photos that had been released of the relic only showed what is considered to be the front, the side with the IHS monogram. It's assumed that the counterfeiter crafted the replica from those news pictures and was therefore unaware of the imperfection.

"The area where the Cup was stored is one of the most secure sections of the Holy City. As yet, investigators have no leads as to how the switch took place."

Thornton turned to the headshot camera. "We'll have more on the theft of the Holy Grail during a special segment of *Close Up* tonight at eight, seven Central. And for continuous coverage of the papal death and funeral, and the upcoming election of the new pontiff, stay tuned to SNN or log onto our Website at satellitenews-dot-org. This is Thornton Graham reporting from Vatican City. Now back to our studios in New York and the rest of the weekend headlines."

Cotten turned off the television. Thornton had looked good. Didn't appear to be pining away for her. Certainly didn't sound like the same man who'd sucked down a half dozen drinks because he was so despondent over their breakup. When Thornton was in front of a camera, he was in his element. She shook her head, got up, and tossed the remote on the couch.

It was a cold, drizzly night, and she wanted to rent *Charlotte Gray* from Blockbuster, have a glass of wine, and curl up in bed to watch the movie. Almost out the door, the phone rang. "Damn," she said, turning back. Cotten peered down at the Caller ID. Thornton's cell phone.

She reached for the phone, but hesitated. "Nope," she whispered. More head games. He'd probably been out drinking and was lonely or horny or both. She'd see him soon enough.

* * *

"How's the Wingate thing going, Cotten?"

Looking up from her notes, she smiled at the SNN science correspondent seated next to her. Along with about a dozen other reporters, they were gathered around a conference table for the 7:00 AM Monday SNN strategy meeting.

"Very interesting, so far." Cotten glanced at her watch. "Are we still waiting on Ted?"

"Yeah," the correspondent said. "I think he's meeting with Thornton first—they're both running late."

"Figures. Thornton doesn't have a sense of time."

"Ouch," he said. "Do I detect a woman's scorn in your voice?"

"Sorry."

"So what's interesting about Wingate?" the correspondent asked.

"Well, for starters," Cotten said, "it looks like someone is trying to blackmail him."

"No shit."

"He's also got a hot temper and a very low opinion of the press, especially SNN."

"He's going to have to get over that real quick," the correspondent said. "He sure hides it well. At the moment, he is the darling of the entire press corps. Everybody loves him."

Cotten flipped through some of her notes. "He certainly took a dislike to me. Called the press piranhas." Cotten glanced up to see Ted Casselman coming through the doorway. His shoulders drooped—he looked drained and spent.

"Good morning," Casselman said, glancing at each of their faces. "I'm afraid I have some bad news." He sat at the head of the table and put his glasses down before continuing. "As many of you know, Thornton has been in Rome this week covering the death of the pope and the Grail theft. He was to have flown back yesterday and planned to brief us at this meeting." Casselman paused, cleared his throat, and massaged his forehead. "Thornton didn't make his plane."

Carousing all hours of the night, it's no wonder, Cotten thought.

Casselman went on, "The hotel's cleaning staff discovered him unconscious on the floor of his bathroom."

Cotten suddenly couldn't get enough air. "No," she whispered, shaking her head as if she could dislodge Ted Casselman's words so that nothing he said would be true.

Casselman stared directly at her with an *I'm so sorry, Cotten* expression in his eyes. "He was rushed to a local hospital but was pronounced dead in the emergency room. A brain hemorrhage."

* * *

Cotten ran through the front door of her apartment and came to a halt in front of her answering machine. Thornton had left a message. She hadn't been able to make herself delete it as she had said she would. Nor had she listened to it. The message was still on the machine—the red button flashing. What had she thought—that maybe one evening when she was feeling particularly self-destructive, she'd want to test herself and play the message to assess her emotional response?

She sat next to the phone and stared at the blinking light. "It's just like you, Thornton," she said. "You go and die on me just when I'm beginning to feel emotionally healthy, not drowning in your back-wash." She wiped tears from her cheeks. "Shit."

Finally she pushed the play-message button.

"Cotten, it's me. You need to pick up. Are you there?"

There was a moment of silence before he spoke again.

"I hope . . . hear me. My cell isn't . . . a good signal.

"Cotten, there's something wrong. Have . . . following this Grail theft story. I stumbled across . . . someone with contacts deep inside . . . There's more to this than . . . As a matter of fact, I think . . . the tip . . . iceberg."

His voice, digitized and at times metallic sounding, faded in and out, making it difficult to follow his stream of thought.

"I'm . . . danger . . . fear for my life. I'm flying . . . I should . . . Monday morning."

Even through the bad connection, Cotten thought she noticed an uncertainty in his voice—one she'd never heard before. "Oh, God," she whispered.

"I think I've found . . . international connections. If something happens . . . still love you."

There was a final bit of static before the call went dead.

In the seas off northern Australia lives an almost invisible killer, the Irukandji jellyfish, Carukia barnesi. *Both the body and the tentacles are armed with stinging cells that inject poison into prey or an unlucky swimmer.*

The initial sting is not usually very painful. However, within five to forty-five minutes, the victim experiences excruciating pain.

In January 2002, a tourist was stung by what was believed to be an Irukandji jellyfish. His preexisting conditions made the sting rapidly fatal. He had recently had a heart valve replacement and was taking warfarin to thin his blood. After being stung, his blood pressure spiked, causing a brain hemorrhage and death.

The poison is not classified, and there is no test available to detect its presence.

GRAVESIDE

IT WAS COLD AND snowing as Cotten Stone and Ted Casselman walked with about three hundred other mourners from their cars to the freshly dug grave. She had not slept well since hearing the news of Thornton's death, and she knew her eyes showed fatigue and distress. Had there been anything she could have done to save his life? she asked herself repeatedly. Even if she'd taken Thornton's call that night, nothing would have changed. But maybe he would have told her what he had found out—what it was that had him so alarmed.

The Italian medical examiner's report showed brain hemorrhage as cause of death. Possibly brought on by a combination of things including hypertension and his medication, it was explained. She just couldn't buy it. He was too young to die of *natural causes*. And as far as the medication, he'd just had his Coumadin levels checked. But mostly what troubled her was his last phone call and the message he'd left on her answering machine.

The pallbearers brought the casket to the grave. Cheryl Graham, Thornton's wife of fifteen years, followed, flanked by her relatives and Thornton's parents.

Cotten watched as the widow took her place graveside. She wondered if Cheryl had been content to be childless, or if that was Thornton's preference. Cotten studied the widow who was dressed in black with a wide-brimmed hat and dark overcoat—large sunglasses hiding her eyes. Cheryl dabbed her nose with a handkerchief.

Cotten's knees weakened at the sight of the coffin. It was hard to un-love someone, she thought.

She had met Cheryl Graham briefly before at SNN when the news department threw Thornton a surprise birthday luncheon. It was a few weeks after their affair had started, and Cotten made it a point to avoid Cheryl, only saying hello as they were introduced.

Now she watched the grieving widow and wondered how much she knew of her husband's womanizing. His extramarital affairs were no secret at the network, but did Cheryl know about them . . . about her? She watched Thornton's wife and felt sick inside. It wasn't fair what Thornton had put either one of them through.

Cotten hadn't told anyone about Thornton's last phone call, yet. Even though the medical report was straightforward and conclusive, it seemed too coincidental that Thornton would say he was in danger and then wind up dead. She knew Thornton was fanatical about keeping notes in his comp book, documenting every detail of his investigations. Perhaps he left something behind in his notebook that could either confirm his suspicions or indicate that he was in no real danger. As much as she wanted to avoid contact with Cheryl, she really needed to ask if his notes were included with the belongings returned from Rome. If so, and she could take a look at them, she could pursue it with Ted or dismiss her concerns. Despite the unpleasantness it might cause, she had to speak to Thornton's wife.

After the service ended, some of the network executives and managers gathered to offer their condolences to Cheryl Graham. Cotten stood back and waited patiently in the biting cold wind and light snow until she saw Cheryl being escorted to the funeral home's limousine. Quickly, Cotten composed herself and rushed to catch up.

"I'm so sorry for your loss," Cotten said, reaching out and lightly touching Cheryl's arm.

"Thank you," Cheryl said, her expression blank, pulling her arm away from Cotten's touch.

Thornton's father took Cheryl by the elbow and began again to lead her to the car.

"Wait," Cotten said, stepping in front of them. "Could I possibly call you sometime? It's important."

Cheryl glared at her before turning and walking away.

"What was that all about?" Ted Casselman asked, coming to Cotten's side.

"I'm hoping they sent Thornton's comp book back with him. I'd like to take a look if Cheryl has it."

"What do you expect to find?"

"I'm not sure."

"Come on, Cotten. I know you better than that."

"It's cold," she said. "Let's get to the car."

They walked quietly to the Lincoln Town Car the network had provided and climbed in the back. The driver steered it out of the cemetery and back toward Manhattan.

"Talk to me," Casselman said.

Cotten hesitated, knowing she could be completely wrong. "Thornton called me a couple of days ago. I didn't pick up. He'd phoned before, trying to get us back together. I didn't want to go through that again. But he left a message. I didn't listen to it until the day you told us he was dead."

"What did he say?"

"He was on his cell and didn't have a good signal, but what I could make out was a little upsetting."

"What do you mean?"

"Thornton said he'd stumbled across something and it scared him."

"You're kidding. Nothing scared Thornton Graham. I've seen him confront terrorists and the Mafia head-on."

"There was something about his voice—something different. He said he was in contact with someone deep inside."

"Inside what?"

"That's a good question. I assume it had something to do with the Vatican because of the stories he was covering."

"But he didn't say for sure?"

"No. It sounded like he didn't want to say too much on the phone."

"What else?"

"He said he feared for his life, and I think he said something like 'the tip of the iceberg' and something about international connections."

"What do you really think?"

"Either it was some kind of pity-me head game he was playing to get my attention, or he was really in danger." Cotten brushed the hair from her face. "Now with his death, I'm thinking—"

"But it was a brain hemorrhage. Nothing suspicious."

"I know, I know. But it just doesn't sit right. There must be some drug or poison that could cause it."

"You're right, and he was on it—warfarin . . . Coumadin. Maybe he had an aneurysm blow—he got excited over the project, his blood pressure went up, the blood thinner kicked in, and there you have it. You're not just feeling guilty about the breakup, are you?"

Cotten huffed out a frustrated breath. "Either way, I need to look at his notes."

"Give Cheryl time—don't push her."

She frowned. "I'm not insensitive, Ted."

"I know you're not," he apologized. "Did Thornton say anything else?"

"He said if something happens, he still loves me."

THE RIVER

COTTEN WAS RELIEVED TO see John waiting for her in front of the restaurant as her taxi pulled to the curb.

He took her hand and helped her out of the cab. Her icy fingers welcomed his warm palm.

"You look a little ragged," he said. "Are you all right?"

Cotten straightened her skirt and fiddled with the collar of her jacket. "I'm a mess. I can't get focused, can't sleep, can't work." She looked at him as he opened the door to the restaurant. "To answer your question, no, I guess I'm not all right."

They slipped into a booth in the back. "I know we've talked about this for hours," Cotten said, "but I still don't think Thornton's death was from natural causes." She pulled a scrunchy from her purse and bound her hair at the base of her neck. A hank of hair didn't get caught in the elastic, and it spilled down the right side of her face. "Shit," she said, yanking the scrunchy free and starting over.

John watched as she collected herself. "Relax," he said.

Cotten forced a smile. "I should have picked up the phone when he called. I keep thinking I might have been able to do something, help him . . . something. I don't know."

"He was a long way away, Cotten."

"It just doesn't make sense," she said. "Thornton was excellent at what he did—probably the best investigative reporter in the business. I've been thinking about the stories he was working on. Since there was nothing unusual about how the pope died, whatever Thornton stumbled upon had to be related to the theft of the Cup. It scared the hell out of him. What if Thornton discovered who stole the Grail, and the thieves were on to him—and he had reason to believe they would kill him. The only thing that gnaws at my theory is who would want the Cup that badly? Who would murder for it?"

John took one of her hands in both of his. "You aren't being rational. We've already discussed this. There's no evidence that Thornton died of anything other than a brain hemorrhage. And you told me he might have been overly dramatic in that phone message just to spark your sympathy. He couldn't accept the fact that you weren't in love with him anymore. You're torturing yourself with guilt."

"I'm not doing that, John. It was over, but I still cared about him. You don't just *uncare* about someone who's been a part of your life like that." She pulled her hand away. "I'm stable." *I'm so frigging stable I've been sitting here holding a goddamn priest's hand, and then I pulled it away like a pouting lover. Jesus, Cotten, he's just trying to console you and you act like an ungrateful ass.*

"I don't doubt you," John said. "I'm trying to help you work through things, make sure you see them as they really are."

He withdrew his hands from the table, and she realized she was sorry she had pulled hers away. For an instant she considered offering hers, open as his had been, in the center of the table—but she didn't.

Instead she fumbled with the scrunchy, again. "I'm telling you, I knew him well enough to know there was something wrong."

John leaned back, his face serious and thoughtful. "All right, then, let's try to make some sense of it. Who would want the Grail? Antiquities collectors. Black market dealers."

"But they couldn't sell it. It's not like they could auction it off on eBay."

"Wouldn't have to. They'd already have a buyer lined up before they did the job. No relic switching on speculation. Most likely the thief would be paid a portion of his fee up front and would get the rest on delivery. There are private collectors who'd think owning the Holy Grail the ultimate prize. To them, money would be no object. There are even those who will go to extensive means to fake an artifact, like the recent Ossuary of James hoax."

"But those kinds of people aren't murderers. They get off by owning a great work of art or in this case, a profoundly religious relic. It doesn't fit."

"So who do you think fits the profile?" John asked. "Who would kill to own the Grail?"

* * *

Charles Sinclair stared out the picture window. He was going to take his time to make his point, he thought, looking past the gazebo and the formal gardens, all the way to the river. "Sit down," he said to Robert Wingate. He heard the soft leather of the chair give way as Wingate sat. "The river never fails to hold me in awe—its sheer power." Sinclair turned to face the man he had summoned.

Wingate shifted in the chair.

Hitching his chin toward the window, Sinclair said, "Ever think about its power?" He stared at Wingate and thought perhaps he detected a nervous tick in the man's left eyelid. Sinclair moved behind the large mahogany desk. "The river has one purpose, one goal. For two thousand three hundred miles it courses, sometimes thundering, sometimes only meandering, but always it flows—driven to carry out its destiny. The current steadily washes over and drowns all obstacles. When it reaches its destination, it empties itself, becoming one with an even greater, more ominous power, the Gulf of Mexico. Oh, men have sometimes thought they could harness it with locks and dams. They've bridged it, they've navigated it, but it's never been controlled. Dams burst, bridges wash out, ships sink, the land floods. All at the river's whim."

Sinclair sat and leaned back in his chair. "The Guardians are like the river, Robert. We have a destiny, a goal we have worked toward for centuries. Nothing will be allowed to stop us. You understand that, don't you?"

Wingate's eye twitched, and he rubbed it. "Of course."

"We've invested our financial resources in you and your counterparts in Europe and other parts of the world. Each of you plays an important role in establishing our new world—the world as prophesied. There's a tremendous amount of money backing you, and more importantly, our mission has been entrusted to you. We can't let anything get in our way. We are like the great river, Robert—we drown all obstacles." Sinclair paused, drumming his thumb on the edge of the desk.

"Absolutely," Wingate said.

"We've got a problem, Robert. And we can't afford problems, can't tolerate them."

Wingate shook his head. "What problem?" His eyelid quivered, and a small muscle beneath his eye seized. He drew his hand over his face, bearing down on eye and cheek.

"This blackmail issue. It's attracted the attention of Cotten Stone. She's not letting go—"

"She doesn't know anything. She's probing, looking for a weak spot. Don't worry, I'll take care of it."

"She's digging up your skeletons, Robert. And she's done it in no time at all. She's as good if not better than her dead boyfriend, don't you think?"

"I told you, she doesn't know anything. I can handle it."

Sinclair took a pencil from a leather canister and twirled it on the desk top. "And the skeleton she dug up, the blackmail matter—it's like a pesky mosquito. You can't swat it away. You have to slap it . . . dead. And you know what? I don't think you've told me everything. You've danced around the details several times, now."

"Because it's not important. I'm innocent. It's just some jerk out there trying to cash in. His kid was in one of my youth camps a couple of years ago. Now the father claims I molested the boy and wants money to keep quiet. He knows it's not true, but he figures I'm running for president and I'll pay to shut him up."

"Robert, Robert," Sinclair said, his voice oozing with southern charm—patronizing. "It doesn't matter whether you are innocent or guilty. The *accusation* will ruin you. You must be beyond reproach. Stone's not going to let this tidbit slip past her. Before you know, it'll be the lead story on the nightly news."

Wingate leaned forward, his hands rubbing his knees through the wool trousers. "Just let me take care of it. It's not something the Guardians need to worry about."

"It's our job to worry." Sinclair studied Wingate, wondering if they had bet on the wrong horse. "Give Stone her interview and tell her there's been a terrible misunderstanding—that there is no black-mail. Apologize for your previous rudeness and move on to the election issues. In the meantime, we'll pay a generous sum to the boy's father to make him go away."

"What if Stone doesn't believe me? Charles, I have friends who could take care of her once and for all."

Sinclair felt the heat rising in his face. "Out of the question. Don't do anything rash, Robert. Don't even think about it."

* * *

The phone rang as Cotten came through the door of her apartment. She slung her purse onto the couch and picked up the receiver, shrugging her left arm out of her coat. "Hello."

"Ms. Stone?"

Cotten froze, her coat dangling off the back of one shoulder. "Mr. Wingate, what a surprise."

FRIENDS

ROBERT WINGATE'S CHANGE OF heart piqued Cotten's curiosity. He'd agreed to the exclusive, so immediately after hanging up with him, Cotten booked a flight to Miami for the following day.

When she arrived at MIA, she picked up her rental car and headed to Vanessa's for a late dinner. They stayed up until the wee hours sipping wine and talking. The morning had come much too early.

Cotten stood at the kitchen counter still perspiring from a morning jog along the beach. She savored a blueberry muffin and cup of coffee while watching Vanessa scurry around the kitchen.

"God, I'm going to be late," Vanessa Perez said. She took a bite of muffin then gulped orange juice from the carton. "Want some?" She held out the carton.

Cotten declined.

Vanessa sat the juice down and spun around. "Where are my fucking shoes? I just had them." She whipped around again, knocking over the carton.

The juice sloshed out and splattered Cotten.

"Oh, shit, I'm sorry," Vanessa said.

Cotten picked up the sponge from the sink and began dabbing at her fleece top and sweat pants. "It won't stain," she said. "I'll throw them in the wash in a minute. Go on and get a move on."

Nessi blurted a sigh. "I'm always a disaster in the mornings."

"You don't think I remember back in college having to drag you out of bed to make your first class? Maybe if you tried going to sleep at a decent hour," Cotten said with a straight face.

They both laughed.

"Wish I could lounge around here all day like somebody I know," Vanessa said.

"What do you mean, lounge? I've got an exclusive interview at noon with a presidential candidate who wants to make up for blowing me off. I'll be able to get ready just as soon as you've relinquished the bathroom."

"You've got such a cushy job," Vanessa said, slipping on her shoes. "Asking questions all day. How hard can that be?"

Cotten moved into the living room and settled on the sofa. "Oh, and looking beautiful while someone pampers you—doing your hair and makeup. That isn't cushy?"

Vanessa appeared to consider the argument. "All right, you win. My cushy is better."

They laughed again as the model grabbed her keys and tote bag, and headed for the door. She stopped short, ran over to the couch, and kissed Cotten on the cheek. "Call your priest friend. He's good for you." She grinned. "Love you."

Cotten waved her off. "Go! You're already half an hour late."

"Yeah, but they can't start without me," Vanessa said. Seconds later, she was gone.

It's a good thing Nessi got paid just to look great, Cotten thought. She'd be hard pressed to make it in the real world.

She leaned back taking a deep breath, deciding to call John later, maybe after she returned from the interview—she knew he must be tired of hearing about Thornton and her guilt trip.

She had to see Thornton's notes, had to know what he was on to and if there had been something she could have done to prevent his death. Cotten leaned forward and covered her face with her hands. "Damn it." Why hadn't she just answered his call? Rocking, she wrapped her arms around her waist as if to hold herself together. "Christ, I've got to stop this." She shoved her fingers through her hair like a harrow.

Cotten grabbed her spiral notebook from the end table. First thing she needed to do was go over her notes for the Wingate interview one more time. Ted Casselman had helped her, suggesting many of the questions. Had she missed anything? Forgotten anything? How would she treat Wingate? Cold and aloof or warm and cozy? She had to get as much as possible out of the candidate without him turning on her. Warm and cozy, that was it. Kill him with kindness—compliments and sweetness. Always dip it in honey, her mother would say. It's easier to pull a chain than push it.

Suddenly, the door burst open and Vanessa bolted in. "Goddamn car won't start, and my cell's dead!" She snatched the cordless phone. "I'll have to call a cab—probably take them an hour to get here."

"Wait, Nessi." Cotten got up and went to her purse lying on the dining room table. "Take my rental." She pulled out her keys.

"How will you get to your interview?"

"I think I can call a cab just as good as you. And I'm not the one who's late."

"Are you absolutely sure?"

"That's what friends are for," she sang in her best Dionne Warwick. She held out the keys. "Here—don't argue."

"You're a sweetheart," Vanessa said. "See you tonight." She grabbed the keys and sprinted to the door. "Good luck with Wingate."

Cotten started to wave, but the door was already closing. She broke off a chunk of blueberry muffin and shoved it into her mouth before strolling out on the balcony. In the distance a handful of sailboats captured the early breeze. Being the height of the tourist season, the snowbirds already sprawled themselves on blankets along the beach, seemingly oblivious to the nippy air. Die-hard tourists, she thought. A chilly wind swept down A1A from the north causing her to shiver as the palm fronds rustled beneath the balcony.

A squeal caught Cotten's attention. Part of the parking lot was directly below, infringing on the scenic view. Vanessa darted across the asphalt. She glanced up and waved, then unlocked the door to Cotten's rental and jumped in.

Nessi was the oldest teenager she knew, Cotten thought. She had many acquaintances, but Nessi was her only real friend. She took a last glance at the beach before turning to go back inside.

In the next instant there was a blinding burst of light and thunderous boom, and she was slammed face down on the floor, her ears filled with a high-pitched ringing. What felt like a sledgehammer had hit her from behind, driving the air from her lungs.

All went black.

Slowly, Cotten opened her eyes but saw only blurred images. Faint pricks of light swirled in a gray haze. The back of her neck, legs, and arms tingled as if they were sunburned.

As Cotten focused, she raised her head and looked around the room. Broken glass from the windows and sliding door littered the floor like chipped ice.

And there was the sound of crackling and popping. Fire.

She heard a chorus of car alarms along with distant shouts as she managed to get to her hands and knees. Heat radiated from the direction of the balcony. Cotten struggled to her feet. A ligature of fear knotted her throat as she looked out at the parking lot. She stood there, numbed by the sight, no longer feeling any chill in the air.

Flames and black smoke billowed from what had been her rental. It wasn't a car anymore—the roof, doors, and hood were gone, metal peeled back. Several nearby cars were also on fire.

"Nessi!" she screamed, hanging over the rail.

Everywhere she looked there was debris—detached car door, mangled hood, swatches of fabric and seat cushion stuffing, an open brief case, bits of paper, prisms of window glass . . . Vanessa's shoe.

"Oh, Jesus. Oh, God," she whispered.

Cotten steadied herself, holding on to the railing as her thoughts came together. This was much more than a gas tank igniting. It had to have been a powerful explosion to do such damage—there were at least five other cars ablaze. And the shockwave had knocked her down, blown pictures from the walls. The windows and sliding glass doors were shattered—balcony furniture overturned.

A bomb.

The realization hit her harder than the actual blast. The bomb was meant for her, not for Vanessa.

Screaming sirens came from the distance.

Blue lights flashed; red lights strobed.

Vanessa was dead. Oh, God, her friend . . . her friend.

She had to get away. Someone wanted her dead.

Cotten grabbed her purse and headed for the door.

At the end of the hall she punched the elevator button. "Come on, come on." She pushed again, watching the floor indicator change numbers in slow motion.

Finally, the bell dinged. The doors slid open and Cotten pressed herself against the metal wall inside. She pushed the lobby button five times, poking it so hard the end of her finger hurt.

"Oh, God. Oh, God."

Her breathing became giant bellows in her ears. She felt blood pumping in her neck, her scalp, even her wrists.

The doors parted, and she was in the lobby. A crowd already gathered, trying to get a better look at the fire. Her eyes jumped from person to person—profiles, faces, backs of heads. Was he here—the person who planted the bomb? Was the man who wanted her dead looking at her right now?

She pushed through the crowd toward the door leading to the patio and pool. Cotten kept her face down, trying to be as inconspicuous as possible.

She fought the urge to run, though panic had her heart thudding heavily and wildly, her lungs sputtering out every shallow and rapid breath.

The door! Get out the goddamn door!

Throwing the door open, she crossed the patio surrounding the apartment pool, rounded the building and burst onto the South Beach sidewalk.

Sirens and emergency horns blasted from all directions.

Cotten fled across Ocean Drive and turned south, racing through the flow of onlookers making their way toward the scene. "Sorry! Sorry!" she shouted, pushing through. She chanced a quick glimpse over her shoulder. Black smoke—red trucks—madness.

She darted down an alley, across Collins Avenue, through parking lots and between buildings, turning south again on Washington Avenue. Past Joe's Stone Crabs she saw a park ahead on her left.

She hurried toward the small concrete block building inside the park—public restrooms. Looking back, she made sure no one followed.

Cotten slipped in the women's restroom and locked herself in a stall. Crouched on top of the toilet she folded her arms across her middle and rocked. "Oh, Nessi, Nessi." She could hear the harmony of Dionne Warwick, Gladys Knight, Stevie Wonder, and Elton John deep in her head.

Knowin' you can always count on me, oh, for sure . . .
That's what friends are for.

Cotten sobbed until completely out of breath and exhausted. Her chest and throat burned.

As she looked down, a drop of blood splattered onto the floor. She raised her hand and felt her face first, then the back of her head—a patch of hair was wet and sticky. She looked at the blood on her fingers. Carefully probing, she found a sliver of glass embedded. She parted her hair as best as she could, pinched the tiny shard and pulled it out. Where else was she cut?

Unwinding a length of toilet paper, she wadded it and pressed it firmly against the scalp wound. She thought of Vanessa again and prayed that there had been no pain, that her death had been instant.

"Oh, God, Nessi. I'm so sorry."

The minutes passed as Cotten waited. The distant sounds of sirens finally faded into the mix of light traffic, seagulls screeching, and kids playing somewhere in the park.

Finally feeling it was safe, she eased out of the stall and cleaned herself at the sink. There were only a couple of bloodstains around her collar. She spot washed it until they were only dull rusty splotches.

She finally had enough courage to walk out of the restroom. A city bus stopped a few hundred feet away—the sharp hiss of its air brakes scattering a flock of pigeons. She hadn't thought to grab her cell phone when she ran from Vanessa's apartment. It had been right there on the nightstand charging. There was no going back for it now.

Across a flat expanse of grass near a water fountain she saw three pay phones. She walked to the phones with her head down. After a few quick looks over her shoulder, she lifted the receiver and dialed a zero.

"I'd like to place a collect call to White Plains, New York," she said. "Saint Thomas College. Dr. John Tyler."

There was a pause before the operator returned and directed her to say her name.

"Cotten Stone. John?"

There was a pause.

Finally she heard John's voice. "Cotten? What's wrong? Are you all right?"

"They tried to kill me!"

In the heart of Hickory Nut Gorge, North Carolina, lies a spectacular lake that National Geographic *has called one of the most beautiful man-made lakes in the world. The sparkling water of the Rocky Broad River surges through Hickory Nut Gap, and through a valley that is shaped like a Croix Patée to form Lake Lure.*

LAKE LURE

Cotten's eyes searched her surroundings as she talked from the phone booth in the park. She finished telling John the details of Vanessa's death. "Whoever blew up my car must believe that Thornton told me what he had discovered. They must think I know whatever Thornton found out. What should I do? I can't go home. They know where I live."

"Do you have any money?"

"Maybe forty or fifty dollars. I've got my debit card and a few credit cards. I could get a cash advance."

"You need to get out of South Florida. Out of sight."

"I don't know where to go, what to do."

"Listen, Cotten, my family has a cabin in the mountains near Lake Lure, North Carolina. No one uses it this time of year. You'd be safe there until we can figure out what's going on. Book a flight to Asheville. That's the closest airport."

"Okay, okay," Cotten said. "Asheville."

"Right. Then rent a car. Call me when you get into Asheville and I'll give you the exact directions."

Cotten twisted around to look over the park again, coiling the phone cord. "All right," she said.

"There's an old friend of the family who lives near Chimney Rock. He keeps an eye on our place during the winter—he's got a key. I'll let him know you're coming."

She swallowed, her throat tight. "I'm scared."

"I know, Cotten. Just hang on until you get there. Let's get you some place safe, and then we'll try to figure everything out."

"John . . ."

"Yes?"

"Will you come . . . be there with me?"

There was a long pause.

"Yes," he said before hanging up.

* * *

"I need a ticket on the next flight to Asheville, North Carolina. Coach. One way." Cotten stood at the Delta counter in Miami International.

The agent stared at her computer screen. "Our next flight departs at 12:55."

"That's good," Cotten said, glancing about but trying not to seem anxious.

"There's a change in Atlanta. Arrives in Asheville at a quarter to five. Would you like to—"

"Yes." She looked up at the clock. It was 11:05.

"Your total with tax and fees is five sixty-one fifty," the agent said.

Cotten dug into her purse and pulled out her wallet. She took her Visa card and handed it to the agent. "Can you hurry, please?"

"I need a picture ID."

Taking out her driver's license from the window in her wallet, she handed it over.

"Is this your current address in New York?"

"Yes."

After typing in the identity information, the agent swiped the credit card and waited for confirmation.

Cotten watched the woman run the card through the processor slot a second time. "I'm sorry, Ms. Stone, but this card has been declined."

"That's impossible," Cotten said. She felt a growing flush spread through her body. "Could you please try it again?"

"I tried it twice. Do you have another?"

Cotten took out her debit card knowing she had enough in her checking account to cover the ticket. "I'm sure there's some kind of mistake."

"The bank's system could be down." The agent swiped the second card and stared at the digital authorization readout. "Sorry."

Cotten was suddenly drenched in nervous sweat as she took the cards back. She knew that no matter how many she tried, they would all be declined. Whoever had tried to kill her had frozen her accounts. My, God, she thought. Who has this much power?

"How about cash?" the agent suggested.

"I don't have . . ."

Cotten turned and walked away, feeling the stare of the ticket agent on her back. *Oh, God, what's going on? How could they have done this to me so fast?* She had about fifty dollars in her purse, and that was all. Even an ATM would be of no use.

She found a pay phone and called John again. There was no answer when the college switchboard rang his office. "Shit. His cell. What's his cell number?" Cotten scrambled through her purse and took out her wallet. She fumbled through the batch of business cards she had tucked away. "Come on, come on." Finally, she found it. She had kept his card from their first meeting. Her hands shook so that she had a hard time holding it steady enough to read as she dialed.

"I couldn't get you," she cried when he accepted the collect call.

"Take it easy," he said. "Settle down and talk to me."

Cotten explained what happened.

"Give me a half hour, then go back to the Delta counter. I'll order the ticket prepaid. And I'll have a car rented in your name at the Avis desk in Asheville."

"I'm sorry I had to . . . I don't know how to thank you."

"We'll get through this, Cotten. Just stay safe. Call me when you land. I'll fly down as soon as I can."

"How soon?"

"Tonight—tomorrow at the latest. Okay?"

"Yes."

Thirty minutes later, Cotten walked up to the ticket counter again, choosing a different agent this time.

"May I help you?" the agent asked.

"You're holding a ticket for me. My name is Cotten Stone."

The woman typed in the information. "Can I see your ID?"

Cotten put her driver's license on the counter.

The agent checked it then handed back the license. "Your flight will begin boarding in about twenty-five minutes, concourse D, gate 23. Do you have any baggage to check?"

"No," Cotten said. "I'm traveling light."

* * *

"Jesus Christ, Cotten, I thought you were dead," Ted Casselman said. "What the hell is going on?"

"It wasn't me in the car. It was my friend." Cotten choked with tears as she whispered into the air phone. "Ted, they murdered Vanessa." She sniffled and wiped under her nose with the cuff of her sleeve.

"Who? What are you talking about?"

"And they killed Thornton, too."

"Cotten, you're not making any sense."

"Ted, they've even canceled my credit cards. They're after me—going to kill me because they think I know something—something Thornton told me. He didn't tell me anything. I don't know who these people are. I'm scared to death."

"Where are you?"

Cotten didn't answer as she stared out the plane's window at the thick blanket of clouds.

"How can I help you if I don't know where you are?"

Silence.

"Cotten, please."

"Find out what Thornton was afraid of, what he was working on, what he had found."

"I'll try, Cotten, I will, but how can I help you now?"

"You can't," she said.

*   *   *

Snow fell as Cotten drove the rental from the Asheville Regional Airport along U.S. 64 through the town of Bat Cave toward Chimney Rock. She remembered watching the movie *The Last Of The Mohicans* and longing to see the area where it was filmed. You're about to get your chance, she thought.

John had given her directions when she called from the airport, telling her that even though the cabin wasn't that far from the city, it would be an arduous drive along the snaking, narrow mountain roads. Once she left U.S. 64 she realized he hadn't lied. She wasn't used to mountain highways, especially with the weather turning nasty. The light snow became sleet and freezing rain—a gunmetal gray twilight veiled the dark mountains.

Cotten followed the country road, from time to time seeing the faint lights of farmhouses barely visible through the sleet. With the windshield wipers flapping to a honky-tonk song on the radio, she strained to see a mailbox with the name Jones on its side. Pulling into a dirt driveway, she drove up to the old two-story farmhouse.

The porch light flicked on when she knocked on the front screen door.

"You must be Ms. Stone," the farmer said, opening the door. "I'm Clarence Jones. Get in out of this before you catch your death."

Cotten guessed he was in his middle to late seventies. He had thick gray hair, leathery cheeks, and worn overalls. He bore the hunched back and bony hands of a man who spent his life working hard.

"Sit right here while I get the key to the place," Jones said. He patted the back of the couch.

"Thanks," Cotten said. The furniture was old and threadbare, but comfortable looking, she thought as she sat on the sofa. Pictures covered the walls, most likely of his family. Jones had been handsome in his youth.

"Is that your wife?" she asked when he returned. She nodded to a gold-framed portrait.

"That's my Lilly. She passed 'bout five years ago. Used to aggravate me from morning to night. Pretty lonesome around here, now. I miss her." He placed the key on the coffee table in front of Cotten. "That's the key to the Tyler place. I've already gone up and turned on the gas.

You'll still want to build a fire, but it'll be fairly warm by the time you get there."

"This is awfully nice of you," Cotten said.

"Owen Tyler's boy said you needed to get away for a while. Well, you sure picked the right spot."

"I hope so."

"You gonna be up there alone?"

"No, John is coming."

"Then I won't have to go checking on you."

"I'm sure I'll be fine."

"There ain't no phone, so if you need anything, you're gonna have to come down to get it. There's a grocery store in Chimney Rock proper, and a gas station, too."

"I'll remember that." She looked at her watch. "I really should be going. I'm pretty exhausted." She stood and walked to the door.

"Gotcha. Traveling does that. You get on up there and kick your shoes off. Road's a little tricky, just take it slow and easy." Jones followed her onto the front porch. "When you leave here, go back the way you came till you see a white sign with red letters that says River-stone. That's the name of the Tyler place. Turn onto the dirt road. That'll be north. It gets pretty steep, but keep on goin' up the mountain. Only cabin up there. The front light should be on. Get that fire goin' soon as you get there and by the time you turn in, it'll be warm and cozy."

"Thanks again, Mr. Jones," Cotten said, shaking his hand.

Cotten got the heater fan blowing on high and turned the rental around, heading back toward the main highway. The sleet had changed to a light snow. Soon, the Riverstone sign came into view.

Taking the narrow road, she heard the gravel crunched under her tires as she headed up the incline.

The trees along the sides were thick, some barren and some ever-greens. Mostly barren. Occasionally, slabs of bare rock became exposed as the road cut back and forth, digging its way up the mountain. Near the peak, the wind picked up and threw sheets of snow across her path. Jones was right; it was steep. She had to gun the engine a number of times. The tires spun in the dirt and skidded over patches of ice.

The cabin appeared hauntingly in her headlights. A yellow light bulb on the front porch flickered like a faint beacon through the falling snow.

Inside there was a light on over the sink in the small kitchen to the right. A musty, closed-up smell met Cotten's nose as she went around the cabin turning on lamps and lights. She found a six-pack of long-neck Budweiser and a few cans of soda in the refrigerator, but not much else. The cabinets held several Ball jars of home-canned vegetables and jams along with a few cans of pork and beans, mixed fruit, and some spices.

After inspecting all the rooms, Cotten started a fire using the kindling she found in a basket beside the hearth—*light wood* her dad used to call it. It didn't take long before she threw a log on and the fire roared, sending warmth into the living room.

For dinner she had a pop-top can of fruit cocktail and a beer. Cotten plopped down on the bench of the trestle table. Great meal, she thought, sipping the Budweiser.

Later, the wind picked up and she stoked the fire—sleet tapped on the windows like nails. She thought of Thornton and Vanessa—her ex-lover and her best friend.

Murdered.

Her life was imploding. John was the only one left she trusted. And maybe she was putting his life in danger as well.

The old cabin moaned in the howling wind, and the trees outside creaked like wooden ships in a gale. Lying on the couch, she watched the fire until she fell asleep.

Cotten dreamed she heard music—its beat pounding louder than the wind. There was laughter, too. Shouts and singing. She felt herself shoved and pulled, caught up in a tide of bodies.

Suddenly, she smelled burning candles and incense. Praying voices hummed like bees. She felt hot breath on her cheek; lips whispered in her ear.

Geh el crip ds adgt quasb. You are the only one who can stop—

Cotten bolted upright. Trying to drive the sleep from her head, she raked back her hair and stared at the fire, now only glowing embers. But something besides the old priestess's words had awakened her. A thump on the front porch.

Through the window she saw orange light from the cabin falling onto the white snowdrifts. In the distance, snow banked against her car.

Cotten inched open the door, and an arctic blast blustered its way inside. In the pool of light from the open door, she saw faint footprints on the porch. Were they hers from hours ago or fresh prints? Had they found her already?

Cotten slammed the door shut, securing the lock and chain. She moved from window to window, checking the latches. Satisfied every entrance was locked, she built up the fire until it crackled and popped —drowning out the wail of the storm.

One by one, she turned off all the lights, then paced, peeking through the drapes and blinds for signs of an intruder. But there was only driven snow and swirling tree limbs in the darkness.

Cotten looked at her watch—three o'clock. The dawn would not come too soon.

She found an old pistol and a box of cartridges on the top shelf of a bedroom closet. After loading the gun, she returned to the couch and sat with the weapon beside her, watching the door. Waiting. Ready.

MAGNOLIA

SINCLAIR SAT IN HIS private plantation estate video conference room staring at the dark monitor screens long after the faces of the Guardians had faded to black. He leaned back his head having grown tired of the endless demands on him. Now that the final phase had begun, he must appraise the Guardians on almost a daily basis. The old man had to be kept pleased and satisfied—all the while meeting the time schedule. Plus, Sinclair was the one responsible for the complex duties—all the way down from procuring the Cup to performing the scientific tasks. Sometimes he thought his dedication to the project was not appreciated or respected enough.

Then there was that goddamn Wingate-Cotten Stone screw up. What the hell was Wingate thinking hiring someone to assassinate the woman? Wingate wasn't good under pressure—that was becoming clear. And he had a real problem following orders.

Out of the corner of his eye, Sinclair spotted Ben Gearhart. "Come in."

"How did it go?" the attorney asked.

"Fine," Sinclair said, keeping his post-video conference thoughts to himself. He swung his chair around and looked at the crest on the wall behind his desk—the crest with the Croix Pateé and the dog rose bramble. "We're so close, Ben. All the planning—all our work is about to pay off."

Gearhart nodded, but Sinclair could see there was something else on his mind. "What is it?" he asked.

"Charles . . . he's here. I saw him outside, on the lawn."

"Fuck." Sinclair closed his eyes and pressed two fingers hard against his forehead, just above the bridge of his nose. He didn't need this right now.

* * *

The old gentleman, his demeanor always composed and relaxed, sat in a high-backed wicker chair in the gazebo.

"Good afternoon," Sinclair said. "You surprise me. I didn't know you were coming." He stepped inside the gazebo. "I just finished another video conference bringing the Guardians up to date."

"Technology is so incredible, Charles. It astounds me."

Sinclair edged to a bench and sat. He thought he knew what the old man wanted to discuss. "The project is going well and on schedule," he said without being asked.

"That is a great relief. You see, Charles, I got the impression that loose ends still weren't clipped. Those untidy things can be bothersome. Perhaps bothersome is a poor choice of words. Treacherous is better."

Sinclair tugged at the knot in his tie. Suddenly, it felt as if there were pressure on his larynx—a sensation not unlike someone's hands around his throat, squeezing ever so softly.

"The good cardinal delivered the Cup just as planned," Sinclair said. "Ianucci has performed perfectly, as predicted."

The old man's face was granite. "The Vatican knows he made the switch."

Sinclair's gut contracted. "We knew they would figure that out. But there has been nothing in the news."

"And there won't be. It would be too embarrassing for the Church to admit that one of their own betrayed them. They will keep it quiet, amongst themselves, and in the next several days I expect they will announce Ianucci's retirement. And that is very fortunate for us." Sinclair knew the old man was leading up to something by the tone of his voice, the deliberate low volume, the expression on his face, the suspenseful pause before speaking again.

"Attention to detail is so important," the old man said. "You know that." The lines around his eyes crimped. "Don't lose sight of the cardinal, not for the smallest moment in time. And you must keep Stone flushed out. You cannot let up. As soon as Ianucci's task is completed, dispose of him."

Sinclair nodded as he glanced toward the river. It surged over anything in its way. "We've begun the work in the lab," he said, changing the subject. "Maybe even a day ahead of the timeline. This is a delicate stage, and we won't rush it at the risk of making an error."

"Oh, I am sure the science is as it should be, Charles. You are the best in the world—just the man to bring about our miracle, are you not?" He paused a moment. "Perfection in everything, Charles. Nothing less will do."

The old man's eyes bored into the geneticist's. Sinclair recognized the fury—he envisioned the flames of hell burning inside.

The grip on Sinclair's throat tightened.

"Now, tell me about the fiasco in Miami."

Sinclair shifted his weight and stretched his spine against the back of the bench.

"Wingate," Sinclair said. "He decided he would take matters into his own hands. He doesn't understand. He operates only on a need-to-know basis. But I did tell him not to do anything to Stone, just give her the interview, charm her, deny the blackmail issue."

Sinclair's stomach felt as if he had swallowed acid as the old man stared at him. "Within an hour of his attempt on her life, we had her immobilized. Her bank and credit card accounts were frozen. Stone was cut off, contained. But her priest friend came to her rescue. When she attempted to purchase an airline ticket to Asheville, we did some background checking and found that his family has property in the area. She's up there now. Arrived last night. We believe the priest is on his way there."

"And?"

"She and the priest are on the run. We've kept the pressure on. It's only a matter of time."

The elderly gentleman crossed his legs and turned to look at a huge magnolia tree nearby. "I am anxious to see that in bloom, again, Charles. Creamy white blossoms. Exquisite fragrance. One of the more perfect creations, don't you think?" His focus returned to Sinclair. "You do open your windows to allow the scent to ride in on the breeze, do you not? It would be a pity not to."

"When it's in bloom," Sinclair said, wondering if this was yet another of the old man's ramblings or—

"A perfect flower has no blemishes. Flawed blooms are an insult to the eye. The horticulturist has no use for flowers with imperfections. He discards them without the slightest hesitation. Wingate is a blemish. I'm sure you follow me."

THORNTON'S NOTES

A THUMPING SOUND JOLTED Cotten out of a light sleep. "Shit," she whispered, snatching up the pistol and slipping across the room to the side window.

She had watched and listened all night, sometimes her hand resting on the gun. When the first hint of dawn came, she'd relaxed enough to doze off.

Now the pale light from the overcast morning seeped into the room. Cotten inched back the curtain just enough to peer out.

A red Jeep Cherokee was parked beside her rental.

Cotten shrank from the window and sat pressed against the wall. She didn't think it was Jones. A red Jeep didn't fit his image, and she hadn't seen one at his farm.

Again the noise. This time she was awake enough to recognize it. A knock at the door.

She held the revolver with both hands and looked through the peephole. A man stood on the porch, his back to her, his head hidden under the heavy hood of his coat.

"Who is it? Who's there?"

He turned and smiled as he pulled back the hood.

"John!" She flung open the door and threw her arms around his neck. "Thank God you're here."

"You weren't going to shoot me, were you?"

"That's a scary thought."

"Inside, before you freeze," he said, turning her by the shoulders and nudging her forward. "Cotten, I'm so sorry about your friend, Vanessa." John closed the door and removed his parka.

Cotten felt a lump in her throat. "Nessi wasn't perfect, but she was kind, gentle, a good friend. She didn't deserve to die like that."

"No one does." He hung the parka up and rubbed his hands briskly. "Is there anyone you can think of who would want to hurt you?"

Cotten shook her head. "No. I mean, I've pissed off my share of people, but not to the extent that they'd want to blow me up." *First Thornton, then Vanessa. They're going to kill me next.* "John, if someone wanted to kill Thornton and make it look like an accident, how hard would that be? Especially with his medical history. I mean, if they're powerful enough to shut me down like they have, then they're more than capable of finding out whatever they wanted to know about Thornton. They made it look like natural causes."

"Well, the car bomb wasn't meant to look like natural causes. Not even like an accident."

Cotten plunked down on the couch and curled her legs up. "That's what has me confused. To be so meticulous arranging Thornton's death, and yet be so crude trying to kill me. I don't get it. One was very clever, and the other a blatant murder. And there's no pattern. Nothing other than the Grail. That's the only common thread that weaves Archer, Thornton, and me together. Vanessa was in the wrong place, wrong time."

"Does anyone know you're here? Have you talked to anyone?"

"No, just you and Jones." Cotten pressed the heels of her hands against her eyes, thinking it might ease the mild headache. "I take that back. I called Ted Casselman from the plane but didn't tell him where I was going."

"Have you had any sleep?"

"Not much. I think I had a midnight visitor, but it could have been my imagination. I can't tell anymore. I'm so wired I jump at everything. I'm glad you're here. Maybe I can let my guard down a little."

"Let's get something to warm up, then you tell me about it."

She followed him into the hall. "I couldn't find any coffee or tea last night."

"Secret stash," John said.

She watched him open the door to a storage closet. He pulled out a vacuum cleaner and a dust mop, revealing narrow stairs in the back.

"The cellar stays cool year 'round, and I don't have to worry about somebody cleaning out the fridge or the cabinets and throwing away my hoard. That way, I know I'll always be able to make a cup of java."

Even though the passage was narrow and the opening small, she could see that there was a lot of clutter at the bottom.

"Be right back," John said before squeezing through the closet and disappearing down the steps. A few moments later, he returned with an old tin can in hand. "Voila."

Back in the kitchen he pulled a percolator from the pantry and lit the flame on the stove burner. "You think it could have been Jones who was here last night?" he asked as he fixed the coffee.

"I don't know. I fell asleep on the couch and woke up to what sounded like someone walking on the front porch. But no one knocked or tried to get in. If it was Jones, he would've let me know he was here, I think." Cotten sat on the bench and placed the pistol on the trestle table. "There were footprints in the snow, but I can't say for sure if they were mine or not."

"But you didn't actually see anyone?"

She shook her head. "No, and that was the end of it. I didn't hear anything else the rest of the night. But I really believe there was somebody out there."

"I saw a few animal tracks around the porch as I walked up," John said. "A fox, maybe. Might have come looking for food. You're not used to the sounds of the mountains, and it could have just been an animal that spooked you."

Steam rose from the percolator's spout as the darkening water boiled and squirted into the small glass tip of the lid.

"Yeah, I guess it could have been. I sat on the couch with that damn gun next to me all night. Every little creak and moan—"

"I hope you were warm enough." John retrieved two mugs. "This place is old—the wind comes right through the walls and floor. There's no insulation between the cellar and us. It's comfortable in the summer, but not this time of year." He rummaged through the cabinet. "I may have some sugar here somewhere."

"You know how I like my sugar," she said.

He set a Ziploc bag of sugar on the table.

"Actually, the fire kept me warm." Cotten watched him fill the two cups, thinking she'd love to snuggle up with him in front of that fire. She missed being held by a man. The thought reminded her of Thornton. He was dead. Vanessa was dead. The moment passed.

John placed a cup on the table and sat opposite her.

Cotten wrapped her hands around the mug.

"We're going to figure this thing out," he said. "I promise. First, we need to find out who *they* are."

Her headache pounded. No sleep, nothing to eat, and her nerves were taking a toll.

John glanced around the kitchen. "I should have stopped and bought some groceries on my way up, but I was anxious to see that you were safe."

"Jones said there's a store in town."

"We're better off going in to Asheville. We can get you some warmer clothes and anything else you want."

"I guess I should call Ted and tell him I'm okay."

"My cell doesn't get service here. If you need to make a call, we'll do it when we get into town."

"I'm ready." Cotten stood and reached for the pistol.

"Plan on shooting your way out of the Piggly-Wiggly?"

* * *

"Hello?"

"Cheryl, it's Cotten Stone." She stood near the Wal-Mart entrance. The suburban shopping center was a few miles outside of Asheville. John leaned against the wall watching the customers come and go.

"With SNN," Cotten said, after a few seconds of silence.

"I know who you are," Thornton's wife answered.

Even with the noisy parking lot and people walking by, Cotten heard the coldness in Cheryl's voice. "I hope I'm not calling at a bad time," Cotten said.

"I knew about you and Thornton—knew all along."

"Cheryl, I'm . . . sorry. I realize there's nothing I can say to make up for the pain . . ." Cotten squeezed her eyes closed. She really meant that. Never had she wanted to cause anyone any pain. She'd just fallen for Thornton so fast. She hadn't had time to think.

"You're right, there's nothing you can say," Cheryl said.

Cotten knew this was hard for Cheryl. It was hard for her, too. "If this weren't so important, I promise, I wouldn't be calling."

"What do you want?"

"Cheryl, it's vital that I know if any of Thornton's notes came back with his personal belongings."

"Why?"

"I . . . I believe they might contain clues to who killed him."

"What are you talking about?"

"Cheryl, I can't go into detail now, but I have my reasons—"

"Reasons? I'm sure you do. Like demanding that he divorce me? Like wanting to get your hands on his wallet? Do you know how much Thornton is worth? I can just imagine your reasons."

There was a pause and Cotten heard muffled sobs.

"Thornton died of a brain hemorrhage, Ms. Stone." Cheryl punctuated the Ms. with disdain in her voice. "So let's just leave it at that." Her voice broke. "At least I didn't have to face the embarrassment of him dropping dead while he was fucking you."

Cotten held her hand over the receiver to hide her sigh. The woman had every right to attack her. Cheryl's crude remarks were aimed to hurt, to make Cotten feel cheap and guilty. It worked, and she knew she deserved it. But Cotten wasn't demanding anything of Thornton when he died. She had broken it off. She swallowed back the bitter taste in her mouth and took a deep breath.

"Cheryl, please. Thornton called me from Rome and told me he was on to something big and he was afraid for his life. It's just too much of a coincidence that he wound up dead. You know as well as I do that for Thornton to be afraid . . ." Cotten didn't know what else to say. She had no proof of anything.

Another awkward pause. "I talked to my husband, too, the day before he . . ." Her voice cracked. "He apologized for all the times he'd hurt me, for the times he'd made me cry. He told me I was a good wife and didn't deserve him. That wasn't like Thornton. I didn't understand why he was telling me all that." She cleared her throat as if regaining her composure. "He was like a drug to women. I know you weren't the first to become addicted. But you were the first one I think he really cared about."

Cotten heard Cheryl blow her nose. She waited.

"So, what do you want?" The widow's voice had become matter-of-fact.

"His comp book. I need to know what was in his last series of notes." She heard a clunk and assumed Cheryl laid the phone down. A moment later there was the sound of footsteps and the rustling of paper.

"They didn't send it," Cheryl said.

"But he always had notes."

"The only thing I have is two sheets of paper that look like they might have been torn out of his comp book. They arrived the other day—Thornton mailed them to himself from Rome."

"Is there any reference to the Grail story?"

"No, just a list."

"Like a to-do list?" Cotten asked.

"Names."

"Can you read them to me?"

Cotten listened for a full thirty seconds before she said, "Wait. Stop. Let me get a pen and paper."

She motioned to John who dug into his coat and pulled out a ballpoint. He grabbed a garage sale notice from a public bulletin board nearby and handed it to Cotten. She turned it over and frantically wrote on the back. "One more time, Cheryl. Just slowly read the names one more time." A moment later, she stopped scribbling and said, "Thank you. Thank you so very much."

Hanging up, she turned to John and whispered, "Holy shit!"

SAINT SUPERMARKET

THE RED JEEP CHEROKEE pulled into the parking lot of the South Asheville Oakley Library on Fairview Road, a half mile west of Interstate 240. Patches of snow partially covered the winter rye grass lawn, and the rusty iron-rich soil sprawled beneath.

"If you log into the SNN site and use their database, can't they track you and know where you are?" asked John as he and Cotten got out and climbed the library steps. "Can't we get background information on Thornton's list just by searching the Internet?"

"Yes, but the SNN archives are much more geared to research," Cotten said. "I'll log into SNN using my Anonimizer-dot-com account. It's a third-party browsing service that totally hides my identity and the IP address of the computer I'm using." Cotten waited as John held the door open. "I use it all the time so nobody can track me. If I'm doing some research, sometimes I don't want anyone to know that a reporter is snooping. People would be shocked to know how much of a trail they leave behind on the Internet."

They checked with the clerk at the circulation desk, and she pointed them to the computers.

There were five PCs lined up along the back wall—one being used by a young couple—the others empty. Cotten chose the one farthest from where the couple sat. Launching Netscape, she logged onto Anonimizer.com, entered her account info, then typed in the URL for the SNN research portal. When it asked, she entered her user name, newsbabe, and password, kentuckywoman. Navigating to the SNN biographies section, she typed in Hans Fritche, the first name scrawled on the back of the garage sale flier. Almost instantly, a list of links came up. She scrolled through them, then chose one and clicked. A picture of the Chancellor of Liechtenstein appeared with a short background summary. Cotten clicked on the print icon.

Ruedi Baumann was her next choice. The first link identified him as the International Bank of Zurich's CEO. She continued until she had printed the biographies for each name—all high-profile world leaders who wielded enormous political, military, and economic power.

"Any idea what those names have in common?" John asked.

"A very big iceberg," Cotten said as they walked toward the Jeep.

* * *

"Maybe whoever stole the Cup is holding it for ransom," John said as he and Cotten sat in the parking lot of a Food Lion supermarket a few miles from the library.

"Or they're trying to sell it on the antiquities black market." Cotten leafed through the printouts, stopping on the French Supreme Court justice. "He could be a potential buyer. Any one of them could." She stared at the bio of the Russian general. "Blackmail? Ransom? Black market art collectors? Was knowing their names so threatening to these men that Thornton had to die?"

John stared at the papers and shrugged. "It's an impressive list, but it could also be just a to-do list of future news contacts."

"You're right. We could be getting all excited about nothing. But Thornton did feel he needed to mail it to himself. Why? He wouldn't have gone to that kind of trouble for a simple list of future news interviews. Did he want to make sure someone would see the list if something happened to him?"

She watched a mother pushing a stroller through the parking lot. "And where are his notes? He was obsessive about keeping detailed records. He used to scold me, complain that I wasn't thorough enough. He made a point many times that reviewing his notes, seeing it on paper, brought clarity."

John leaned back. "Well, think of it this way—the missing notes could be confirmation that he was murdered because of the story—because of the Grail theft. The killer must have taken Thornton's notebook."

"So we're back to the list."

"What do you want to do now?"

"I'm going to call my Uncle Gus. Let him take a shot at tying these names together. If anyone can do it, he can. I need to check in with him anyway on the Wingate thing."

"While you do that, I'll go into the market and get some supplies." John looked at the scribbled list in Cotten's hand. "There's one more thing you wrote here that you haven't mentioned." He pointed to her notes. "S-T, S-I-N."

"Yeah, I have no idea about that one. Cheryl said Thornton had circled something at the bottom of the page. She said he'd circled it so many times that the pen lines ran over it and made it impossible to read the whole thing. All she could make out was the beginning. S-T period. Like in the abbreviation for Saint. Saint Christopher. Saint Louis. Might as well be Saint Supermarket." She motioned to the

Food Lion and shrugged. "Then beneath it again he wrote S-T but followed it with a slash and the word SIN and something else. Cheryl tried to describe what it looked like and said she couldn't really make sense of it.

John stared at the notation. "I have no idea." He shook his head and looked at her. "Go make your call and meet me back here in twenty minutes."

"Deal." He started to get out, but she touched his sleeve. "There was one other thing Cheryl said, but I didn't write it down."

"What?"

"I thought she said grandmother at first, but I had her repeat it. She said Thornton had written Grand Master."

John's mouth dropped open. "Cotten, the Knights Templar referred to themselves as the Guardians of the Grail. Their leader was always called the Grand Master."

13 DROPS

"Do you think the Knights Templar are still around today?" Cotten asked from the kitchen as she stirred the pot of spaghetti sauce on the old gas stove.

"There are a number of organizations that have their roots in the Templars. The Freemasons are a good example."

"Oh, yeah, like the DeMolay boys' club. I just heard about that one the other day."

John stoked the fire. Heavy snow clouds had returned in the afternoon and the temperature took a dive. "Many historians trace the Mason's beginnings to the Templars. Now that I think of it, the head of each Masonic Lodge is called a Grand Master." He stood as the fire roared to life, and the heat poured into the room. "By the way, that sure smells good."

"Thanks. This was one of my father's favorites."

"I can understand why if it tastes as great as it smells." John came into the kitchen and looked over her shoulder at the thick red sauce.

Cotten scooped a small amount onto the tip of her wooden spoon and offered it to him.

"Excellent," he said, sampling.

"How about fixing us a glass of Chianti while we let this simmer."

John found the corkscrew and opened the bottle of Italian red wine. He pulled two mugs from the shelf. "Sorry about no wine glasses. We rough it up here."

"It won't be the first time I drank wine from a coffee cup." She placed the lid on the pot of sauce. "What would the Masons want with the Grail?"

"I don't think they would. Even though they're somewhat of a secret organization, they're into supporting charities, not murdering news reporters. Tons of notable people have been Masons—George Washington and Winston Churchill for example, and famous celebrities like Clark Gable and Red Skelton. The list is a mile long." John handed Cotten a mug of wine. "Cheers," he said, raising his.

Their cups clinked. Cotten took a sip. "Let's go out on the deck."

"And freeze to death?"

"Just for a minute." She took a long drink of wine, then grinned and nodded toward his cup. "It'll warm you up."

"That's why drunks freeze to death. They think they're warm."

"Be right back," Cotten said, heading for the hallway. A moment later she returned with a heavy woolen blanket. "Come on." As she opened the back door, a rush of frigid air struck her face.

John followed onto the deck and closed the door behind them.

"It's beautiful," she said, looking out over the mountains. "Twilight is magical, don't you think?"

He agreed, briskly rubbing his upper arms.

"Come here," she said, wrapping the blanket around herself and holding one side open in invitation.

He stood close beside her and pulled the blanket around his shoulders.

"Better?" she asked.

"Much."

Taking another mouthful of wine, she hooked her arm in his. The land behind the cabin dropped off sharply—rocks jutting out in ledges and ridges, the winter-barren terrain exposing the raw earth.

"There's a creek at the bottom," John said. "Not very big, but when you're a young boy, it's an incredible playground every day during the summer. I used to spend sunup to sundown roaming these mountains. I knew every rock, cave, and hollow tree for miles around. I'd make my father let me out of the car way below. By the time he and mom would drive up to the cabin, I'd be standing on the porch with my arms crossed and a victory smile on my face. There was no better place for a kid—a million adventures."

Cotten looked at him, seeing the innocence of a boy and the wisdom of a man. She found that disparity charming.

"Where did you live your adventures as a young girl?" he asked.

Cotten laughed. "Feeding the chickens."

"Come on. Every kid makes up adventures. Didn't you have a fort or a secret hiding place?"

Cotten wondered for a moment. "A tree. A huge oak in the middle of the back pasture. I nailed foot-long two-by-fours on it to make a ladder and wedged a few boards between the limbs for a platform. I was always running away to my tree house. Got my first kiss in that tree. I must have been about twelve. Robbie White. We were sitting up there hiding from Tommy Hipperling when all of a sudden Robbie just leaned over and gave me the biggest smooch, right here." She tapped her lips. "When it was done, neither one of us said anything for a long time. I think it might have been his first kiss, too. We never discussed what happened, but we found ourselves up in that tree quite a few times that spring—practicing. Then he moved away, and I never saw him again. I don't think I got another kiss until I was sixteen, and that one couldn't compare to the memory of Robbie White's."

"So while I was scaling these mountains and chasing pollywogs in the creek, you were getting kissed by Robbie White."

"I was a tomboy, except for when it came to kissing. Then I felt real girlie. I loved to kiss as much as I loved climbing trees with the boys."

John drew in a breath and opened his mouth as if to speak, but apparently decided against it.

Suddenly, they were hurrying for the door as the wind drove them inside.

"This is delicious," John said, after his first mouthful of spaghetti.

"Thanks." Cotten's mind wasn't on dinner, it was back on the Cup. "If the Templars consider themselves the Guardians of the Grail, then maybe they would steal it to protect it, not to sell it."

"Maybe."

"The Cup could already be stowed away in some bank vault or part of a private collection by now, and we may never see it again."

John pointed his fork toward her. "That doesn't explain killing Thornton and trying to murder you. Someone is very scared of you—scared you know their secret."

With a tentative smile, she said, "More wine?"

"Sure." He held out his mug, and she poured the last of the Chianti.

"Know what I read one time?" Cotten said. "It was in a book about keeping a writer's notebook. The author, Fletcher was his name, said he had overheard a waitress tell a story about how much wine was left in an empty bottle. The waitress said there were always thirteen drops left. Fletcher jotted that down in his notebook because he thought it was a wonderful metaphor for when a person feels like there's nothing left—like they're totally empty and drained, but still they always have thirteen drops in reserve." She sat the bottle down and looked at John. "I hope if I ever need it, I have my thirteen drops left."

Both glanced at the dark window as a gust of wind made the cabin shudder.

"I can't believe how fast night falls up here," Cotten said.

"Just the opposite from the summer. On a cool summer night, the twilight seems to go on forever. My grandfather and I would sit on the front porch for hours counting fireflies until they faded into the stars."

"When you were growing up, did you ever fall in love?"

"Actually, I did. Jones has a granddaughter that used to come up here and visit us. I was madly in love with her for the whole month of July."

"What happened?"

"Not much. We were only kids."

Cotten lifted both eyebrows in a playful expression. "Did you kiss her?"

"Did Robbie White like sittin' in trees?"

They laughed, then Cotten said, "Ever hear from her?"

"No. She became a firefly and faded away."

"What about since you grew up—falling in love, I mean?"

John leaned back in his chair, sipped the wine, and stared across the table at her.

"What?" she said.

He shook his head, then after a moment, stood. "I say we crack open another bottle and clean up."

* * *

The wind roared up the mountain and pushed against the cabin. It groaned under the attack, but held firm.

Once the dishes were done, Cotten and John refilled their cups and moved to the couch in front of the fireplace. For a long time they sat in silence watching the flames biting at the air, sending small sparks shooting up the chimney.

"I wish we could shut out the world, right now, and stay just like this." She sat with one leg tucked under her, half turned to face him.

"You know we can't."

"Well, why not?" she said. "I hate this always being afraid—thinking about Vanessa's death, Thornton's death—this emotional turmoil."

"Don't let it swallow you. You aren't in this alone. I'm here with you."

Cotten put her mug on the floor. How could she explain how this was eating her up inside? "Look at me, John. Look hard. Somebody killed my best friend and wants to kill me. They murdered Thornton. I don't even know why. And everybody keeps telling me *I'm the only one*. The only one to do what? I don't have a clue what that means. I'm supposed to stop the sun from rising?" She glanced at the fire, then back. "What kind of insane life have I made for myself? Look at the pattern. I only want what I can't have, and whatever I touch turns to shit . . . or dies."

"Their deaths weren't your fault. I know this is a tough time," he said. "Ease up on yourself."

She stared into his dark sapphire eyes. "I've dragged you into this nightmare, and I'm afraid you're going to wind up dead, too."

John held both her hands.

Cotten laughed through her tears. "On top of everything else, I'm trying not to fall in love with you." She immediately regretted her words. "Shit, I'm sorry, John. I shouldn't have said that."

She felt his warm hands squeeze hers.

"Cotten . . . You're getting your feelings all mixed up. You're in danger, you're scared, all that makes you very vulnerable. We've been through some unusual times together—we've formed a bond, a kind of love, but not the kind you think."

She hung her head. "I'm sorry. I put you in an awkward position." She was silent a moment. "I feel like an idiot. Too much wine. It was wrong for me to say that. I'm so screwed up. God, I'm sorry, John."

"There's nothing to be sorry for, and you're not screwed up, just confusing your feelings. You're an amazing person who is decent and honest. Have you ever thought that when you believe you've fallen in love with a man you think you can't have, that protects you from having to choose between marriage and your career?"

Cotten sighed. Images of her mother flooded her. She could still picture her standing at the kitchen sink, expressionless, passionless, staring out the window for long periods. Deep lines carved her mother's face, the skin abused, not by the sun, but by the absence of purpose and joy. And the eyes—no sparkle, the sense of wonder sapped from them. Sometimes that same vision came in dreams, and like watercolors exposed to rain, the image ran and changed, and she would see herself aged in the same way. That's when Cotten would wake with a start and promise to push herself even harder at work so she wouldn't one day find herself used up like her mother.

No thirteen drops left.

John lifted her chin with the crook of his finger. "If I weren't a priest . . . you are the woman I would fall in love with. You're the one I would spend my life with."

Cotten couldn't take her eyes from his. "You don't have to say that to make me feel better. I know I was tangled up in a fantasy."

"I said it because I mean it. I'm speaking the truth, telling you what's inside."

"You are always so . . . stable, so grounded. You see things as they really are. I wish I was like that."

"Remember I told you that I'm on a leave of absence because I don't know what it is I'm supposed to do? My life is unclear. You know what you want, Cotten. Do you know how blessed you are?"

He was right in one respect—she desperately wanted a successful career, a life different from her mother's. But she always managed to want what she couldn't have—at least when it came to men.

"When the right guy comes along, you won't need to make choices or sacrifice one thing for another. You'll find a balance." He smoothed her hair back from her face. "And he'll be the luckiest man in the world."

Cotten wrapped her arms around John's neck. "I still wish you weren't a priest," she whispered.

THE CELLAR

THE DARKNESS CLOAKED THE mountains in a tight embrace as a dusting of snow drifted down.

Cotten came out of the bathroom wrapped in the long white terry cloth robe they had bought in town. Her hair spilled down her back, dripping wet. "Hi," she said, seeing John lighting a candle on the dresser. She noticed the aroma of mulberries filled the bedroom and realized there was an array of burning candles scattered around the room. "Where did you . . . ?"

"We use them when we first open up the cabin each summer," John said. "It can get pretty musty after being closed all winter."

"They're delicious, like you could eat the very air."

"I thought the scent might help you relax. My attempt at new age aromatherapy."

She wrapped her arms around herself. "Thank you, for everything."

"I'll be in the room next door. If you need anything . . ."

Cotten lifted the gold crucifix on the chain around his neck. Taking his hand, she pressed the cross inside his palm. "You'll find a balance, too. We both will."

When the lights were out and all she could hear was the sigh of the wind, she lay awake thinking. John was probably right about having her feelings confused, but still there was a pang, a small ache inside her. With John, there were no pretenses, no masquerades. With him she was completely herself, a freedom she hadn't enjoyed in a long, long time. He had opened a door in her heart that had been sealed shut when her father died.

* * *

The dream was disturbing. She saw Vanessa, then Thornton, then Gabriel Archer—all through a haze, thicker than fog, like frosted glass. Then she saw her father kneeling on one knee, his hand outstretched, beckoning her to come to him. He spoke, but his words sounded like the rumble of distant thunder. She moved toward him, gliding rather than walking. The closer she got, the more he sank into the fog.

Suddenly, a voice broke through the mist. Her eyes flashed open, but the cloud of the dream still clung.

"Cotten!" John called. "Get up, quick." He shook her and pulled her arm.

"What?" she said, blinking awake. The room was dark except for a single candle that still burned. John had one arm through his flannel shirt and was madly shoving his other arm through the opposite sleeve.

"Hurry," he said, yanking her up and off the bed. "The cabin is on fire!"

Cotten bounded to her feet. She could smell it now, the acrid stench of smoke from burning wood, fabric, plastic.

John grasped her wrist. "Come on," he said, pulling her behind him into the hallway.

The remaining grogginess vanished as she followed, clutching the robe together at her chest. The thickness of the smoke increased, and she felt the heat radiating down the hall. An eerie, flickering orange light came from the living room—the direction they were headed. Cotten balked. "No, you're leading us straight into the fire." She pulled back, resisting.

He tugged on her arm. "Stay with me." His voice was hoarse.

The smoke would suffocate them even before the flames had a chance to burn them, she thought. Cotten nearly lost sight of John in the darkness as she coughed, the smoke stinging her mouth and nose.

Near the end of the hall he stopped and opened the door to the storage closet. He cleared the way, then led her down the narrow stairs to the cellar.

Cotten hugged the wall, wishing for a railing she could hold. The cold sliced into her, but she was thankful there was less smoke in the darkness of the cellar.

They dodged old furniture—stumbling over chests, bumping into large rubber trashcans, and plastic bags stuffed with what she guessed were clothes or linens.

Cotten tripped on a stack of heavy steel pipes, sending them rolling and clanking across the bare concrete floor. She fell to her hands and knees. "Shit." Pain exploded from the top of her foot where she had smashed it into the pipes.

John clasped her forearm and helped her up. "There's a window," he said. "Over here."

She couldn't see it, couldn't see anything as she hobbled behind him.

"Here," he said, climbing up on an old workbench beside the wall. He unlatched the window and tried to shove it open, but it didn't give.

The basement brightened slightly, and Cotten glanced over her shoulder toward the source. The opening at the top of the stairs glowed with the light from the fire, and a river of heat channeled down the steps. She heard the crackling and popping followed by the thud of falling timbers. The fire raged and would soon eat its way down the wooden stairs, blast into the basement, and feast on the contents.

"We're going to die," she cried.

John shoved again.

Cotten felt around on the workbench, finally coming up with a crescent wrench. "Use this," she said, handing it up to him.

John took the tool and punched the glass. After the first shatter and tinkle, he ran the wrench around the perimeter of the window clearing out the remaining shards.

"Give me your hand," he said.

Cotten reached up, and he helped her climb beside him. The bench wobbled, and she heard the wood crack. It wasn't going to hold them much longer.

"I'll boost you up," he said. He laced his fingers. "Put your foot in my hands."

Cotten planted her right foot in the center of his hands, and he lifted her up to the window. She wedged her torso through, then grabbed at the earth with her hands and forearms, pulling forward, her robe snagging on the window frame. She worked herself onto a small rocky ledge just below the back deck of the cabin.

The rush of icy air instantly dried out her eyes and pricked her skin like needles.

In a moment she saw John's hands on the outer frame. She latched on to one of his wrists, tugging, helping him rise high enough to finally get his shoulders through.

Quickly, he heaved himself onto the stone ledge. "You all right?" he asked.

"Yes."

"We're going to have to climb up. Think you can do it?"

She glanced at the jagged mountain that seemed to rise almost straight up. "I have to," she said.

Cotten followed him up the steep incline that would lead them to the level ground around the side of the cabin. She seized fistfuls of dry brush, some ripping out of the ground. Losing her footing, she slid backward, the hard ground scouring her skin. Again she attempted to follow the slippery ledge, digging her feet in the frozen ground, clawing at the earth, fighting to keep the robe from entangling her. With each yard of progress she seemed to lose two. "I can't," she said. "It's too steep."

"Get up," John said. "You can make it. It's just a few more feet." He slid down toward Cotten, then moved behind her and heaved her upward. "Keep going."

Cotten stared up. The fire lit the sky to her right. Her hand found an outcrop of rock, and she got a foothold on a trunk of a mountain laurel.

When they reached the level ground, she looked at the cabin. The snowdrifts glistened with the reflection of the fire. Flames erupted from the roof and roared out the windows; the porch caved and collapsed. The cabin burned as if made of kindling—nothing more than tiny splinters of light wood. Sparks from the roof jumped to the branches of a barren hickory that grew close to the house.

John shoved her low to the ground and clapped his hand over her mouth. "Shh," he whispered, pointing. "Look."

Reflections from the fire revealed shadows of two men, hazy silhouettes, standing in the distance along the tree line watching the cabin burn. About thirty yards away sat John and Cotten's rental cars. To reach them they would have to cross in front of the men.

"We can't get to the cars," she whispered.

"We don't need to," John said.

LILLY'S CLOTHES

"JONES!" JOHN POUNDED ON the farmhouse door while he supported Cotten with his other arm. "Open up, Jones!"

Cotten's teeth chattered as she desperately hugged the torn robe to her. The ends of her fingers had at first tingled, but now were numb. And she hadn't felt her toes in the last five minutes.

John rapped on the door again just as the front porch light flashed on.

"Who is it? What's going on out there?" The voice was aged and shaky.

"Jones, it's John Tyler. We need help."

"John?" The door cracked open and Clarence Jones peered through. "What the—" The old man's mouth gaped as he looked at them. "Blankets. I'll get some blankets."

John carried Cotten to the couch and began vigorously rubbing her hands and feet.

"Here," Jones said, dumping the blankets beside them. "Let me get you some hot chocolate." He headed for the kitchen.

"I'll never be warm again," she said, her voice rattling, her body shivering.

John threw both blankets on Cotten, then sat next to her. He lifted her feet onto his lap, blew his breath in his hands, and put them around her right foot. "Any life coming back to these toes?"

"Slowly," she said, curling her body and leaning her head on the arm of the couch.

All she could think of was the horrific flight from the cellar, then down the side of the mountain. Because she had no shoes, John carried her when possible—running, stopping to rest, lifting her, trekking over the rocky ledges that dropped in back of the cabin toward the creek far below, through the darkness, dodging boulders and jagged outcrops of stone, sliding over iced rocks and into fallen trees. Every time they stopped and she tried to stand on the frozen earth, her feet burned as if ablaze.

Fleeing down the mountain, John had retraced a route memorized from hundreds of childhood journeys. He told her not to worry, that he knew the side of the mountain well enough to maneuver down blindfolded.

As she tried to gather her thoughts, Cotten strained a weak smile, watching John wrap her like a mummy in the thick blankets, tucking the cover especially snug around her feet.

After giving his visitors steaming mugs of Swiss Miss, Jones got a cup for himself and sat in his rocker near the fire. "Now that you folks are warmin' up, you gonna tell me what the hell happened?"

Cotten glanced at John.

"The cabin caught fire," John said. "We barely made it out. Electrical problem, I think."

Jones rocked, sipping his hot chocolate. "My God." He stroked a weathered hand across a stubbled face. "And you and the lady here ran down the mountain to my place?" He sipped again, staring at the fire, then turned to them. "Hmm. Seems it would've been easier to drive." He covered his mouth and coughed. "Don't mean to be prying. See, not much excitement happens 'round here, so . . ."

John let out a long breath and moved Cotten's feet from his lap. He leaned forward, bracing his elbows on his knees. "I can't explain it all to you, Clarence. I would if I could. Let me just say that Cotten is in real danger. I thought she'd be safe at the cabin, but I was wrong. The fire was a deliberate attempt on her life."

"What?" Jones's eyes grew large.

"Arson," Cotten said. "Two men set the fire. Then they stood by and watched the cabin burn. We couldn't get to the cars without them seeing us. Hopefully, they think we're dead."

Jones scrunched up his face, obviously shocked. "Let's get the chief on the horn." The old man pushed down on the rocker's arms to get out of the chair. "Police ought to get up there right away if they're gonna nab—"

"No," Cotten blurted. "Nobody can know where we are. We've got to get out of here, first." She explained how her credit cards were canceled, and how John arranged for her to fly to Asheville. "We thought it would be safe. But they still tracked me down. We can't trust anyone. Not even the police. Not yet. Once the authorities trace our cars, they'll know soon enough that we were there."

Jones dropped back into the chair. "What are you gonna do? How can I help?"

"We need to borrow your truck, if we can," John said. "And we're going to need some clothes for Cotten. Then we'll drive down to Greenville. So you can find it easy enough, I'll leave the truck at Bob Jones University, in the parking lot of the university's museum. I hate to do this to you, Clarence, but you'll have to find a way to get it back on your own."

"I can do that." He laughed. "But I could drive you m'self."

"We don't want you to risk your life," John said. "If they catch up with us, we don't want you in the middle. Will borrowing your truck be too much trouble?"

"No, sir, no trouble. Got the old Buick out back anyway, case of emergencies. Bob *Jones*, huh? Isn't that a coincidence . . . or *coin-keedink* as my Lilly used to say?" He blew across the surface of the hot chocolate before taking another sip.

"What made you think of the university museum?" Cotten asked.

"I know the museum. I've been there. It's got one of the most highly recognized religious art collections in America. Dolci, Rubens, Rembrandt, Titian, VanDyck. And it seems like an easy place for Clarence."

"Who'd have thought—Rembrandt in Greenville, South Carolina?" Cotten said.

John smiled. "We can catch a flight from there."

"How? My cards are no good. Yours probably aren't either."

"I'll try to make a withdrawal from an ATM. If there's a problem with my card, we'll know they're tracking me, too. And if that's the case, I'll get in touch with a friend back in White Plains. He'll wire enough cash for us to fly out of the country, maybe Mexico or South America."

Jones rocked back. "Gotta call the fire department. There's nobody up by your place to report it. Even if there was, they'd be sleeping. The whole mountain might catch if the fire's as bad as you say. Save for the recent snow, it's been mighty dry."

"But you've got to wait until we're gone," John said.

"They'll ask you how you knew about the fire, Mr. Jones," Cotten said. "It's three-thirty in the morning—not like you were out taking a stroll."

Jones thought a minute. "How 'bout I tell 'em I got an anonymous call. They'll ask me why this anonymous fella didn't call them direct, and I'll say I was wondering the same thing. Thought it kinda funny myself, is what I'll say. That'll get 'em thinking something's fishy, too. They'll start looking for who did it, and maybe get them bad folks off your tail."

"But they could think you started the fire," Cotten said. "We don't want to cause any problems for you. Heaven knows I've already—"

"Shoot, we all know each other up here. This isn't the big city. Most of us grew up together. Everybody knows everybody and everybody's business. Sometimes that's bad. Most of the time that's good." Jones used a forward rock of the chair to boost himself to his feet. "Give me a minute and I'll get some clothes for you, little lady." He studied Cotten for a second. "You're on the skinny side. Lilly was a tad heftier. She didn't like that word. Nope, she preferred fluffy." He took two steps then stopped. "Isn't that a silly expression? But she liked it." He nodded. "I'll give you one of her belts to cinch up the waist. Height's 'bout right, though. But I don't know how the shoes will do." He continued the conversation more to himself than John and Cotten as he left the room.

"They're going to find us, you know," Cotten said. "We'll have to use our real names and ID to buy airline tickets. It doesn't matter where we go. They'll trace us. And then they'll kill us, John. Both of us."

COME NOVEMBER

CHARLES SINCLAIR WAS PATIENT, letting Robert Wingate fume. He watched Wingate, knowing the man was about to come undone. As Grand Master, Sinclair's decisions were final. It didn't matter what Wingate said now.

The camera tracked Wingate as he paced the floor of the video-conference room in Sinclair's plantation estate, shaking his head, wringing his hands—moving in panicked animation. From the wall of monitors, every Guardian's face glared at their presidential candidate.

"But I've explained to you," Wingate said, "there is nothing to the accusation. Yes, the kid went to one of my youth camps, but I never touched him, or any other child for that matter. Never even met him. The father is a scam artist and sees a fast way to make a buck. Anybody in the public eye is subject to this kind of thing by the low-life out there. The world is filled with their type—vultures. It happens all the time." He panned the room, looking first at Sinclair and then the monitors. "Come on. This is nothing new to men of your stature. Just pick up any supermarket tabloid and look at the cover." Except for the tapping of the soles of his shoes on the marble floor as he paced and his heavy breathing, the only response was silence. Obviously frustrated, Wingate thrust up his arms. "What else do you want from me?"

Sinclair spoke in a calm, quiet tone. "Your statement will be that you've decided to drop out of the race for health reasons. You've recently learned that you have a serious kidney condition with resulting debilitating anemia, compounded by high blood pressure. We'll arrange for medical confirmation. You and your family made the decision together that you would not continue to pursue the presidency. You love your wife and family and want to spend more time with them. You appreciate all the support you've received. Public sympathy will pour in. The people will embrace you and then tearfully send you off to live a stress-free life somewhere out of the limelight. No questions. The press will also handle you compassionately. After all, you're such a young man to be so ill. And in the fickle American way, they'll forget about you in a couple of months and move on to our next choice."

Wingate stood with a stunned expression. "Charles, you can't ask me to drop out. I've made a good run so far. Everything is working and—"

"No, that's the thing, Robert—it isn't working. The blackmail issue will always be an albatross, a millstone that gets heavier and heavier."

"But I didn't do—"

"I told you, when dealing with an allegation of child molestation, it doesn't matter whether the accusation is factual or not—once it's made public, it becomes embedded in the subconscious—a blemish that can't be removed."

"Nobody knows about the blackmail except that Stone woman. You said you know where she's hiding and you're going to take care of her. That means there's not going to be any—"

"She's no longer your concern. You were told not to take any action—not to do something rash. But you did. And it's created a mess we have to clean up. We can't risk the bomb being linked to you."

"But I made sure it couldn't be connected to—"

"You're an amateur, Robert. You should have left these matters to us. It's taken valuable resources to cover your sloppy trail. Besides, there are things about the Stone woman you don't know." Sinclair started to explain further but realized it would make no difference. "I want you out of the public eye where there's less of a chance anyone will dig deep enough to unearth your ties to that . . . fiasco. As of now, your political career is officially over. You've become a liability."

"But you need me," Wingate said. "Have you seen the latest polls? I'm way out in front. And it's not just your political machinations that have done that. I've fucking charmed and captivated the American public. Even the press."

Sinclair's eyes performed a long, exaggerated blink. "Charisma, like talk, is cheap. Do you know how many charismatic men are out there who would jump at the chance to run for the presidency of the United States with the unlimited backing we could give them? And of course from your own personal experience, you do know how easy it is to launch a political career from out of nowhere—with the proper support."

"Please, Charles. I'm one of you. My family has a long history."

"Then you know we sacrifice for the Order."

"But there is no need for sacrifice. Please, Charles."

The man was begging now, and it made Sinclair's stomach roil. "Most unbecoming, Robert. Sit down and collect yourself."

Wingate stood behind a high back chair, his hands squeezing the stainless steel frame at the top.

"Relax, Robert. Your future won't be so awful."

Wingate remained behind the chair.

"You've been loyal, and we do value that quality. Tell me where you want to go. Belize? Barbados? Fiji? We'll see to it you're taken care of."

Wingate tugged at his collar and straightened, like the last rally of a terminally ill man. "I can pull this off . . . even without you."

"But you won't."

"I don't need any more campaign money. The press loves me, so I'll get all the coverage I want. Americans believe in me, they trust me, and they'll take that straight into the voting booths next year in November."

Sinclair forced a smile. "Are you sure you don't want to sit?" His jaw muscles tightened, and his teeth clenched.

"What the fuck is with you, Charles? You know I can finish the race and win. Come November, you'll see. I'll be President Elect Robert Wingate. There's nothing you can do to stop me."

Sinclair folded his hands, his patience exhausted. "What about the spray of roses?"

Wingate stared at Sinclair. "What roses?"

"The ones wilted on your grave, come November."

TIMESTAMP

THE SUN HAD NOT yet stolen above the horizon as the '66 Chevy pickup sped along U.S. 25 out of the mountains toward Greenville, South Carolina. Cotten watched the bleak landscape rolling by. In the headlights, the glare of snow patches shone like white islands in the fallow brown fields and skeleton forests. Bare, bony tree branches reached up and picked at the thick sky.

She felt a trickle of warm air on her legs, but not warm enough to remove her coat. She wore one of Lilly Jones's long work dresses and her herringbone wool jacket. The shoes fit better than the clothes, she thought, as she glanced down at the simple brown lace-ups. Even the dim light of the dash couldn't hide that they were sturdy work shoes, but certainly more comfortable and practical than the heels she wore everyday at SNN.

A semi-tractor trailer rig moved past, throwing up a shower of grime. The pickup's worn-out wipers only smeared it across the windshield.

"I know," John said, glancing quickly in Cotten's direction. "Needs a new set of blades."

"That's not what I was thinking."

"Then what?"

"I was thinking how lucky I am."

"To be sporting around in this fancy retro truck or donning that Blue Ridge designer outfit?"

"Lucky I have you. Despite everything that's happened, you're still here."

Another huge truck swept by, spraying more slush. John leaned forward as if a few inches would improve visibility. "Nobody can say you don't look on the bright side. Have I told you I'm a sucker for adventure?"

"You'd have to be." He was trying to lighten up the situation, and she appreciated his effort. "How we doing on gas?"

He checked the gauge. "We'll fill up in Hendersonville. There's a Skyway Truck Stop there."

"Good. Then I can check my answering machine and call Uncle Gus."

"It's Saturday." John looked at his watch in the headlights of a passing truck. "And five thirty in the morning."

"Gus is a workaholic. He's up and at it before the dawn—Saturdays included. If he's not in the office, my call will be routed to his house. We need to know if he's put together some connection with those names on Thornton's list."

"Cotten, what if I get you out of the country? Maybe fly to someplace like Costa Rica."

"It's not just me anymore. They want you, too," Cotten said. "Whatever they think I know, they must believe I have told you. We'll never be safe, never have any peace until we unravel this whole mess."

They rode in silence for a while before John said, "There's the Skyway."

As the endless parade of 18-wheelers swept by, John steered the pickup into the truck stop's parking lot and pulled beside the first available gas pump. "I'll fill up while you make your calls." He took his wallet out and gave her a ten dollar bill.

Cotten slipped out of the truck and after getting change made her way past shelves of junk food and soda cases to a line of public phones. She called Gus.

Waiting for him to answer, Cotten dumped the rest of the money in her pocket and looked back in the direction of the cashier. She could see John beyond the front window in the glare of the service center lights pumping gas.

A sleepy voice came on the line—a man, but not her uncle. "Hello."

"Hi, this is Cotten Stone. Can I speak to Gus, please?"

The line was quiet for a moment. She already knew something was wrong.

"Ms. Stone, my name is Michael Billings. I'm the operations manager for Ruby Investigations. I've had the calls forwarded to my home."

"I've never heard my uncle mention your name."

"I just recently joined the agency."

"I need to speak to Gus right away." She hoped Gus was out of town on business or taking a few days vacation.

Billings sniffed, obviously still trying to wake up. "Ms. Stone, I hate to be the one to give you bad news, but I'm afraid your uncle was in an accident last night."

Cotten sensed the all-too-familiar chill sweep through her body. "Accident?"

"Driving home, his car ran off the road."

"Is he . . . all right?"

Billings' long sigh sounded like air escaping from a punctured tire. "It's pretty bad. What we know so far is that Gus suffered a severe head injury, his liver is lacerated, and there's internal bleeding. He's got some broken bones, but that's the least of it. Doctors won't speculate on his recovery, or if he recovers what kind of brain damage there might be."

She wanted to scream. Everything she touched . . . Yes, she had a touch all right. Not a Midas touch, but the touch of a mortician. Everyone she loved wound up dead. God, please don't let him die, too, she thought. Raw rage built inside her. "How did it happen?"

"The road was icy. Apparently he lost control and ran off the highway into the river. Because of the weather, there weren't many people on the road, so the accident didn't get reported right away. He's lucky he's even alive."

"He just ran off the road?"

"Apparently."

Cotten looked around the service center. It wasn't yet daylight, and only a handful of truckers moved about, mostly filling large Styrofoam cups from the self-serve counter or shoving an egg 'n' bacon sandwich into the microwave. Her thoughts came like splinters that brought needles of pain. Her life was coming unstitched, and all the things that were good were spilling out and dying. How could these people in the truck stop just go about their business slugging down black coffee and eating Krispy Kremes while she was unraveling? Their lives went on like long, flowing rivers while hers was tumbling over cliffs—out of control.

"Ms. Stone? Are you still there? If there's anything—"

"No." Cotten hung up. "Gus had no fucking accident," she mumbled, gritting her teeth.

She braced herself, palms flat against the wall, her forehead resting on the phone, her body shaking. Pretty soon there would be no one left. They were getting to everyone around her and eliminating them all, one by one.

She looked back toward the cashier and caught a glimpse of John cleaning the pickup's windshield. He was all she had left. How long before she lost him, too?

Digging into her pocket she pulled out quarters and dimes, picked up the phone again, and dialed her apartment. In response to the automated system's message, she successfully fed the phone a quarter, but the second coin clanked in the return slot. She punched in another quarter and hit the phone with the heel of her hand. The telephone accepted the rest of her money, and in a moment she heard her answering machine pick up.

"Hi, this is Cotten—"

After entering her retrieval code, she heard a synthetic voice say, "You have two messages."

Beep.

"Cotten, this is Ted. It's imperative that you call me immediately. Day or night. The authorities want to talk to you right away."

The synthetic voice announced the digital timestamp, "Thursday, 9:10 AM." Two days ago.

Beep.

"Ms. Stone?"

The voice was odd and muffled, disguised as if spoken through an electronic distortion device. Cotten strained to hear, to understand.

"Please listen to me. I can save your life, yours and the priest's if you do exactly what I tell you. I'm willing to give you the whole story on the theft of the Grail and more . . . much more. This is bigger than you can possibly imagine. Follow my instructions and meet me where I say. Here's what you must do."

Cotten pressed the phone harder to her ear and listened to the remainder of the message. Then she heard the timestamp, "Saturday, 2:20 AM." Today.

Beep.

"End of messages. Press one to save or two to erase."

Cotten pushed the number two button on the phone then hung up. She looked around suspiciously as she hurried to the front of the store. Was anyone watching her? She threw open the doors and sprinted across the parking lot. John had just climbed into the truck when Cotten jerked open the passenger door.

"What's the matter?" he said. "Is everything all right?"

"They got to Gus. Get us out of here!"

"Where are we going?"

"New Orleans."

REVELATION

"THAT NAILS IT," JOHN said, withdrawing his card from the ATM. It was midmorning as he and Cotten stood in the Greenville-Spartanburg International Airport.

"They've canceled your accounts, too," Cotten said, shaking her head. "That means you're as much of a target as I am." Her voice trailed off. "John, I never intended—"

He pressed his fingertips to her lips. "I'm here because I want to be."

"They're shutting us down."

"Not completely. I still have a trick or two." He motioned to a bank of pay phones along a wall. "I've got an old friend who can help."

"Archbishop Montiagro?"

"No, someone harder to connect to me. My rabbi friend I told you about—Syd Bernstein. He can purchase the tickets at his end and wire us some money. I've still got a little cash, but not enough to get us very far. And with no credit cards, we'll have to pay cash. So don't expect the Marriott when we get to New Orleans. It'll be more like the No-Tell Motel—pay by the hour in advance."

This brought a smile to Cotten's face. "And how would you know about such things?"

He rolled his eyes. "I'm a priest. The confessional—remember? People tell me everything."

She grinned but then turned serious. "Can you trust your friend?"

"Completely.

"That's how Vanessa was for me."

There was a moment of awkward silence as John dug for pocket change. He dropped quarters and dimes into the slot and dialed.

How wonderful it must be to have such a fertile life, she thought. Hers seemed shallow and sterile in comparison. He was the only other person besides Vanessa who added richness to the threadbare tapestry of her life. Not even Thornton had done that.

She remembered a close friend from high school and how they kept in touch for a couple of years after Cotten left home. But their lives took on such different dimensions—Cotten in college studying journalism, and her friend at home raising three children—that they soon found little in common. Gradually their friendship came down to a few scribbles on the inside of Christmas cards. John and his friend managed to maintain a strong bond even though they lived in different worlds. Cotten hadn't thought about it before, but she regretted purging so much from her life. She could hardly complain about winding up being so isolated when she was the one who had let it happen. Self-inflicted wounds were the most painful.

"Right," John was saying into the phone. "Try the two-twenty flight on US Air. If there aren't any tickets for us at the counter in an hour, I'll call you back. And Syd, thanks. *Shalom*."

* * *

US Air flight 319 touched down in New Orleans at 4:51 PM. Cotten and John caught a shuttle to the French Quarter, then a taxi to Checkmate Services on Canal Street where they picked up the money Syd had wired. An hour later they checked into the ten-room Blue Bayou Motel a few blocks from the Quarter. They paid cash in advance for two days.

"I thought we had a choice of a smoking or non-smoking room," Cotten said, wrinkling her nose at the heavy smell of cigarette smoke that seemed embedded in everything.

John left the door open to the outside letting the breeze in. "Can't say I didn't warn you."

Cotten looked around the drab, shabby room. There was a double bed with a faded gold spread—over the headboard a framed poster of dogs sitting around a table playing cards—beside the bed, a dark-colored wooden nightstand with a cheap gooseneck lamp. The bulb couldn't have been more than 40 watts. A small desk and chair sat under the blackout-drape-covered window. The closet was only an alcove with a solitary wire hanger on a rod. "About the only thing that would help this place is arson," she said.

"We've already been down that road," John said.

Cotten laughed. "Or down that mountain. Guess that's what brought it to mind." It was the same kind of humor that often came up at funerals, she thought. Even during the bleakest situations, the human spirit attempts to uplift itself.

John switched on the TV and sat at the foot of the bed. He tried to adjust the volume with the remote but nothing happened. "No batteries," he said, holding it up to show Cotten the battery connector dangling like an empty fishhook. He reached out and turned up the volume on the set as the weather report segment of the local news started. The young, attractive girl with a slight Cajun accent swooped

269

her hand over the map of the country, as the screen behind her zoomed in on the Crescent City. She explained that high pressure brought fair weather just in time for Fat Tuesday, but warned that it was still winter and parade-goers should keep a sweater or jacket in tow.

The news anchor appeared—a shot of St. Peter's Square at the Vatican shown over his shoulder. It dissolved into a procession of red-cloaked men walking two abreast past the camera. "Coming up next, the ancient ritual known as a conclave got underway today in Rome as the College of Cardinals gathered from all over the world to elect the next pope. Stay tuned for details."

The station went to commercials.

"So it begins," John said.

"Maybe my friend Mikey from the Rathskeller is a contender," Cotten joked.

"You are incorrigible."

"I've been thinking about the message on my answering machine. The voice. It was disguised, but there was something vaguely familiar. I just can't place it. And why wouldn't this guy tell me everything on the phone instead of all the stupid intrigue?" She stared at the numerous leak stains on the ceiling.

"No idea who he was?"

"No. He sounded nervous, though. I could tell that much. What if this is a setup?"

"I'd be surprised if it wasn't. But we don't have much choice. It's the only thing we've got to go on."

The news was back and the anchor said, "To recap our top story, front-runner independent presidential candidate, Robert Wingate, put to rest the rumor that due to his health, he would drop out of the race. His recent health scare proved to be just that, only a scare. In an impromptu news conference held during his visit to the Crescent City, Wingate announced he has gotten a clean bill of health."

Cotten leaned toward the TV screen, watching the clip of Wingate. He stood in front of a bank of microphones—the Tulane University Hospital in the background.

"I have no intentions of letting down all those who have supported me, and I definitely plan to stay in the race," Wingate said.

The clip ended and the newscaster wrapped up the segment. "Stay tuned to News Central for complete coverage."

Cotten jumped to her feet. "Did you hear that? Health scare, my ass. He must have paid off the blackmailer." She read the parade schedule that appeared on the TV screen. "What is the Krewe of Orpheus parade, anyway?" Cotten asked. "I thought everything was on Fat Tuesday, but this one is supposed to be tomorrow, Monday."

John flipped through a brochure he'd picked up in the airport. "Lundi Gras parade. One of three on Monday. The floats will carry over twelve hundred costumed riders. Says here they'll pass in front of almost a million parade-goers along the route. And our mystery man thinks we can find him among a million people?"

Cotten closed the door to their room. She would rather smell the staleness than be chilled. "He said he'd be dressed as a pirate, and he explicitly said the northeast corner of St. Charles and Jackson. That should narrow it down a bit. I don't think we'll have to look for him, anyway. He'll find me."

John opened a city street map and held it close to his face in the dim light. "You'd think they could put a slightly larger bulb in that lamp."

"You don't need a lot of light to do what most people rent this room for." She sat beside him on the end of the bed.

"Yeah, I guess you're right. That's probably the original bulb." He put down the map and picked up a phone book, turning to the yellow pages. "Costume shops," he said, leafing through. "At least your friend on the phone didn't tell us the kind of costumes to wear. We know how he'll be dressed, but he won't know which ones of those million people we are."

"But he said when I get to the corner, I'm supposed to remove my mask," Cotten said. "That's how he'll know it's me. And, John, not us—only me. He said I had to come alone."

"I don't like it. That's not going to happen. If we're both in costume, as far as he knows, I'm just another parade-watcher. I can't let you go alone, Cotten. It's way too risky."

"No," she said. "If it's a setup—"

"There's no argument you can give me. Nothing you can say. I'll stay back a short distance, don't worry."

She put her arms around his neck and hugged him tightly. "John, I couldn't do this without you."

He returned her embrace, then said, "Why don't you try to take a nap."

Cotten let go and parked herself on the edge of the bed. "I am tired," she said. As soon as her head touched the pillow, she slept.

When she awoke, it was dark. John sat at the desk by the window—a second dim lamp barely illuminating its surface. He studied an open book while making notes on a small pad of paper.

Cotten lay watching him for a long time. It was hard remembering anything about her life before John. She wondered what his destiny was, and hers.

"You hungry?" John asked, looking up from his notes.

"Starving," Cotten said. "I crave pizza. Sloppy with cheese and covered in pepperoni."

"It's a deal." He pointed to the nightstand. "I put the phone book back in the drawer. Should be a place around here that delivers."

Cotten sat on the side of the bed and pulled out the directory, thumbed through it, and found a Dominoes. After placing their order, she stood behind John and peered over his shoulder. "What are you working on?"

"Some things about this mess we're in that have been nagging at me."

Cotten saw that the book on the desk was a Gideon's Bible. Beside it, he had filled a couple of pages in the pad with notes and diagrams. "You think the answers are in there?"

"I think the Bible contains the answers to everyone's problems, Cotten."

"You believe it's that simple? Want to share the enlightenment with me?"

John turned to face her. He sat quiet a moment, just looking at her. Finally he said, "Not yet. In a little bit."

She could tell he didn't want to talk. At least he didn't seem offended by her flippant remark. If reading the Bible made him feel better, she shouldn't spoil it for him. "I think I'll go shower before the food arrives," she said.

John nodded without looking up.

Everything about the shower, the whole bathroom, she found seedy. The toilet seat slid to the side when she sat on it, the mirror needed resilvering, and the tile was held together more by mildew than grout. Even the toilet paper was slick and stiff like gift wrap tissue.

Under the water trickling from the showerhead, Cotten finally let go and cried. It seemed unfair that she was alive while Vanessa and Thornton were gone. And Uncle Gus, fighting for his life—all because of her. John sat in the next room searching for answers in the Bible.

He said it gave him understanding and strength. Would it have the answers she needed? Would it help her understand? Give her strength? *Don't hold your breath, Cotten.*

Her life had come down to this moment in a dank, seedy motel—her only friend, a man searching for his destiny, trying to find answers in a book written thousands of years ago.

She held her face up to the sprinkling water. "If you're really there, God, then how could you—"

John rapped on the door. "Pizza's here."

Cotten turned off the water and climbed out of the shower. Her hair would have to drip dry. There were no amenities like a hairdryer mounted on the bathroom wall at the Blue Bayou Motel. She dried herself, then turbaned her hair in the thin white terry towel and wondered how much water it would be able to wick away.

She threw on a pair of jeans and T-shirt they had bought on the way to the motel. "That was fast," she said, coming out of the bathroom.

"Apparently, they're just around the corner," John said. "The guy told me he walked over here."

"Ready to eat?"

"You go ahead."

He seemed pensive, and she asked, "Is everything all right, John?"

"I think so. I mean, I'm starting to put things together. And it's caused me to lose my appetite."

"Like what?"

He hesitated, obviously gathering his thoughts. "Let me preface by saying I believe that God speaks to us through the scriptures. Whenever I need answers, I turn to this book. One way or another, it always gives me what I'm looking for." He paused and glanced at her. "After you fell asleep, I decided to pull it out of the bedside drawer and read.

As I opened the book, this was the first thing I came across." He lifted the Bible. "It's from the book of Revelation. *I saw a woman sitting upon a scarlet beast that was full of names of blasphemy, having seven heads and ten horns. The woman was arrayed in purple and scarlet, and adorned with gold and precious stones having in her hand a golden cup full of abominations.*"

"I don't get it."

"I didn't at first, either. But then I started thinking about the list that Cheryl read to you. Thornton put that list together because he believed those people are connected to the Grail theft. Thornton ends up dead. Then you give the list to your uncle; he somehow makes a connection and winds up almost killed in a car crash. And then there's Archer's death at the start.

"There are seven names on the list, all of them powerful world leaders. They cover the entire gauntlet of politics, economics, communications, and the military. Remember the Bible quote—the seven heads—the seven world leaders. The cup, full of abominations. The Grail. Someone, some group, with enormous resources managed to switch the real Cup with an almost-perfect replica right out of the Vatican's Secret Archives. I think the Templars are alive and well, and they are the seven heads. The ten horns puzzled me for a while, but then I realized the list probably didn't include everyone, only the world leaders. There must be a core, those who are directing the chorus. My guess is there are three more, one of which is the Grand Master. I think Thornton figured it out, set off some alarms, and he had to be stopped."

"But if the Templars are Guardians of the Grail, why would they be such bad guys in the Bible?" Cotten toweled her hair. "And why abominations? If the Grail contains Christ's blood, how could that be considered an abomination?"

"That's the part that really rocked me. It's not the blood, it's what someone could *do* with the blood . . . that's the abomination."

"I still don't understand."

John turned the pages in the Bible until he came to one he'd dog-eared. "You might want to sit down for this."

She sat on the edge of the bed, and he joined her.

John didn't say anything for a few moments.

"Come on, tell me."

He heaved out a sigh. "I think I have some idea of what God has planned for you . . . for us—why we have been brought to this place at this time. I believe that you *are* someone extraordinary."

Cotten's stomach clenched. He was leading up to something that she felt sure was going to scare the hell out of her. "Just tell me," she said, closing her eyes.

"You are very special," John said. "I believe you are more than special. Chosen. Gabriel Archer thought so, too. He said you were the only one. The old priestess told you the same thing. What if they were messengers? Delivering a message from God? And they did it by speaking to you in a language only you could understand—the language of heaven, the tongue of angels. You thought they told you to stop the sun, the dawn. But you misunderstood them. Cotten, it has nothing to do with stopping the sun from coming up. In fact, that would prove easy compared to what lies ahead."

She held her breath as she watched him open the Bible again to the page he had marked.

"It's not *something* you need to stop, it's *someone*." He scrolled his finger down to Isaiah 14:12, and held it up for her to read.

Cotten scanned the single sentence. She looked back at John—her mouth agape, her breath catching in her throat, her palms dampening.

The room iced.

Looking back at the text, Cotten read it again, this time aloud, "How have you fallen from the heavens, O Lucifer, Son of the Dawn."

For false christs and false prophets will arise and show great signs and wonders, so as to deceive, if possible, even the elect. (Matthew 24:24)

THE FALSE PROPHET

"Lucifer? Like in the devil, Lucifer?" Cotten said. "I don't understand. What I'm thinking can't be right. Can't be . . ."

John sat patiently while she tried to keep up with the hundreds of thoughts rolling through her mind like marbles spinning over tile.

"Son," Cotten said. "So it's not the *sun* in the sky, but the *Son* of the Dawn . . . Lucifer . . . Satan? I'm supposed to stop Satan." Her head shot up. "Jesus Christ, are you insane?"

Visions of Archer and the Santeria priestess swept past her like a flock of blackbirds. The box. The Cup. The Crusader Cross. John sipping coffee talking about the Knights Templar. Thornton. His list. Vanessa waving goodbye. Her shoe. The Guardians of the Grail.

The Son of the Dawn!

Cotten's hands flew to her temples as she shook her head. "No, this is crazy. It makes no sense. I feel like I'm watching a horror movie like *The Exorcist* or something."

"Cotten," John said, taking her wrists and lowering her hands. "It does make sense. Everything makes sense now. Don't you see? Gabriel Archer was there in the tomb, not to keep the Cup, but to give it to you. He was there to pass the task on to you, a task given to you by God."

"Bullshit," she said, pulling away and getting to her feet. "He was just an old man, not a messenger of God. And now he's dead! I heard him take his last breath."

"Yes, but not before he fulfilled his task—to deliver the message that you are truly the only one."

"That's a bunch of Catholic crap. I don't believe there is a God." She whipped around, turning her back. "And if there were, He'd have to be nuts to pick me. I don't even go to church. I'm nobody." She plowed her fingers through her hair. "Nobody."

John stood and placed his hand on her shoulder. "Let's back up," he said, "step-by-step."

She turned to him and forced herself to listen. Cotten felt as if her bones were dissolving, and the structure that kept her upright was collapsing.

"Lucifer was the most beautiful angel in heaven—so beautiful that his name meant Son of the Dawn. But he was cast out of heaven for leading a rebellion against God because he thought he was God's equal. After he was defeated, his name on earth became Satan. Down through the ages, he has waited to get back at God for casting him out. I believe that time is now. Are you with me so far?"

"I think," she whispered.

"Good," John said. "The Cup that held Christ's blood was preserved, and inside that vessel beneath the layer of beeswax is Jesus' DNA."

Cotten took a step back, and he slowed down, holding his hands up like a warning for her to listen and hear him out. "I know this part is going to be a leap. It was for me. But this is the crux of the whole thing, the link that puts it all together. Someone, guided by Lucifer, stole the Grail and wants to use the DNA to recreate the body of Christ. That person, the one under Satan's influence, is called the False Prophet. I believe that person is the current Grand Master of the Templars. He prepares the way for the Antichrist. He is the one organizing everything—the leader of the seven heads. It will be Lucifer's ultimate revenge on God, to use God's own flesh and blood to do the bidding of the devil. That's the abomination."

John picked up the Bible. "I reread the Book of Revelation while you slept. All the clues, the answers to everything, are here." Locating the passage, he said, "Revelation 13:14: *And deceiveth them that dwell on the earth by the means of those miracles which he had power to do in the sight of the beast; saying to them that dwell on the earth, that they should make an image to the beast, which had the wound by a sword, and did live.* Not so many years ago, no one would have toyed with the thought of creating a *real* image to the beast. But with today's technology, and given the fact that we have Christ's DNA, it will be easy for the False Prophet to create the Antichrist through the *miracle* of cloning Christ's body, a body that rose from the dead after being crucified and wounded in the side by a spear.

"And here," he said. "Revelation 13:15: *And he had power to give life unto the image of the beast.* By cloning the body of Christ, the False Prophet is able to give life, to create life. Other than natural childbirth, how else but by cloning could any human have the power to give life?" John took a deep breath. "And Cotten, you are the one who has been appointed by God to stop it."

"Why me? Why not some Mother Teresa, or Billy Graham, or the pope?"

"I can't pretend to know why God does some things, but for whatever reason, He chose you. You were given the knowledge of the language of heaven—the tongue of the angels. All things are led by the Divine hand. Think about this, Cotten. You were led to me, but if it had been a different woman, maybe I would have taken no interest, and the box would not have been delivered to the Vatican. A different woman wouldn't have found me on old news footage, wouldn't have looked for me. A different woman wouldn't be a reporter. There would have been no news story to follow, no Thornton and Vanessa to drive that other woman to uncover the mystery. The Cup could have just disappeared, landed in evil hands, and Satan's plan would have unfolded without obstacles.

"God and Satan are at war; they battle every moment of every hour. We can't possibly understand it all. We are only His instruments. God moved you through your life in ways that brought you to that crypt in Iraq on that given day, and at that hour. When Gabriel Archer handed you the box, he passed on the task of defeating Satan for the second—"

"Stop! I don't want to hear anymore. Stop it!" Cotten collapsed into John's arms, sobbing. "No," she whimpered. "I can't do this. I can't. There's been a mistake."

John held her close. "God wouldn't have chosen you if He didn't believe in you. And if it were a mistake, why would they be doing everything possible to stop you?"

She breathed into his chest. "But why haven't they stopped me? Why Vanessa and Thornton? Why not me?"

John lifted her face in his palms. "Because He has something for you to do. You are His—chosen, Cotten."

"I don't know what to do."

"So far it looks like you've done everything He's asked." John cleared the hair from her eyes. "You told me once that your father said you were meant for greatness. I think he was right. I believe you're special. Now you have to start believing it, too."

Cotten's voice was weak. "I'm just Cotten Stone, a simple Kentucky farm girl, daughter of Furmiel and Martha Stone—simple farm folks. I'm definitely no one special. You'd be a better choice. That would make sense. Why weren't you given the job of stopping this thing—whatever it is?"

"Maybe He knows I can't. He didn't choose me, but He let me decide to help you. Maybe He knows neither of us can do it alone."

"You're the one with all the faith. Shit, you talk to Him on a regular basis." She touched his crucifix with the tip of her finger. "I haven't prayed since I was a kid."

"Praying isn't something you whisper on your knees in church. Praying is simply communicating with God. I'd say He's found a way to open up a pretty good line of communication, wouldn't you?" John's words came in a low voice. "He can see all the flaws in my faith. There's never been anything I wanted more than to serve God, but I've floundered, never wholly giving up my life to Him. No matter how profoundly I've thought I wanted to live my life for God, I haven't managed to find a way, so I've wandered from one endeavor to another. I've even buried doubts when they've arisen. But we can't hide from God."

"Stop it. John, I've seen your strength, your solid faith. But me, I've never believed in anything, not even myself. I've always wanted the things I couldn't have. Look at you, look at all the ways you've proven your devotion to doing God's work. I've done nothing!"

She felt her stomach turn sour. Had she destroyed his faith? It wouldn't be fair; he was a good man. If the two of them had never met, if she'd never dragged him into her screwed-up life . . . Everything she touched . . .

"I have to trust in Him, trust that He has brought me to this moment, brought me to you." John's eyes searched hers as if he hoped he could read her thoughts. "Cotten, there's one more thing . . ." He drew away.

Cool air replaced the warmth of his closeness.

"John? What is it? Don't keep anything from me, now. There is nothing else you can tell me that could be worse than what you've already said."

* * *

It was the middle of the night, but light sleep plagued Charles Sinclair. He had dozed for twenty or thirty minutes, then eyes flashed open, his mind clear and alert. This was not a time for the passive state. His brain and body were fed a continuous charge of energy knowing what was taking place only a few steps from where he slept.

Sinclair slipped from the bed, rearranging the covers, putting a down pillow against his wife's back so she wouldn't notice his absence. There was no need to disturb her. He wandered down from the family quarters to the lab to satisfy himself that all was well—that the process was safe and proceeding on schedule.

Sinclair pressed his finger in the DNA analyzer before entering the code. In a moment he heard the familiar heavy metallic thump as the magnetic locks released, and the door to the lab unlocked. He pushed on the stainless steel door and entered.

The molecular biology lab was dark—only a few security lights and the glow from a handful of computer monitors lit the room. Sinclair smiled as his gaze fell on his prized possession. Walking past a centrifuge and a few incubators, he approached a long counter—on top sat an acrylic case containing the Cup—beside it the silver titanium travel case.

In the state-of-the-art surroundings of gleaming chrome, stainless, brass, and glass, the Grail looked out of place—an anachronism. The ancient beeswax, meticulously removed from the Cup, lay in a separate sealed container. In its place, a thin, specially created polymer, clear as cellophane, adhered to and conserved both the inside and outside of the Cup.

Sinclair moved to a second polycarbonate container a few feet away. But this one was extraordinary, developed and produced for this purpose alone. The container was mounted to a microscope so its precious contents would not be disturbed during observations— tubes and hoses attached to its sides provided a controlled environment of air, humidity, and temperature. Inside, within a small glass petri dish rested the miracle. But unlike all the previous clonings by other scientists, there would be no human surrogate mother. Instead —and perhaps this was his most exquisite invention, he thought— the virgin to carry this Christ-child would be a synthetic womb. He'd experimented for years with women who, for a price, offered to be surrogate mothers. And then later he'd experimented with *donated* uterine organs, but the failure rate with both was unacceptable. Embryos often divided properly at first, then stopped. Those he managed to encourage to divide appropriately, most often failed to implant. And those that did, terminated in miscarriage.

It was during this time of haunting frustration that the old man had come into Sinclair's life. Within months, he guided the geneticist in a creation that rivaled that of nature's—a perfect synthetic uterus. And, he had solved the mystery of primate cloning—why there was chromosomal chaos during the last stages, and better yet, how to remedy it with a key protein-rich chemical soup. The thought brought a satisfied expression to his face.

The hum of computer cooling fans and mini-pumps filled the room as Sinclair looked into the microscope and adjusted the focus. "The world is about to change forever," he whispered. "The Son of God belongs to the Son of the Dawn."

Behold, I come as a thief, and thou shalt not know at what hour! (Revelations 3:3)

THE RED HEIFER

"WHAT DO YOU MEAN, there's more?" Cotten said. Her hands trembled in anticipation.

John moved from the window. "Like I said, while you slept, I reread the book of Revelation. It seemed so clear that we are dealing with evil in its purest form. But then I read more passages—the words of Ezekiel, Matthew, and others, all describing the Second Coming.

"You have to realize when these men described the event, they thought it would happen soon, perhaps even in their lifetime. Their writing related to customs, beliefs, traditions, and ways of life they were familiar with—they used the terminology of their time. They had no idea what was to come hundreds, even thousands of years later. If you had described the concept of cloning to any of them, they would have considered you insane—perhaps even a heretic for thinking you had the power of God to create a human. When I reread their words describing how Christ would return to Earth, I could clearly see that maybe, just maybe, this is how it is supposed to be."

"What do you mean?" Cotten said.

"This might really be the Second Coming."

"You've lost me."

"The book of Revelation—the Apocalypse—is filled with the visions of John the Apostle, a man who had no knowledge of the science we know today. He predicted the events as best he could, relying on the depth of his information at the time. Tonight, I used his words to convince you that this whole thing is an attempt by Lucifer to get revenge on God—that we are about to see the creation of the Antichrist. But consider for a moment that there's something even deeper here. What if using the DNA from the Grail and the cloning of Jesus Christ *is* in fact the Second Coming? The time is right. The signs are present. What if we pursue this and though we think we are stopping something evil we really become responsible for stopping the true Second Coming?"

John looked up at the ceiling, then back at her. "Okay, I'm going to reach out to the farm girl in you. We're going to talk cows."

Cotten offered up a confused laugh.

"One of the last signs in the Bible that the end is near, that it is time for Jesus to return, is the rebuilding of the Temple in Jerusalem. But first, those who would rebuild the Temple must undergo purification. According to the book of Numbers, a perfect red heifer—no defects, and on which a yoke has never been placed—has to be slaughtered and burned, its ashes made into a paste to be used in the purification ceremony."

"That should be easy enough."

"Except that no flawless red heifer has been born since Herod's Temple was destroyed in A.D. 70—about 2,000 years ago. That is, until last April. They thought one was born in 1997, but white hairs popped out on the tip of her tail, so she was ruled unacceptable for sacrifice. But the calf born in April looks like she might just be the one. So you see, if the purification can take place according to the directions given Moses, the Jews will certainly take over the Temple Mount and begin rebuilding. The red heifer means the time is at hand."

Cotten's eyebrows furrowed as she strained to put it all together. "What you are saying is it could go either way—the cloning might be the work of Satan, or it might be that the Second Coming is supposed to be happening right now, and it might be happening by way of cloning?"

"What if Satan's real mission is to use you and me to interrupt God's plan?"

Cotten sat on the bed. "I'm so confused, I can't think straight. You just finished convincing me someone is going to create the Antichrist, and now you're turning it completely around."

He held her by the shoulders. "I'm relying on my gut feeling, here. I could be wrong. But I think we are on the brink of coming face to face with those who stole the Grail and are attempting to clone Jesus. We are going to find out who they are and try to stop them. But what if I've got it all wrong?"

Cotten took his hands from her shoulders and held them, shaking her head. "No. God wouldn't let that happen to you. He wouldn't. You're too good. There isn't the tiniest cell in your body that could be made to do anything evil." She looked deep into John's eyes—the intensity, the turbulence, the dark blue of the sea during a storm—and prayed she was right.

THE KREWE OF ORPHEUS

AFTER A RESTLESS NIGHT and only a few hours of sleep, the next morning Cotten and John took a cab to MGM Costume Rentals. They had first tried stores that sold costumes, but found the prices too steep. Renting would be much more reasonable.

John started with a realistic Henry the Eighth, but because of his slim build the costume draped in folds where it should have billowed, hung loose where it should have clung. He didn't look kingly, Cotten told him. When he appeared as King Tut, she bent over with laughter, sending him back to the changing room. But when she saw him reappear as Elvis singing "Blue Suede Shoes," her laughter pealed through the store.

She tried Marie Antoinette, Peter Pan . . . and an angel. Standing in front of John as the angel, white feathered wings, silver threads woven through the gossamer white robe, she heard him suck in a breath.

Cotten raised her brows. "Thought I should a least give this one a try."

"You look so . . . beautiful," he said.

It sounded more as if he were thinking aloud than meaning to speak, so she didn't respond. Looking at herself in a full-length mirror, she thought of Motnees and wondered if angels really had wings. The costume was lovely, but she needed something less cumbersome considering she might end up having to make a quick exit if she were walking into a trap.

Like a sudden slap, the reality of their predicament jerked the fun out of the moment.

John eventually chose a Phantom of the Opera black cloak with a mask made of a translucent plastic, while Cotten selected an Alice in Wonderland dress and the same kind of translucent mask devoid of color except for the dark rose lips.

"Great choices," the clerk said. "As you can imagine, our selection has been picked over, but I think you both looked terrific." She handwrote the bill. "That'll be one hundred four dollars."

John handed her two fifties and a five, and the clerk gave him change.

"I'll need a credit card for the security deposit," she said.

"But we paid cash," Cotten said.

"I know. But sometimes our customers don't return the costumes. Store policy. We don't charge your card unless the costume doesn't come back after forty-eight hours."

John put his arm around Cotten's waist, pulled her close to his side, and put on a wide grin. "Jan and I are making a clean start," he said.

Jan? Cotten repeated the name in her head, holding back the urge to elbow him.

John went on. "When we were first married, we got into some financial difficulty. When we finally got out of debt, we cut up all our cards. If we can't pay for something in cash, then we don't buy. It's our rule. Right, honey?" he said, smiling at Cotten.

"Right," she said.

"How about we leave you another hundred dollars for the deposit?" He joggled Cotten's waist, rocking her against his side, making her lean into him, then pecked her on the cheek. "We've made a promise," he said. "We aren't ever going to find ourselves in debt again."

The clerk watched as John slid a one hundred dollar bill across the counter. "The store manager isn't here to decide," she said, looking around. "Oh, I don't know if—"

"We're honest people," John said. "And this is our first Mardi Gras. We've saved all year. We're really stretching our budget just to be here."

"Please," Cotten said. "Buddy and I have looked forward to this for so long." As soon as she spoke, she couldn't help but glance at John. *Jan and Buddy.*

The girl sighed. "All right, but swear you'll bring them back tomorrow."

"Absolutely," John said. "Thanks."

"Honey? Jan?" Cotten said when they were on the street. "You're a con-artist. A silver-tongued—" She stopped herself.

"Devil?" he said.

Cotten looked down, wishing she had thought before she spoke. "I could use a little sugar on my foot to make it taste better."

"That reminds me, I'm hungry, too," John said. "But I think I'd prefer a beignet or some pralines."

Carrying their costumes, they walked a few blocks, stopping at Mulates Cajun restaurant for a sandwich before hailing a taxi and heading back to the Blue Bayou.

* * *

293

"The Krewe of Orpheus parade starts about three o'clock," John said as he read the Mardi Gras brochure in their room. "But you aren't supposed to meet this guy until six thirty?"

"I guess he wants it to be dark. The parade goes on for five-and-a-half hours."

"Cotten, I'm only going to be a few feet behind you, so—"

"You know I don't want you to go. If anything happens to you because of me . . ."

At five o'clock they got dressed, then studied the street map.

"He'll be wearing a pirate costume. That's all we know," Cotten said. "There will probably be a dozen pirates on the corner of St. Charles and Jackson at six thirty."

"Go first," John said. "I'll give you enough time to get to the end of the first block before I come out. This guy already might know where we are and follow from the start. At the third intersection, wait on the corner long enough for me to catch up. Fiddle with your costume or something to buy me a few minutes. Don't look back or you'll give me away. Are you ready?"

"No," she said. "But I'm going anyway."

John stood behind the door, and Cotten walked out. A few moments later he followed.

Throngs of people jammed the streets as they got closer to the parade route.

At the third corner, Cotten stopped, adjusting the lay of the flimsy white organdy pinafore over the blue Alice dress. She retied the sash, using the opportunity to sneak a glance behind. The crowd was too thick for her to see how close John trailed.

Suddenly, she was swept up by the current of people, whisked along like a leaf on a river. The closeness, the constant jostling and bumping, had her heartbeat pulsing even in her fingertips. She thought of the street festival in Miami, and her stomach tightened. The man on her answering machine who told her to come to New Orleans, the one who disguised his voice, the one who might be hell bent on killing her, could be standing next to her, even brushing against her.

A burst of fireworks popped nearby. Cotten jumped, and her mouth dried as if someone had sprinkled alum inside. Beneath the mask her skin turned damp, and a bead of sweat rolled down her spine.

She continued on, weaving through the multitude. A giant float decorated with gargoyles crawled by—glittering strands of braided beads, fake gold doubloons, and garland necklaces rained down. Hundreds of parade-goers' hands scrapped and clutched at the souvenirs. A spatter of cold liquid splashed her back. Cotten spun around.

"Sorry," the grinning man behind her slurred, lifting his plastic cup of beer above the crowd.

Cotten sidestepped and crabbed another several yards, slowly fighting her way to the rendezvous point. She wanted to look back for John, but she resisted. Cotten prayed that he'd been able to keep her in sight. Funny, she thought, she'd prayed in one fashion or another more times in the last few days than she had in the last ten years.

Finally she stood at the corner of St. Charles and Jackson. The crowd became oppressive—smothering. Not everyone wore a costume—some only masks, others just in street clothes with gobs of Mardi Gras beads dangling around their necks. And there were the quirky—like the man who stumbled past her with the seat of his jeans cut out to flaunt his naked rear end, or the girls who were topless—except for their beads. Everyone wore beads.

Cotten removed her mask and slowly turned in a circle, searching the faces around her, letting her face be seen.

She first noticed the eye patch, then purple pants, white shirt, beard, mustache, buccaneer hat—and somewhat out of place, a pair of thick work gloves. Her heart broke its rhythm as the pirate pushed his way to her and grabbed her arm.

She resisted, wrenching away.

"Walk with me," he said. "Don't be afraid."

Cotten followed, risking the chance to look behind for John. If he was there, the swarm of people kept him hidden. But someone else did get her attention, a large man in a monk's costume and mask, lumbering and shoving through the crowd, heaving people out of the way.

The pirate yanked her forward. "Come on," he shouted, apparently noticing her hesitation.

Cotten's eyes locked on the monk whose bulk prohibited any agility as he forced his way toward them.

The pirate glanced over his shoulder at her and tracked her line of vision. He froze.

Another sudden burst of fireworks startled Cotten, and she shrank, drawing her shoulders together, shielding her face with her arm. In the same instant, the monk pulled a gun from a slit in the brown robe just below the rope belt. She heard the rapid popping—louder and closer than the fireworks. She saw the spark of flame at the end of the pistol and felt the grip on her arm loosen. The pirate slumped to the ground.

Cotten screamed as fear ricocheted through the crowd. Who had been the target, her or the pirate?

Bodies dropped, knocked down by others trying to get away from the gunfire.

One of the bystanders jumped at the armed man, attempting to wrestle the pistol away. The monk jabbed his elbow into the man's face, then waving the gun, clambered over those who had fallen in the melee.

From out of the dense mass, Cotten caught a glimpse of John battling his way toward the shooter. With a long leap, he dove onto the monk's back, driving him to the pavement. Others caught in the crush of the crowd faltered and went down. People screamed as they scrambled in every direction.

She lost sight of both John and the monk as they were swallowed in the confusion. Cotten dropped beside the pirate. Blood trickled from the corner of his mouth and onto the fibers of the artificial beard. His white shirt had turned crimson.

Finally, the terrified crowd thinned, fleeing the corner of St. Charles and Jackson.

"Help will be coming," Cotten told the pirate. "You're going to be all right." She strained to look for John. "Oh, God, please don't let him be hurt." She found herself rocking. "Please. Please."

The pirate coughed, but the sound was more like the gurgle of air blown through a straw into a glass of water.

"St. Clair," he mumbled. "Stop Sinclair."

Cotten slipped the beard and mustache off his face and removed the buccaneer hat.

"Oh, my God," she said, recognizing him.

"Cotten! Are you hit?" John called as he came behind her, a bloodied lip and out of breath.

Cotten shot to her feet and flung her arms around him. "Thank God, thank God," she said. "No, I'm fine. You're all right. What happened to the monk?"

"He broke away and disappeared in the crowd. I tried to follow, but there were just too many people."

"It doesn't matter," she said, putting her palm to his cheek. Cotten looked down at the wounded man at her feet. "John, it's . . ." she said in almost a whisper.

John bent over and looked at the pirate. "Holy Mother of God."

In 1442, in Scotland, Sir William St. Clair, a member of the St. Clair/Sinclair family who were a part of the Templars since 1118, began building a collegiate church dedicated to St. Matthew. The church was laid out in the shape of a cross, but only the chapel was ever completed. The chapel, an enigma to even modern scholars, was based on the floor plan of Solomon's Temple. Engraved in the masonry are maize and aloe, which are New World plants—but the chapel was built before Columbus's voyage. Everywhere inside the chapel are Christian, Islamic, Celtic, pagan, and Masonic pictures, hieroglyphs, and symbols. It has been conjectured that the Knights Templar hid treasure and other sacred relics there. The name of this Gothic structure is Rosslyn Chapel.

INVITATION TO THE BALL

"You are the one who called me? Told me to come to New Orleans?" Cotten used the underside of the hem of her dress to dab blood from the face of the man who had disguised himself as a pirate. "Why? What is it that you know?"

"I have sinned against my God. A grievous sin. I'm ready to accept my fate." Lying on the sidewalk, Cardinal Antonio Ianucci stared at the night sky. "Oh, God, forgive me." His words sputtered. "You . . . you must stop Sinclair. What he does is an abomination." He clutched Cotten's arm, struggling to raise his head.

"Cotten! Thornton's list," John said. "Saint. Sin. St. Clair. St. Clair was the French name. They became the Sinclairs. Famous early Templar family. That's it. Sinclair is the name of the Grand Master," John said. "Where is he? How do we stop him?"

From the inside of his shirt, Ianucci struggled to pull a blood-stained envelope. "Take it and—" A wet, bubbly cough erupted. He gasped for air, and it rattled into his lungs.

Kneeling beside the cardinal, John read the contents of the envelope before looking at Cotten. "It's an invitation to a masquerade ball tonight at the estate of Dr. Charles Sinclair."

"Oh, shit," Cotten said. "Charles Sinclair."

John leaned in close to Ianucci. "You want us to go? We should use this to get in?"

The cardinal nodded and tapped his pants pocket.

John reached in the pocket and withdrew a small plastic box. He cracked open the lid, then snapped it closed and stared at the cardinal. "Sweet Jesus, what have you done?"

The wail of sirens blared, growing closer.

The cardinal opened his mouth as if to speak, but then grimaced.

"We'll stay with you," Cotten said.

Ianucci's eyelids fluttered, and the grasp on Cotten's sleeve relaxed. His hand fell to the ground; his labored breaths grew quiet, then still.

Cotten dragged her hand over her face. "He's dead."

John blessed the cardinal, then looked up at Cotten. "We've got to get out of here."

"Shouldn't you give him the Last Rites or something?"

"Cotten, that guy might have been shooting at you, not Ianucci. We've got to go, now."

John gathered Cotten to her feet, pulling her along even as she kept looking over her shoulder at the dead cardinal who lay in a sprawl of blood.

Quickly, they took to the side streets and narrow dark alleys until the sound of the sirens faded into echoes of Dixieland Jazz and the call of street vendors and barkers.

Winded, and the pain in her side growing intense, she had to stop. She darted into a recess that formed the entrance to a small antique shop closed for the night. Towing John in with her, she leaned back against the door, panting. "I can't go any farther."

He pulled off the Phantom mask, breathing hard.

"Should we go back to the motel and ditch these costumes?" Cotten asked.

He shook his head as he bent over in the small alcove with his hands on his knees. "We need them to get into the masquerade ball."

"But what about this?" she said, pointing to the blood splotch on the hem of her dress.

"We'll find a bathroom and wash it out as best we can." Still catching his breath, he looked at Cotten. "Sounded like you've heard of Sinclair."

"Yes," she answered, closing her eyes. "What you said about the cloning—it must be really happening. Charles Sinclair is a geneticist, a Nobel Prize winner. His research is on human cloning. SNN has covered his accomplishments many times."

John straightened and paced, still breathing hard. He slapped his palm to his forehead. "Why didn't I see it before with the Saint and Sin on Thornton's list? It should have rung a bell."

"But you didn't know about Charles Sinclair, that he was a geneticist."

"No, but I know about the St. Clairs, Sinclairs. That's what I should have picked up on. Back in the fourteen hundreds William St. Clair built Rosslyn Chapel near Edinburgh, Scotland. It has strong connections to the Templars and today's Freemasons. The chapel is thought to have been built to hide a sacred treasure. Rumors said it held the Ark of the Covenant—even the mummified head of Christ Himself, if you can believe that. The St. Clair family has a long, distinctive line of succession. I'll bet you anything, it ends with Charles Sinclair as a direct descendant of William St. Clair. The Grand Master."

"What are we supposed to do at this ball?" Cotten asked.

John shook his head. "Hopefully, it'll become clear once we get there. Believe me, Ianucci had something specific in mind." He took the small plastic box from his pocket and opened it.

As soon as Cotten saw the contents, she gasped.

* * *

"Step out of the car, please," the private security guard said as he opened the taxi door.

John got out, followed by Cotten, both still in costume.

"Invitation, please," a second guard said, extending his hand. John gave the man the white embossed card, and the guard shined his flashlight on it.

"Extend your arms out to the sides, sir," the first guard said.

John complied, and the man scanned him with a handheld metal detector wand. He then moved to Cotten and performed the same routine.

The guard returned the invitation. "Enjoy your evening," he said, stepping aside.

John paid the taxi driver. Then he and Cotten walked through the security checkpoint at the iron-gated entrance to the Sinclair plantation. They moved down the driveway onto a great expanse of manicured lawn that gently sloped to the river. Costumed guests sipped champagne from crystal flutes and walked among torch-lit paths, fountains, and gardens. A string quartet played Mozart, and the sweet sound drifted on the Mississippi River breeze.

Judging by the rows of limousines and exotic cars they passed coming in, Cotten guessed that the elite of New Orleans society were in attendance.

John squeezed her hand, nodding at the ornate carving stretching across the entrance to the house—the Cross Pateé with twining roses in recessed gold leaf below the name of the estate.

"Rosslyn Manor," John read. "Sinclair named this place after the chapel."

Despite the tight security at the gate, Cotten noticed little in the way of guards or security uniforms as she and John wandered toward the gardens. "I'm surprised they didn't check our IDs," she said.

"Picture IDs would be useless at a masquerade ball," John said, motioning to a woman walking past them whose face was painted like a rainbow.

"Keep your eyes open to anything odd," John said. "Out of the ordinary."

"Are you kidding? This whole shebang is nuts," Cotten said. "For starters, you can't tell who's who." They passed a boy-on-a-dolphin fountain. "This reminds me a little of the place I told you about in Miami," she said.

"Vizcaya, where you first met Wingate?" John asked.

Cotten nodded and looped her arm through his.

Soon, they stood on a wooden dock on the bank of the Mississippi. A beam from a tugboat's searchlight swept across them like a blind man's cane as the vessel pushed a long line of barges through the darkness. The string quartet stopped playing, and a voice came over the PA. "I'd like to welcome everyone to my annual Mardi Gras celebration."

"That must be Sinclair," Cotten said.

"Please gather beneath the veranda so I can see all of the spectacular costumes," the voice said.

Cotten and John walked up a stone path, joining those gathering beneath the balcony.

A man stood on the balcony dressed as a crusader with sword at his side. On his chest was the red Cross Pateé. "Welcome to Rosslyn Manor."

Enthusiastic applause broke out.

"That's him, I'm sure," Cotten said. "I've seen his face on our science segments."

Their host continued. "We've planned a wonderful evening of food and entertainment. Until dinner is served, feel free to wander the grounds and enjoy the beautiful starlit sky. I think you will all agree Louisiana is God's country."

Another roar of applause washed across the lawn as Sinclair waved, then disappeared inside.

"He doesn't look all that menacing," Cotten said.

"Remember the story of the wolf in sheep's clothing."

The two watched until the knot of people dispersed.

"Now what?" Cotten asked.

"Time to scope out the mansion."

"Are you crazy? How?"

"By doing exactly what they won't expect. We'll walk right in the front door."

"And I will give power to my two witnesses." (Revelation 11:3)

IN PLAIN SIGHT

JOHN RAPPED THE BRASS doorknocker, and Cotten pushed the doorbell.

"Ready?" John asked.

She nodded.

As the door opened, Cotten started. "I told you we need a cell phone now that we have the baby. A beeper isn't—"

Cotten turned and faced the man standing in the doorway. He was tall, balding and formal, dressed in a white tie and tails.

"Good evening," he said.

The butler, she assumed, and mentally named him Jeeves since he could have posed for the cartoon character on the popular Internet search website.

"Dinner will be served at nine," Jeeves said. "Doctor Sinclair will not be receiving guests until then."

"No, no," Cotten said. "We need to use the phone. The sitter just beeped us."

"The baby's been sick," John said. "My wife's a little nervous. First child and our first time away from him."

Cotten flipped her hair back and said to John, "I told you we shouldn't have come." She turned to the butler. "Could we use the phone? Please?"

Jeeves hesitated, then stepped back, clearing the doorway. He gave a slight motion of his arm allowing them entrance.

"Thank you," Cotten said.

They followed the butler through the marble-tiled foyer and past the double spiral staircase.

"This way," Jeeves said. He showed them into a study—dark wood paneling, a large desk with hand-carved legs, a high-back leather chair, several occasional chairs and tables, and floor-to-ceiling bookcases swelling with hundreds of volumes. Thick draperies shadowed the windows that stretched the height of the room.

Cotten watched the butler turn on the banker's light beside the telephone on the desk.

"We appreciate it," John said.

Jeeves strode back across the room but parked himself in the doorway.

Cotten picked up the cordless phone and dialed, never pressing the *talk* button. She held the receiver to her ear and waited, then rolled her eyes and put it down. "Busy."

"The sitter must be on the Internet," John said, looking at the butler. "We're the last of the dial-up diehards."

She glared at John. "You'd have us living without electricity . . ." Her voice was cold. Cotten leaned against the desk. "Do you mind if we wait a few minutes and try again?"

John sat in a leather wingback. "Don't let us keep you," he said to the butler. "As soon as we get in touch with the sitter, we'll show ourselves out."

Jeeves cocked his head as if calculating his responsibility. "Very well," he said with a bit of hesitation. "You can find your way out?"

"No problem. And thanks so much." Cotten gave her most grateful smile. As the door closed, she said, "Damn. I didn't think he'd ever leave us alone."

John cracked the door. "Let's start on the second floor. There's going to be too much activity down here."

They slipped out of the study and crept up the staircase—Cotten cringing at every sound.

The first three doors they tried led to bedrooms, and the fourth to an office suite equipped with an entertainment center—plasma TV, DVD player, the works—covering one entire wall. "Impressive," Cotten said. There was also a desk with a computer which she assumed was for the convenience of any visitors staying at the plantation. Guests could get on the Net and surf or check their email.

Cotten went to a window, pulled back the sheer curtain and peered out. "So these are the riches you get when you sell your soul." She turned to John. "Any idea what we're looking for?"

John shook his head. "Hopefully we'll know when we see it."

They explored several other rooms that turned out to be additional bedrooms—all extravagant, but of no help. Cotten wondered if the cardinal had sat on the edge of one of those beds in the middle of the night contemplating his deed.

At the end of the hall was a door smaller than the others.

"Storage closet?" Cotten said.

"Probably."

The door opened to a cramped media room outfitted with a video projector sitting on a tall stand. Its lens was aimed through a glassed rectangular window looking out onto an expansive, high-ceiling conference room below. Tall racks of audio gear and other electronic equipment stood beside the projector. Muffled voices came from beyond the window.

John and Cotten squeezed between the projector and equipment rack, and peered through the window. Cotten saw that the room below had a richly polished ebony conference table in the center and ten high-backed chairs ringing it. Only two men were seated. One was Sinclair; the other she didn't recognize. On a far wall, seven video monitors glowed—each filled with a different face.

"My God," Cotten said quietly. "I recognize those men. They're the ones from Thornton's list!"

"The Guardians—the seven heads," John whispered. He motioned at Sinclair and the other man seated at the table. "And two more of the ten horns. The gang's almost all here."

"Who's missing?" Cotten asked.

"Don't know."

Sinclair spoke to Gearheart, but the soundproofing of the media room reduced the transmission of the conversation between the two rooms.

"Here," John said, rotating a wall-mounted knob labeled *monitor speaker*. As he slowly turned it, the voices from below could be heard.

Sinclair said, "Gentlemen, welcome. All of you know my associate, Ben Gearhart."

Cotten recoiled. *Gearhart . . . Gearhart.* She nudged John. "Ben Gearhart, that's the name on the card—the business card given to Robert Wingate that night at Vizcaya. Shit, he's Sinclair's right-hand man." The words spooled from her lips, but not as fast as her thoughts came together. "Wingate's tied into this, too." She closed her eyes. John's theories about God and the devil were scary enough, but in a removed surreal way. She couldn't comprehend Lucifer and God engaged in battle other than in some distant ethereal place or on the movie screen with Linda Blair's heading spinning. But this . . . The presidential candidate's involvement brought what had floated in the foggy realm of fantasy smack into the bright light of reality. All of this was becoming too real.

"You okay?" John whispered.

Before she could answer, she heard Sinclair's voice and turned back to the window.

"I wish to take a moment to celebrate all of our hard work. We are on the crest of the wave that will surge over mankind. We will finally achieve the rewards that our bloodline deserves. Our plan has been effective and efficient down to the smallest detail. Even the good cardinal played his part and behaved as predicted. He has served his purpose and is now stricken from the flock."

A low mumble circulated through the men on the screens.

Sinclair said, "Only the purest of us gather tonight as we start the most important journey in history—the journey toward bringing about the Second Coming of Jesus Christ, the Lamb of God. Just a few steps from this room the miracle is taking place right now."

"Miracle?" Cotten whispered. "Do you think he's creating the clone here at Rosslyn Manor?"

John turned the speaker volume knob down. "What would be more appropriate? It has to be," John said. "He must have a lab somewhere in the house—that's why Ianucci wanted us to come here—to stop the cloning, to destroy it."

"But why would Sinclair have all these guests here, if that were the case?"

"Maybe he's arrogant and doesn't think he can be stopped. And if you think about it, there was elaborate security before we could even get on the grounds. He could use the events of nine-eleven to justify it. Sinclair is probably a major player in this community, and if he has this party every year he wouldn't want to cancel and arouse any kind of curiosity as to why. Finding the lab might be easier than we thought. You know, sometimes the best place to hide something is to put it in plain sight."

Cotten's mind raced, weaving everything together. "There's something wrong."

"What do you mean?" John asked.

"You said finding it will be easy. Getting in here was easy—too easy." She put her fingers to her temples. "We weren't so clever getting into Sinclair's party. We were lured here. We did exactly what they wanted. We're the moths, and this place is the flame."

John's expression darkened.

"Did you hear Sinclair?" Cotten said. "Ianucci served his purpose. It wasn't only to switch the real relic with a fake. They knew he would lead us to them. He was the bait. He gave us the invitation."

John slipped his hand into his pocket and removed the box given to them by the cardinal. "Do you think they know about this."

A soft click caused John to drop it back into his pocket. The door to the media room opened—a large man was silhouetted in the light from the hall.

"*Solpeth*, Cotten."

For an instant, just a flash that passed through her, she wanted to jump up and run to him, throw her arms around his neck, and give him a big hug. But then Cotten Stone's heart tumbled, and her mind made its best effort to comprehend. He had said *hello* . . . like Motness, in Enochian. "Uncle Gus?"

What was he doing here . . . in a monk's robe with a gun pointed at her? Cotten shook her head in disbelief. She looked hard at him. "I thought you were—"

"In intensive care from a terrible car accident? No, I'm fine. We had to tell you something to keep you frightened and on the run— keep you distracted until we could get things underway here."

Cotten could see his familiar smile—his words sounded soft and gentle.

"We tried to hold you in New York. That would have been simpler. But Father Tyler screwed that up, coming to your rescue." He looked at John. "You weren't in the original plan. So we had to slow you down a little, like we did Cotten. Cut off the money. But at the same time, keep you running. When one is desperate he lacks clarity."

"Thornton . . . Vanessa?" Cotten said, awash in betrayal.

"Your boyfriend was a hell of a reporter. He got way too close. We were sure he had told you everything. But the fashion model . . . that was unfortunate. Wingate panicked. He was way out of line. He could have injured you."

Cotten swallowed—her throat was so dry it pained her. "And the cabin fire? You did that?"

Gus said, "We kept our fingers crossed on that one. For a time there, we were afraid you wouldn't get out. I almost came and banged on the door to wake you."

"Why? What's going on, Uncle Gus?" Her voice broke.

"Sorry, sweetheart, but I need to make sure you and the priest go no further. It stops here."

Cotten glared. "I trusted you. Always have, since I was a little girl." She paused before speaking again. "Did you kill the cardinal?"

Gus sighed. "He served his purpose."

"I can't believe Cardinal Ianucci was willingly involved," John said. "He couldn't have known what was going on here—the cloning."

"Oh, on the contrary, Father Tyler. He knew. Though he was duped just a bit, thinking he was helping bring about the Second Coming.

Ironically, he was half right. It really will be the Second Coming—after all, Christ is about to be born again . . . with a twist."

"But Ianucci repented," John said. "He realized what he had done and asked God to forgive him."

Gus rolled his eyes. "Perhaps. Who knows what's really in a man's heart. But the cardinal was predictable. We knew that from the start. That's why he was chosen. Sinclair let Ianucci *discover* our true plan, then *allowed* him to escape and contact you—invite you to the ball. He was just a pawn."

"Why didn't you kill me when you murdered him?" Cotten asked.

"Much cleaner this way. We knew you would be coming here—you and Tyler. A *twofer*, so to speak." Gus Ruby paused as if reluctant to go on. "Your priest friend has to be taken care of, but the fact of the matter is, I can't kill you."

"Because you're my uncle?" She struggled to accept his explanation.

"Well," Gus said, drawing out the word to an exaggerated length. "How should I explain? I'm your father's brother, just not quite in the same sense as you might normally think. But part of a family, just as well."

Cotten's eyes blinked rapidly as she shook her head. "I don't understand."

"Of course you don't. It's just like you didn't understand when Archer said you were the only one. Now, there's an understatement. I suppose this is as good a time as any," Gus said.

Cotten reached to clutch John's hand.

Gus nodded to John. "Perhaps introductions are in order."

"Father Tyler, do you realize whose company you keep? Meet Cotten Stone, daughter of Furmiel Stone. I'm sure you've heard of Furmiel—the Angel of the eleventh hour? Furmiel . . . one of what you call the Fallen, the Watchers, my brother."

Cotten felt as if she were hallucinating. "Stop, stop," she whispered. "What are you talking about?"

"Your father was with us from the beginning. He fought in the Great Battle. When we were defeated, we were cast out and have been condemned to wander this place forever. Eventually, your father weakened and begged God's forgiveness. He deserted our ranks . . . a traitor. He groveled, shaming us. God took pity on him and granted him a life as a mortal man. He was permitted to marry and procreate. You and your twin sister are his offspring—half breeds, Nephilim. But your father had to pay for God's mercy. Selfishly, God took your sister and left you on earth to fight His battles. Of course, your father splintered under the pressure of mortality, and always feeling guilty at the burden placed on you. And for what? A life of misery. He chose to end his life, disappointing God once again. As I said, he was weak."

Gus shifted his gaze to John. "And, priest, your God is not what you think. He is not the all-merciful, all-forgiving god you pray to. Not Furmiel, not any of us, can ever return to our home in Paradise.

"Fortunately for you, Cotten, all of my brothers have sworn to never harm any of our own kind—your kind—as our number would dwindle and diminish our legion. To do our work, we have recruited mortals—egotistical, power-hungry men, the likes of Charles Sinclair and the Templars. But you, dear Cotten, are different—a one of a kind. For not only are you of this place, but part of you is of a higher order. You are one of us."

His expression softened, and Cotten saw the same familiar smile she had loved for so long—now a repulsive mask of evil and betrayal. It sickened her.

Lowering the pistol, Gus Ruby said, "I'm not here to kill you, Cotten. I'm here to bring you home."

THE LAB

As Gus Ruby lowered the gun, John sprang forward, slamming the big man full in the chest, knocking him backwards into the hall. Dropping his weight onto Gus, John gripped his wrist and wrenched the weapon away. Fighting for breath, Gus tried to rise up but stopped as John aimed the gun at his face.

"Don't move," John said. "Not a sound."

Wind knocked from him, Gus coughed and struggled to talk. "You haven't been listening, priest." His lips warped into an arrogant grin. "You're wasting your time. You can't kill me."

Cotten stepped beside the two men. "You're right, Uncle Gus," she said. *Geh el Grip. You are the only one.* It was all becoming so clear to her.

"*He* can't hurt you," Cotten said as she slowly reached to take the gun from John's hand. She pointed it at Gus. "But I can. Isn't that right? You said you can't kill me—that there is a pact not to harm another of your kind—*our* kind. That must mean we have the power to harm each other . . . that I have that power."

John rolled off of Gus and stood.

Cotten motioned with the gun. "Get up, Uncle Gus."

With great effort, Gus Ruby managed to pull himself to stand. He looked at Cotten, his chest straining the buttons on his shirt as he breathed. "You're not going to shoot me."

His confidence seemed to ebb.

"But you don't know that for sure, do you?" she said. "You don't know which part of me controls the pressure on the trigger."

"Cotten, you've done enough to pay your father's dues," Gus said. "It's time you were set free. We want to bring you into the fold."

"Don't listen to him," John said.

Gus laughed. "You're out of your league, priest. You have no say in this matter."

Gus glared at Cotten. "How has your life been so far, sweetheart? Has God shone his glorious grace on you? Hmm?"

"Leave her alone," John said.

"Unlike your god, Father Tyler, the Son of the Dawn is forgiving. Cotten, your father was never allowed to return to Paradise, no matter what he did, no matter how he begged. And his punishment never ended, did it? His day-to-day battle to survive, to provide for his family, to live as a man, crushed him. God never let up on him. Remember the drought? All the hardship? Poor Furmiel finally broke. Why would anyone choose to honor that kind of a god? But we are opening our arms to embrace you. You will be given anything you want—wealth, fame, contentment—there is no limit."

His voice turned soft, tender, the old Uncle Gus that she had loved all her life.

"Come home, Cotten."

Tears streaked Cotten's cheeks and her arm trembled as she raised the gun. "I am home . . . and I'm the one who has to end this." She pointed the gun at Gus's head.

"Don't make the biggest mistake of your life, sweetheart."

Cotten shook her head. "Where's the lab?"

"That's your problem," Gus said.

"Turn around," she said. When his back was to her, Cotten nosed the gun into Gus's shoulder and said, "Down the hall."

They guided the big man to a guest bedroom they had entered earlier. Cotten nudged Gus inside the closet.

John stripped the king-size sheet off the bed, wound Gus inside the top sheet, and then tied the contoured sheet around him.

As he did, Gus said, "How many times do I have to tell you that you're wasting your time?"

"We've got to keep him quiet," Cotten said. She took off her pinafore and ripped a broad swatch from the cheap material. "Here, jam this in his mouth and tie it with the rest."

When John was done, Cotten stared at Gus for a moment, wondering if all their effort would be in vain. "Think that will hold him?" she asked. "Or does he have some kind of special—"

"It will hold the flesh. That's all I can guess," John said.

"All right, let's do it," Cotten said.

They descended the staircase, veered opposite the study and entered a room as elaborate as the lobby of a Park Avenue hotel. It opened to the dinner hall. They froze at the sight of servants scurrying about, adding last minute touches to banquet tables.

Cotten suddenly stopped short, hearing the clatter of pots, the tinkle of crystal, the voice of what was probably the head waiter ordering about the servants. "Not that way," she said. "That must be the kitchen. She broke down a passageway to a closed door at the end. Cotten turned the knob and pushed the door open.

This part of the house looked barren and sterile. She peered up into the eye of a security camera.

"Go, go," John said, almost pushing her down the empty corridor. The lighting here didn't come from Strauss or Waterford chandeliers, but from recessed fluorescents. The walls were stark and the doors stainless steel.

"See what's in there," Cotten said, pointing to the first door.

John opened it. "Looks like laboratory supplies," he said.

"Then we must be close. This wing has got to be Sinclair's private lab suite."

The remaining doors they passed stood open, revealing what appeared to be rooms for surgical procedures, pharmaceuticals, general laboratory operations, more storage, and even a collection of medical and science reference materials. The hall made a turn to the right, ending with an imposing steel door.

They stood before it.

"Looks like a bank vault," Cotten said. "This must be it."

John pointed to the combination keypad and a device shaped like the bowl of a spoon.

"Oh, shit," Cotten mumbled, realizing what it was for.

John reached into his pocket.

She watched him open the cardinal's box. Inside rested a human index finger severed at the second knuckle.

John turned and glanced around the corner, down the hall. "I think I heard something. They're bound to be coming any second."

Cotten motioned to the box. "Do it."

John took the finger from the box.

She fought back a gag as she saw the trail of dangling tissue and ooze from the severed end.

He positioned the pad of the finger in the *spoon*. The device hummed faintly, bringing the keyboard to life, each key backlit in soft blue. The readout scrolled the message: *Cardinal Antonio Ianucci.*

Identity confirmed. The screen darkened and then displayed a new message. *Enter code.*

Cotten looked at John. "What code?"

"I have no idea," he said.

"We're dead."

Just south of Scotland's capital city of Edinburgh is the village of Roslin, the home of Rosslyn Chapel and Rosslyn Castle, the home of the St. Clairs (Sinclairs). In that small village is a state-of-the-art research center, Roslin Institute. It is here that Dolly the sheep was cloned.

The God of peace will crush Satan under your feet. (Romans 16:20)

THE CLONE

"A CODE, A CODE," Cotten whispered. "Why would the cardinal get us this far and not tell us the code? If he knew about the security, he must have known we needed a code."

Suddenly, in her mind Cotten heard Archer's mumblings. A rush of heat swept through her. As if inspired, she said, "Oh, my God! John, I think I know what it is! I've known it all along—Archer told me." She reached to the keypad. "Please let this be it. Please." She looked at John. "Matthew," she whispered, then pressed 2-6-2-7-2-8.

The keypad turned from blue to green, and the display read: *Code accepted. Entry authorized.* There was a heavy metallic thump as the magnetic locks released, and the motor-driven door slowly opened.

On the inside wall was a red rectangular button the size of a pack of cigarettes labeled *open/close.* John slammed it with his palm, and the mechanism reversed. With a heavy thud, the door closed and locked.

Cotten whirled around, catching a panoramic view of the laboratory. "Where is it?"

Her eyes fell on a silver travel case, and then next to that, a transparent container. The Cup. She approached the acrylic container in awe of the beauty and simplicity of the remarkable relic inside. Two thousand years ago, Jesus Christ drank from it and the next day it caught His blood as He died on the Cross. Carefully, she removed the Cup. Her finger traced the rim, then made a long stroke down the outside of the bowl and the stem to the base. It was completely encased in some sort of thin, clear coating, but even with the protective veneer, touching it gave her chills. Cotten placed it in the silver travel case, closed the lid, and hugged it to her chest.

The Cup of Christ had come back to her.

She turned to watch John as he walked to a stainless steel cart near a far corner. He stared at an incubator with a microscope attached. Digital displays flashed above it showing temperature, levels of oxygen saturation, CO_2 concentration, humidity, and other vital indicators. Inside was what appeared to be an ordinary petri dish. He peered through the lens of the microscope and became still as if spellbound.

"John?" she whispered.

Slowly lifting his head, he made the sign of the cross.

"Is that it?" she asked, standing beside him.

He faced her, his eyes hazed, a thunderstruck expression.

"Hurry before someone comes. Destroy it," she said.

John didn't move.

Cotten placed the silver case on the counter and put her eye to the microscope. There in the dish she saw four cells like tiny bubbles clumped together.

"Blastocyst," she whispered. It looked exactly like every picture she'd ever seen of a fertilized egg growing and dividing—the beginning of a human life.

"What if it's really . . ." John faltered. His words sounded painful. "We could be murdering the Son of God."

Cotten's lips parted to speak—*Geh el crip* resonated in her head.

"But what if we're wrong?" He stared at her, but his eyes were filled with doubt. His voice cracked. "How could I ever live with myself knowing I was no different than those who drove the nails into his hands?"

She reached to touch his face. Here in the final moment, John wasn't going to be able to destroy the clone. He was on fire inside, she realized. His entire being burned with dread. All the doubts and concerns he had expressed must be ripping him apart. Was this thing the Antichrist? Or was John about to stop the Second Coming? Would destroying the clone be the equivalent of committing abortion? Murder?

"I can't," John said. "I can't play God."

A chorus of voices echoed in Cotten's head. "*Geh el crip.*" She took his hand. "We aren't playing God. He chose us—brought us together and led us to this place." She choked. "Thornton. Vanessa. I can't believe they were sacrificed for no reason. John, you made me see reality. Why did I wander onto that dig site in Iraq at just the right moment? Why did my twin die at birth only to talk to me in a language you said is the language of heaven? Why have you searched for the way God wants you to serve? John, this is it."

Her mind cleared. She was the only one who could stop the Son of the Dawn. John's very faith gave him doubts—and God knew that would happen. That was why she was chosen. She was part of the contract her father had made with God.

Geh el crip.

John gripped her arm and took a step back, pulling her away.

"I'm sorry," she said, pushing him aside. "But I have to do this." She ripped the hoses and wires from the incubator, then picked up the entire apparatus and smashed it on the floor.

As if in slow motion, the box split open on impact sending jagged transparent shards across the tile. The microscope tore loose and spun on the floor at her feet. But the petri dish miraculously landed upright and intact.

Cotten glared at it for an instant, and then stomped down, crushing it under her heel.

The dish shattered.

"It's over," she said. "It's done."

Suddenly, the lab filled with the blare of alarm horns. Cotten covered her ears. Red and white strobes flashed.

"Come on," John yelled, the noise appearing to startle him back to life.

"Wait," Cotten said, spotting a row of oxygen canisters along the wall. Her eyes searched the room. Near the door was a workstation with pipes leading to it. "Gas lines." She recognized the Bunsen burner on the counter.

She rushed to the canisters, yanked the hoses from their attachments, and opened their valves. Oxygen hissed into the room.

The Bunsen burner had a hose running from its base to a gas outlet on one of the pipes. She flipped the control handle, turning on the gas flow. She rotated the knurled knob at the base of the burner, funneling the gas up through the barrel.

"Light, light, light," she yelled over the screaming alarm. "Find a match!"

John grabbed a Duraflame lighter gun from a nearby shelf.

She took it and ignited the burner. It flickered pale and weak. Quickly she adjusted the Bunsen's air vents, and at last the luminous flame turned orange and yellow. She wasn't after the kind of flame the burner was most often adjusted to produce—not the controlled compact flame with a pale violet-blue halo around a dark core.

She wanted fire—the fires of hell.

Quickly she retrieved the silver case that contained the Grail. "Let's get out of here," she said, grasping John's arm.

They turned toward the door. It was already opening.

Then the beast was captured, and with him the False Prophet who worked signs in his presence, by which he deceived those who received the mark of the beast and those who worshiped his image. These two were cast alive into the lake of fire burning with brimstone. (Revelation 19:20)

FACE TO FACE

COTTEN CLUTCHED THE TITANIUM case, and was set to run, every fiber in her body, every strip of sinew and thread of muscle on the ready. But then she caught sight of the man standing just outside the open door.

A flash of heat blew in, and the air sizzled. Cotten shuddered.

An old gentleman gazed at her, his eyes piercing.

John stared at the man in the doorway. "The missing tenth horn," he said.

A debilitating pain just above Cotten's eye sockets wracked her—similar to the pain that follows eating ice cream too quickly. But this was more intense, like glowing hot spikes driving through her skull, the muscles to her eyes—her very brain—cramping, burning. Cotten pressed the heel of her left hand to her forehead and cried out. "John, get us out. I can't see."

She heard a snap, and then John took her hand and put an object between her thumb and forefinger. His crucifix from the chain around his neck.

He lifted her hand by the wrist. "We've got to do this together," he said.

John spoke while moving her forward.

"In the Name of the Father, and of the Son, and of the Holy Spirit. Amen.

"Most glorious Prince of the Heavenly Armies, Saint Michael the Archangel, defend us in our battle against principalities and powers, against the rulers of the world of darkness, against the spirits of wickedness in the high place."

The pain slackened for an instant, and Cotten fluttered her eyes briefly to see John. Sweat beaded above his lip and on his brow. But there was confidence in his face and his voice. His eyes bore down on the old man who was now more a mirage, a quavering image like heat rising from pavement. The pain in her eyes made her close them.

"Cotten."

The voice shot nerve impulses through her, and the room flooded with the distinct aromas of fresh cut hay, shucked corn, Kentucky soil.

"You haven't forgotten me, have you?" the voice said.

"Daddy?" Cotten said, a wave of emotion washing over her.

"It's not your father, Cotten," John said. "He's a liar." John inched forward and continued the liturgy. ". . . take hold of the dragon, the old serpent, which is the devil and Satan, bind him and cast him into the bottomless pit that he may no longer seduce the nations."

Again the voice—this time in the language only she could understand. "*Cri sprok inhime. Sprak dien e vigo*. Listen to me. You are my little girl."

She felt John use their joined hands to make the sign of the cross. Three steps forward.

"In the Name of Jesus Christ, our Lord."

"*Gril te*." It was Vanessa. "Put your trust in me, Cotten. I'm your best friend. I died for you. Step away from the priest. He is the one who lies."

"Stop!" Cotten shouted, pressing a hand to her ear. "Nessi, forgive me."

"Don't listen to the voices, Cotten," John shouted. "It's a trick. He's trying to weaken you."

"No!" Cotten screamed.

The old man's voice thundered. The glass beakers trembled. "*Tunka tee rosfal ee Nephilim*. You belong to the Fallen. You are one of us."

John gripped Cotten's wrist even more tightly. "Don't listen!"

A hiss, like steam escaping a boiler, sounded, and her flesh seared with the heat of the old man's breath.

"Behold the Cross of the Lord, flee bands of enemies," John said. "May Thy mercy, Lord, descend upon us."

Sign of the cross.

Hot wind blasted her—a gale spun out of hell.

"We drive you from us," John said, "whoever you may be, unclean spirits, all satanic powers, all infernal invaders, all wicked legions."

The pain in her head grew with a fury. Cotten balked and stumbled. She feared she was going to vomit and felt herself heave.

John edged her onward. "God the Father commands you."

Sign of the cross.

The floor seemed to vibrate. The hot wind, the quivering, her body shaking to its core—she was losing touch. Again she stumbled, one leg collapsing beneath her.

"God the Son commands you."

Sign of the cross.

"God the Holy Spirit commands you."

Sign of the cross.

John reached around her, pulling her to her feet.

The air pressure in the lab throbbed—pounding, crushing.

"This is not where it ends." The voice was harsh like stones scraping. "You are weak like your father."

The heat boiled Cotten's strength from her. Another stab of pain made her rip her hand from John's.

"By the God who so loved the world that He gave up His only Son, that every soul believing in Him might not perish but have everlasting life." John grabbed her hand again.

The heat was so intense now, Cotten felt her skin blister.

John's voice echoed above the wind that nearly shattered her eardrums. "Holy, Holy, Holy is the Lord, the God of Hosts. Oh Lord, hear my prayer. God of heaven, God of earth, God of Angels, God of Archangels—"

The crescendo of the wind.

The blast of hair-singeing air.

The boom of John's powerful voice.

The stabbing pain.

Cotten heard crashing sounds as tables overturned, the shattering of glass, the clanging of steel on steel. She wanted to give up, to fall on her knees, to beg for mercy, but John held her to him, more carrying her now than leading her. She hadn't the strength or the will to continue on herself. For an instant she tried to break from him and flee, but he held her firm.

"Oh Lord, hear my prayer. And let my cry come unto Thee."

Cotten twisted away. "I can't. I can't."

John yanked her back and enfolded her.

"We beseech Thee through Jesus Christ Our Lord. Amen. From the snares of the devil, deliver us oh Lord."

Sign of the cross.

"In the Name of the Father—"

Sign of the cross

"And of the Son—"

Sign of the cross.

"And of the Holy Spirit."

Sign of the cross.

Suddenly the wind died to a trickle, and the heat in it cooled. The unbearable pain in her head seeped away. She opened her eyes in time to see a flare of light and a whirl of dust where the old man had stood.

John and Cotten passed through the door. She leaned on him, drained, her throat scorched raw.

He held her to him as he slammed the push button panel, making the door close.

Before it shut, Cotten caught a last glimpse inside the lab—she could see a slight swirling of smoky air, papers drifting down, the flicker of the flame from the Bunsen burner.

John cradled her face between his palms. "It's going to blow any minute. We've got to get out of here."

They ran, John pulling her as her strength slowly returned. Behind them, the door to the lab sealed in the deadly combination of pure oxygen and an open flame.

Cotten tried to focus, but everything still blurred—her vision—her awareness. A thick mist clung inside her skull, her thoughts jumbled, foggy, and disconnected. John pulled her down the hall leading from the lab, and she could hear their footfalls, echoing their way into her ears.

The alarm horns shrieked like prehistoric creatures in mortal combat. The fire-like sensation on her skin faded, but she feared it left blisters behind. The unusual smell of sulfur filled her nostrils while she ran, hugging the travel case.

Panicky voices rang throughout the house as she and John burst into the foyer at the base of the huge staircase. Servants, caterers, and guests ran past them toward the front entrance.

"Come on," John yelled, guiding her into the rush of bodies.

Suddenly, she sensed fresh, damp night air, and stumbled down the porch steps and across the drive—her shoes sinking into the soft earth. Cotten choked back a cry. A breeze off the river swept over her, and tears spilled down her cheeks.

In the next instant, the ground and the air convulsed—a shockwave. The blast struck from behind.

The lab had blown.

The explosion pushed her and John a half dozen yards through the air and landed them in a flower garden. John hit first, face down in the soft loam. But Cotten smacked her head on one of the decorative stones. She lay still for a moment, dazed.

Finally, she lifted her head and looked back at the classic antebellum architecture of the estate house. Smoke billowed from the roof of the east wing—flames shooting from broken windows, lapping at the eaves. The sound of a nearby fountain merged with the crackle of fire.

The earth shook again with smaller explosions.

The noise in her head, like the buzzing of swarming locusts, a violent vibration, grew louder, deafening.

"John?" She saw his distorted face, as if looking up through the water from the bottom of a pool.

Cotten felt herself fading into darkness. Her fingers loosened their grip on the silver case, and a moment later her hand fell away.

"He who endures to the end shall be saved." (Matthew 24:13)

RECOVERY

"I THOUGHT I WOULD never see you again," Cotten said as she looked up into the face of her sister, Motnees, who was framed in a brilliant light.

"I'm always here."

"Is it really over?" Cotten asked.

"For now," Motnees said, stroking her sister's forehead. "Our father is proud of you."

"So he is at peace?"

"Yes," Motnees said.

Her image faded, and the light paled. "Never forget."

"What?" Cotten said, reaching.

"*Geh el Grip*." The radiance barely illuminated Motnees and her smile. Then she was gone.

Ted Casselman's voice transcended the mist and lifted Cotten up to consciousness. Suddenly, she felt like a diver returning from the depths.

"I think she's waking up," Casselman said.

Cotten blinked.

John took her hand. "Welcome back."

The room was bleak, sterile, and smelled of disinfectant. She lifted her arm and stared at the attached IV. The memory of their escape flooded back.

She wanted to speak, but her tongue seemed stuck to the roof of her mouth, and her lips felt glued together. She looked at the plastic pitcher and cup next to her bed.

"Are you thirsty?" John asked.

Cotten nodded.

He poured her a glass and held it for her.

The water cooled her mouth and freed her tongue and lips. The light streaming in through the hospital window made her squint. "What time is it?"

"Four thirty," John said. "You've been in and out over the last couple of days. You look more alert, like you are going to stay with us this time. The doctor says you're going to be fine. Only a bad concussion."

Cotten's stare locked on John. "Where is it?" she whispered.

"FBI," John said.

She closed her eyes. It all seemed so unreal, more like a dream she had gladly awakened from, even though some of the vestiges of the nightmare held fast. Her body hurt, and her skin felt sunburned. No, it had all been real—from the tomb and Gabriel Archer to the cloning lab and Charles Sinclair, to—she shuddered, recalling Gus's revelations and then the old man blocking their escape from the lab. She tried focusing on her boss. "What are you doing here, Ted?"

"You're both all over the news. As soon as the first reports hit the wire, the production crew and I were on a plane to New Orleans. You know the old saying about someone having a nose for news? Well, honey, you've outdone yourself."

Cotten wanted to laugh, but she didn't have the energy. It was more like the story had chased her until it finally ran her over.

"Uncle Gus?"

"No sign," John said.

"No, there wouldn't be."

"It's all over, Cotten," he said.

"Thank God."

"Yes, you should do that."

The nurse came in and checked Cotten's vitals, rendering the room silent for a few minutes. When the nurse finished, Cotten directed her gaze back at John. "By the way, that was quite a tackle you threw on Uncle Gus," she said.

"I was saving it for the next student-faculty game, but it seemed like the right time to give it a shot."

"I ever tell you those eyes are wasted on a priest?" Cotten said.

Casselman thumped the bed rail with his knuckles. "What's up? Anything I should know about you two?"

"We're just good friends," Cotten said.

"This is one special lady," John said, speaking to Casselman, but his eyes on Cotten.

"That she is," Casselman agreed.

Cotten's expression turned somber. "What happened to Sinclair?" she asked.

Casselman pulled a chair to her bedside but didn't sit. "He didn't make it. There were about a dozen people injured, and four dead, so far. Sinclair was one of them. The whole deal is outrageous—what Sinclair was up to, stealing the Grail, the cloning. Then to top it off, they found that cardinal you interviewed at the Vatican—Ianucci—murdered right here in New Orleans. They're saying he's the one who switched the relic." He glanced at both of them. "Either of you know anything about that?" When they didn't respond, he went on. "That and the Sinclair story are on the front page of every paper in the country. And, my dear Ms. Stone, you are going to be the darling of every news broadcast and talk show. The world isn't going to be able to get enough of that beautiful face." He reached out and tweaked her chin almost like a relative would pinch a youngster's cheek. "I smell a Pulitzer on the horizon, Cotten, once you write the whole story."

She was only half listening to Casselman. "Are you all right?" she asked John.

"A few cuts and bruises," he said, shrugging. "You're the one who took the brunt of it."

"And the old man?"

"What old man?" Casselman asked.

John shook his head, casting his eyes to the floor.

"Who are you talking about?" Casselman asked.

"Someone we ran into on the way out," John said.

"Oh. Well, I'm sure we'll be getting a complete list of all those injured or killed. What was his name?"

"Son of the Dawn," she whispered, turning away.

"What?" Casselman said.

"It doesn't matter," Cotten answered. "Robert Wingate is involved in this, too," she said.

Casselman seemed to reel back on his heels. "No shit," he said. "Well then, listen to this. This has been a hell of a week. Monday morning Wingate was found dead in his car in the garage. Carbon monoxide poisoning. Looks like suicide. Guess the guy couldn't handle the scandal. Same day that he announced he was back in the presidential race, some kid came forward and accused him of child molestation. After that initial allegation, four other boys came forward. Seems Wingate had a fetish for young boys. That accounts for the boys' ranch. Always turns out to be little league coaches and scout leaders or priests—excuse me, John. No offense."

"None taken," John replied.

Casselman dropped down in the chair. "It's amazing how far the tentacles of this Grail thing reach—like somebody spit in the pool and the ripples just keep on spreading." He patted Cotten's hand. "We're sending you to Rome to cover the Grail's return to the Vatican. Of course not until you're on the mend. And there's a big fat promotion in this for you, Cotten. Thornton will be missed, but the public will love you in his spot. Not only are you the rising star, the whole backstory will have everyone clamoring to sit in front of their televisions when you're on."

She didn't want any more notoriety. The quest for the big story wasn't high on her list anymore. "Not me." Her voice was small.

"But Cotten," Casselman said, "of course you'll cover it. Think of the publicity for both you and SNN. Young female reporter saves the most important religious relic of all time." Casselman grinned. "Twice!" He rubbed his chin. "In the meantime, I've got a million questions for you two, starting with this cloning business."

"Let somebody else go to Rome, Ted," Cotten said.

Casselman chuckled. "No way. You're the only one who can do it—the only one."

Cotten gave a half-hearted laugh. "Yeah, I get that a lot."

Movement in the doorway made them all turn.

"Felipe," John said, surprise in his voice.

A tall man in a black suit with a Roman collar entered the room. His dark complexion matched his eyes. He extended his hand. "John, it is good to see you." A faint Spanish accent coated his words.

"And it's good to see you again." John took the priest's hand in both of his and gave it a strong shake. "I'd like you to meet someone," he said. "Your Excellency, this is Cotten Stone, news correspondent with SNN. Cotten, this is Archbishop Felipe Montiagro, the Vatican Apostolic Nuncio to the United States." He nodded toward Casselman. "Archbishop, this is Ted Casselman, news director for the Satellite News Network."

Casselman got to his feet. "It's a pleasure, Your Excellency." He stepped away from his chair. "Here, please."

Montiagro waved his hand. "No, no." He moved next to the bed and studied Cotten's face for a few moments. "You are a courageous young woman. I hope your recovery is going well?"

"Thank you," she said. "I don't know about courage. John is the one who got us out."

He blessed her and whispered a quick prayer. Then he turned to John. "I received a call late last night. You've been summoned to the Vatican to document the extraordinary events that have taken place here."

"Whoa, that's incredible," Casselman said, raising both hands high. "An audience with the new pope!"

Montiagro smiled at Casselman. "There is no guarantee of that. As you can imagine, everyone wants to meet the new Holy Father."

"How soon?" John asked.

"They are anxious."

"Give me a few days."

"I'll relay your request," the archbishop said. "And John, I have a feeling the Holy Father has something special in mind for you."

The archbishop turned to Cotten. "Miss Stone, the authorities are making arrangements to return the blessed relic to us. We would be honored if you could be there to take part in the ceremony."

"She accepts!" Ted Casselman said.

A small idiosyncrasy in Montiagro's expression made her realize he understood that the final decision would be hers. "We will see you in Rome, then. May the Lord speed your recovery," he said.

"Archbishop," John said as Montiagro walked to the door. "Thank you for everything."

Montiagro placed his hand on John's shoulder. "It is you we must thank—both of you."

When the archbishop had gone, Casselman grabbed Cotten's toes through the sheets and wiggled her feet. "This just keeps getting better."

THE HALL OF CONSTANTINE

"THEY'RE READY, MS. STONE," the priest said. He motioned with his arm, and Cotten rose from her chair in the Vatican Museum antechamber. Standing nearby was an FBI agent, a group of clergy, and a handful of plainclothes members of Vatican security. Two Swiss Guards were positioned on each side of the tall, ornate door—their colorful armor and plume uniforms dating back to Michelangelo. The FBI agent held the silver travel case.

As Cotten stepped through the doorway into the Hall of Constantine, the first of the museum's Raphael Rooms, she gasped at the splendor. The room, chosen for this ceremony because of its theme of the triumphs of Christianity, displayed scenes from the life and battles of the great Roman emperor.

The hall was packed with clergy, dignitaries, and members of the world press—a sprinkling of red and purple designated many of the Roman Curia who were present, including the Secretariat of State, along with other heads of the Vatican and Italian governments. Cotten also recognized the U.S. ambassador to the Vatican, and the president of SNN. Beside him was Ted Casselman.

The priest escort ushered her to the center aisle where she turned and took the case from the agent.

The room was so quiet that Cotten could hear the rustle of her crisp gray suit against her stockings as she walked alone up the aisle. Ahead, on a platform riser, stood a solitary man—the newly consecrated bishop and papal appointed prelate of the Pontifical Commission for Sacred Archaeology—John Tyler. Her eyes fastened on his—still the bluest she'd ever known.

Suddenly, she felt a knot in her stomach—a pang of dread that a chapter in her life was ending—a door was closing forever. Seeing John in the purple cassock of his new office confirmed it.

But everything she needed to know was all there in his eyes.

"Hello, Cotten Stone," John said softly, extending his hand as she came to stand before him.

"Hello, John Tyler," she said so only he could hear. Accepting his hand, they stood in silence for a moment.

The Hall of Constantine erupted in applause, becoming awash in flashes and the brilliance of video camera lights.

Then she let go of him for the last time.

Cotten held the silver case out to John. "Your Excellency, I have the honor of presenting to the Universal Church, this blessed relic known as the Cup of the Last Supper, the Cup of the Crucifixion, the Cup of Christ, the Holy Grail."

Lynn Sholes (Florida) leads fiction workshops and trains educators in teaching writing. Her extensive work with the Broward County Archaeology Society sparked the idea for *The Grail Conspiracy*, her seventh novel. More information can be found at www.grailconspiracy.com and www.satellitenews.org.

Joe Moore (Florida) is a marketing executive with twenty-five years' experience in the television postproduction industry. As a senior audio engineer, he received two regional Emmy awards for individual achievement in audio mixing. He drew from four years of theological seminary training to write this book. *The Grail Conspiracy* is his second work of fiction.

WWW.MIDNIGHTINKBOOKS.COM

From the gritty streets of New York City to sacred tombs in the Middle East, it's always midnight somewhere. Join us online at any hour for fresh new voices in mystery fiction, book club questions, author information, mystery resources, and more.

Midnight Ink promises a wild ride filled with cunning villains, conflicted heroes, hilarious hazards, mind-bending puzzles, and enough twists and turns to keep readers on the edge of their seats.

MIDNIGHT INK ORDERING INFORMATION

Order by Phone:
- Call toll-free within the U.S. and Canada at 1-888-NITEINK (1-888-648-3465)
- We accept VISA, MasterCard, and American Express

Order by Mail:
Send the full price of your order (MN residents add 7% sales tax) in U.S. funds, plus postage & handling to:

> Midnight Ink
> 2143 Wooddale Drive
> Woodbury, MN 55125-2989

Postage & Handling:
Standard (U.S., Mexico, & Canada). If your order is:
> $49.99 and under, add $3.00
> $50.00 and over, FREE STANDARD SHIPPING

AK, HI, PR: $15.00 for one book plus $1.00 for each additional book.

International Orders (airmail only):
> $16.00 for one book plus $3.00 for each additional book

Orders are processed within 2 business days. Please allow for normal shipping time. Postage and handling rates subject to change.